ENTWINED
THE DRAGON CAPTURED

BRIDGET E. BAKER

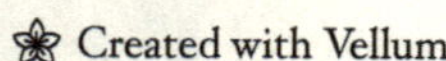 Created with Vellum

PROLOGUE: LIZ

Monsters can be scary, imaginary creatures like vampires, werewolves, or succubi. But they can also be people who do terrible, unspeakable things.

Most of the world thinks of the Donner party, the ninety-person group of pioneers who got caught by an early blizzard at Donner Lake around Halloween of 1846, as monsters. They may not be the most famous group of cannibals in the world, but they certainly are in the United States.

You probably can't study them without wondering whether you'd do the same as they did in those circumstances. Most people today can't even imagine what it would be like to endure the starvation, hypothermia, and deprivation they did. For those who left the camp on December 16 to seek help, seventeen of their strongest members, things only got worse. Much worse. As a blizzard froze many of them to death, and a wrong turn sent them down a funnel in the center of the Sierra Nevada mountains, it was even odds on whether they'd die of hypothermia or starvation first. Only seven of them survived that month-long trek, and only because, after consuming their own shoes and snowshoes, they consumed all but one of those who didn't make it.

On February 18, the first relief party finally returned to the two camps at the base of the mountains, but due to difficulties of both weather and animals, they were only able to save a scant handful of the seventy people still waiting. By that point, most the survivors had nothing left to eat. They were also nearly out of wood to burn, and those left largely lacked the strength to even locate or cut more wood.

On March 3 another rescue group came, but thanks to the onset of another brutal blizzard, more than a dozen of the people they set out to save wound up at the bottom of a twenty-four foot deep snow pit instead. They were left there with three days of firewood, no shelter, and no food. Two died almost immediately—an older brother and a mother. The despair those remaining eleven emaciated and frozen pioneers must have felt is practically unfathomable.

But that's not the end of the story.

Not one, or even two, but four separate paid rescuers walked by that pit and just kept going. They must have decided that the people yet alive at the bottom of that macabre pit were a lost cause. Or perhaps they were worried that any attempt to save the hopeless, godforsaken people below would simply cost them their own lives.

They were out of fire to burn. Out of energy to cut it. Out of hope for the future. They had all but given up when the last few rescuers made it to that terrible pit. Two desperate fathers who had made it over the summit in that horrible December trip had paid two men to help them go back, in the hope that they might rescue their remaining sons. They passed the pit, hopeful that when they reached the lake camp, they would find their children.

They didn't know that both their sons had already perished.

The eleven people in that hole, two adults and nine children, were alive in part because the adults had begun to feed the flesh of the deceased mother and brother to the children.

The rescuers saw the two partially consumed corpses at the top of the pit, and they saw that none of the eleven remaining survivors had the energy to climb out of the pit, much less travel any distance. Two of the rescuers had been offered money from the fathers to bring a child back out—fifty dollars was a lot of money at the time. They each chose a small child and carried them out on their back.

They can't be blamed for taking only one—anything more would have seriously jeopardized their own lives.

But John Schull Stark was the third man, and he was not your average twenty-year-old. He was massively large, extremely strong, and he was a man with strong morals. He would not leave without taking every last survivor out with him.

They had ninety miles yet to travel, through mountains covered in deep snow. A blizzard could hit any time, and traveling with any nine people would be difficult, but most of the survivors could not even walk. John Stark could have decided those people were *monsters* for consuming their fallen companions in those desperate circumstances, and returned home alone. He hadn't come for a monetary prize. He had come to do what was right.

But when he saw that the father, mother, and seven children (several of whom were not theirs, but whom they were caring for) were about to be left behind to die, he resolved not to leave a single one. He carried all nine of the remaining survivors out of that pit, along with his pack of supplies for one. He could only carry two of them at a time, so during long stretches, he picked two up, climbed ten or fifteen yards, dropped them off, and went back to do the same with the others.

Alone, he saved them all.

The accounts of the survivors say that Mr. Stark made jokes the entire time, never once complaining or criticizing them. When they apologized for being a terrible burden, he joked that they were so light that he could carry them all, if only God had given him a broader back.

Monsters and heroes, you see, often go hand in hand. In fact, no hero truly exists without a monster to slay. It's the reaction to the situation that determines who is a monster and who is a hero.

I've lost count of how many times I've referred to the dragons who invaded Earth as monsters.

The moniker certainly fits the creatures who have burned, electrocuted, and attacked mankind without provocation. But recently, I've begun to wonder about monsters with increasing frequency. When desperate times come, to what lengths will I really go? What kind of person will I reveal myself to be?

A monster?

A hero?

Sometimes I worry that the only thing determining the answer is who's telling the story.

LIZ

Girls don't like me.

They never have.

Maybe it's because I'm not very girly. I don't understand the point of nail polish. I never wear makeup. I'd rather punch a guy than flirt with him. And I'm much more comfortable doing burpees than I am trying on clothes at the mall.

When I got older, I hoped this might change, but when I met the wives and girlfriends of the guys at the gym, they hated me too. They never said that specifically, but I could hear their snide comments, and I saw their glances. Their feelings were clear.

How to fix it wasn't.

The only girls in my life I've been close to are my mother and my sisters, Jade and Coral. My mom's a hippy, my sister Jade is a girly-girl, and my youngest sister Coral's just like me. Thirty pounds of angry in a two-pound bag. No matter how different they all are from one another, they all like me just fine, because that's what family does. They take you as you are, and they appreciate the things about you that make you unique.

I wasn't surprised when Ocharta, the electro dragon who bonded my mother, hated me. She is a female, dragon or not. On top of that, she hated Axel for being Azar's weakness, and I was bonded to Axel—despised by extension.

The real surprise is how much I like Asteria, Ocharta's sister.

When Azar's brother Hyperion showed up, she came along with him, like a miserable two for one deal. She's the electro dragon who's supposed to *marry* and *mate* with my bonded dragon, Azar, and I do hate her on principle. But she started our acquaintance by acknowledging how awful her sister is, and while Hyperion and Azar are arguing, she's been chatting with me, even though I'm human. Most of the dragons aren't too impressed by us, seeing us as nothing more than useful tools in subjugating the other humans on earth.

But now, it appears she's ready to move on from the mundane topics of climate and resources in Houston. *What do you think of Axel?*

"I like him," I say. "As much as I like any dragon."

She half-smiles. A dragon's half-smiling about my distaste for dragons. *I imagine our return hasn't been easy for you.*

"You can say that a dozen more times," I say, "and not even begin to cover it. Three and a half million." I shake my head. "That was the humans' estimate of how many humans you'd killed when last I checked."

You liked Axel, and yet, you let Azar take your bond.

Like everyone else, she sees Azar and Axel as completely different dragons—the red fire dragon prince who can eat nukes, and the golden, wingless earth dragon prince. "Right." To all of them, it's a big deal that my bond 'transferred' from Axel to Azar, when in fact all that happened was I discovered Axel's secret and started guarding it along with him.

Did it upset you? Was it hard?

"Actually, I just wish I could replicate it," I say.

Her eyes widen.

"Not for me," I clarify. "I'm happy to be bonded to Azar, but not every Ensnared is bonded to a dragon they like."

So you do like Azar, too.

"We're entwined," I say. "I don't think that happens when you hate each other."

She looks. . .contemplative. I can't say that I've ever seen a dragon look contemplative, not in the month they've been here.

"More specifically, your sister's bonded to my mother." I'm not sure why I told her that, except that she almost seems to be reasonable, and I'm guessing she'll find out soon enough on her own. It's not a secret.

You wish she wasn't.

"Azar was going to kill your sister," I whisper. "The only reason he didn't—"

Was because you entreated him not to, so your mother's life would be spared.

I nod.

But you wish he could *kill her.*

I could lie, but I don't bother. Instead, I shrug. "My mom does, too."

Tell me how you passed your bond, and I'll attempt to take your mother's from my sister.

Her offer floors me. "You. . . You'll what?"

She'd still be bonded against her will to a strike blessed, but I vow to try and make amends for my sister's actions.

She's trying to win me over, because I'm bonded to Azar and she's his fiancée. Of course she wants me to like her, because he might listen to what I say.

Actually, I reinforced her suspicion that he might like me by telling her I'm the reason he spared Ocharta. "He only wanted to kill your sister because she kept challenging him." I sigh. "It's not because—"

She tried to kill you. That's how she challenged him.

I can't argue with that.

And you were Axel's bonded at the time, but shortly after, Azar took your bond. He cared enough about your life to steal you from his best friend, so that he could better care for you.

Not exactly, but I'm not sure how I can clarify without revealing the Axel-Azar connection, so I just shrug again. "It was a little more complicated and accidental than that."

Is Axel upset?

I glance at Azar and Hyperion, pacing up and down the street, clearly talking to one another on a frequency we can't hear, both agitated.

"Why are they fighting?" I ask. "Do you know?"

Probably the same as always, she says. *Hyperion thinks Azar's too small because he doesn't eat properly.*

Of all the things in the world I expected her to say, that was not it. It makes me laugh. So much for Azar's claim that dragon families are different. If I counted all the times my mom and dad stood over us, trying to lecture us into eating our dinner, they'd be almost infinite.

I'm no expert on dragon expressions, but I swear Asteria's reaction to my laugher isn't conspiratorial. It's. . .more like confused. Maybe I misinterpreted her. Was it not a joke after all? Is Azar really not eating enough?

Before I have a chance to follow up on her answer, Azar spins around and stomps toward us. He may be much smaller than his massive brother—who can barely fit on the four-lane road they're standing on—but Azar's still gargantuan. I think he's eating plenty of pigs or cows or whatever he flies away to consume.

Speaking of—he hasn't left to eat anything since we

entwined. He probably *is* hungry. I'll have to ask him about it. The one time I asked what dragons eat, he kind of evaded the question. Maybe he was just distracted, but it feels odd now that Asteria's mentioned it. Either way, I can't help my cringe when I think of the mangled cow carcass he brought as Axel, then roasted, and then dragged off at my behest right after we bonded.

Even thinking about that makes me laugh. He clearly had to disappear, shift into Azar, roast it, then switch *back* to Axel and return, all without Gordon or Rufus knowing. His life is a strange one, made more complicated by my presence.

I've offered to take Elizabeth's mother's bond from Ocharta, Asteria says, no preamble whatsoever.

Azar freezes. *What?*

She informs me that her mother does not wish to be bonded to my sister, and that Ocharta's life was spared only to save her mother's.

Azar's expressions are a great deal easier to read, probably because of the bundle of sensation that lives in the corner of my brain, which is now a very buzzy yellow.

He's annoyed.

"It's true," I say. "You'd have killed her otherwise."

Which would probably have served us all much better. Asteria huffs.

Is she serious? Does she actually want her sister dead? Maybe Azar was right about dragon families not being close. "I mean, it's not like you'd have to kill her after she releases my mom. I was just saying—"

No. Azar tosses his head, indicating I should climb onto his back.

"No?" I drop my hands on my hips. "That's hardly polite. You could at least—"

The Prince of the Flame isn't polite, Azar snaps. *Get on. Now.*

"If you think I'm going to climb on your back because

you ordered me to, you've lost your scaly mind." My next move will be drawing my swords. "You can be polite to me, or you can fly home alone."

The buzzy yellow softens to a mild gray, but he looks exactly the same. It's not the apology I wanted, but it's something. I sigh dramatically. He's being watched by Asteria and Hyperion, but that doesn't make it okay.

"Maybe I'll have her take my bond, too."

Asteria's eyes widen.

Azar laughs, tiny flames shooting from his nostrils. *Get on my back, you stubborn human. We can talk about the bond shifting later.*

"Fine," I grumble. "You should at least let Asteria try. Whether you kill Ocharta or not, my mom shouldn't be abused by her. None of the humans should, for that matter."

If you could just tell me how you took Elizabeth's bond, then I could—

No, Azar says again.

I thought maybe you'd changed my brother. Hyperion's smiling. *But he's just as rude and unyielding as he ever was.*

He certainly hasn't changed for me. That's the biggest lie girls tell themselves about men the world over—that they'll change.

Not that Azar's a man.

He's a dragon.

I'm not delusional. I know he's a dragon. I take the two steps to reach Azar's shoulder, and then I bang on his leg. If he thinks I'm going to try and scramble nine hundred yards up to his back in front of these two, he really has lost his mind.

Azar drops his shoulder and flattens out his leg so I can climb up more easily. "Still no saddle, though," I mutter.

That makes the bond go light green, which means at least he finds me slightly amusing.

Where's my sister? Asteria asks. *I should see her.*

"She's trapped under a red bubble." And the bond is back to yellow. "What?" I hiss. "She was going to find out. We're leaving for Iceland soon, and we still don't know what to do with her when we go. Right?"

Asteria's now staring at me. Clearly she's getting no answers from Azar.

"He stuck her under there so she couldn't keep doing dumb things, but when we leave, we'll have to either let her out, or leave her stuck. I doubt the humans will let her just go free when they return."

Asteria blinks.

"But, if we could get my mom's bond passed to your friend here." I gesture. "That would be an easier thing to navigate. Right?"

Azar launches into the air with no warning, and I slide sideways, nearly falling off.

Note to self: don't irritate him right before flying. "Whoa there, big red. Humans, even strong ones, can't cling at these kinds of speeds." I frown, the wind whipping my newly-turned-scarlet curls into what I'm sure is going to be an epic wad of tangles. "Or is it velocity? I think that means speed plus direction. I didn't pay much attention in physics."

Your bond wasn't passed, Azar says. *Or did you forget?*

"I remember." I just sort of momentarily overlooked it.

So what exactly do you think Asteria's going to do if she tries to take your mother's from Ocharta, other than fail miserably?

And in the process, get my mom's hopes up... and then let her down again. "I—"

But in that moment, Azar lands with a loud thump in the woods.

Next to Ocharta.

My mother's leaning against a nearby tree, her eyes open and staring, her expression blank. When Asteria and

Hyperion land off to the side of us, her head pivots slightly to take them both in, but she doesn't even look shocked at seeing another fire dragon.

Sister. Ocharta doesn't sound very happy to see Asteria.

That only improves my opinion of Asteria, to be honest.

You're the same as ever, taking things that don't belong to you. Somehow, even saying such bitter things, Asteria manages to sound amused.

He's not yours, Ocharta says. *He left you behind.*

I'm not talking about Azar. Asteria's beautiful, long silver head turns slightly and peers curiously at my mom. *You bonded someone against her will. Why doesn't that surprise me?*

Ocharta slams against the red dome, her lip curling to reveal her teeth. *As if human feelings matter. They're easily overridden. They're a tool, and you're a fool if you believe anything else.* Now Ocharta turns her face upward, toward me. *But the biggest fool of all is our Return Leader. He's allowed a* human *to entwine him.* She shakes her head and huffs. *You're welcome to him.*

And am I welcome to take the bond of your human? Asteria straightens, turning fully to face my mother. *As far as I know, a bond cannot be dissolved, but it can be transferred.* She looks like she's smiling. *Will you allow me to try to take your bond?*

No, Ocharta says. *I don't allow it.*

I'm less concerned about your refusal, Asteria says. *You didn't have permission in the first place.*

Mom stands up. I had begun to think she wasn't allowed to move. "Why would you take my bond?"

She won't, Ocharta snarls. *You're mine forever.*

That's why, Asteria says. *My sister can't be allowed to ruin things that could otherwise be beautiful.* Asteria's head swivels upward, staring at where I'm sitting on Azar's back. *A bond between blessed and human can be a powerful thing, but only if it's voluntary.*

My mother drops to her knees, her face falling into the dirt.

I forbid it, Ocharta hisses.

"I've begged for death." I can barely hear my mother, with the way she's facing the ground.

I realize that Ocharta must be forcing her there.

Mom raises her voice. "No one will grant my wish. I suppose having a different blessed might be my only other option."

What did you do? Asteria asks. *How did you take the bond?*

She's asking Azar a question he can't answer.

"He felt for my bond," I say, "just as you'd feel for the capacity in any human, and then he pulled as hard as he could." I shudder. "It was not comfortable."

Mom's laughter is dark and hollow. "Nothing about this ever has been."

Asteria shifts and her eyes narrow as she stares intently at Mom. And then I feel it, the soul-sucking feeling, like an enormous vacuum's pointed at me and turned to maximum.

My hands tighten on the ridges on Azar's back.

She can't take you, Azar says.

"She's not even trying," I say.

But as the feeling intensifies, I almost wonder.

Is she?

The feeling moves quickly from uncomfortable to painful. It seems like the trees around us should be bowing, their branches whipping toward the source of the vortex-feeling—Asteria. The pain grows slowly, but steadily, until my hands are trembling where they're gripping Azar's red scales.

My mother, however, is shrieking, her body rigid and trembling. Her skin's pale, her eyes rolled back in her head, and her muscles are taut.

"Stop," I say. "It's killing her."

The suction-feeling disappears, and I breathe a heavy sigh of relief. Mom collapses against the dirt, completely spent.

That's not how it felt for you? Asteria looks entirely fine, totally unbothered.

I lean against Azar's back. "Not like that, no, but maybe because Ocharta's fighting it."

Her lovely face sags a bit. *I'll think about it and try again.*

Ocharta's laughing as Azar launches into the sky. I hate leaving my mother like that—prone and lying in the dirt, with her tormentor now free and apparently healed—but I'm not sure what else to do. I didn't even wave at my mom before we bolted.

"Don't you need to, like, tell them you're leaving or something?"

Do what? Azar's head whips around, his left eye studying me.

"Never mind."

Have you considered letting your mother have her wish?

It takes me a moment to realize, with the wind whipping past my head and all, what he's asking. "Do you mean, have I considered letting her die?" I can barely even say the words.

She's miserable, and she wants it—it's probably her only way out.

"That we know of," I say. "She hasn't even seen my siblings yet. I haven't told her they're alive. My mom should've asked about them first thing. She should be fighting tooth and nail for us, but she's not. The worst thing about it is that Mom looks like she's just given up."

That's why I'm asking.

Oh. "She's not herself, that's for sure. But I'm not ready to throw in the towel on freeing her, and—"

You'll torture her until you're ready?

"You're in a bad mood." I think about that. Sure, our attempt there wasn't what Azar wanted, and it didn't go well, but it's not like that was unexpected. "Even if they can't transfer her bond, it's not like people won't believe that you shifted yours. You're a fire dragon, and—"

That's when it hits me.

He's been in a bad mood since before our idea. He was in a bad mood when I was talking to Asteria earlier, but I was too distracted to realize that. "What did Hyperion tell you? What were you arguing about?"

He drops just a hair in our flight path, and my butt lifts up off the seat. That's not uncommon, but it felt like a reaction to my question.

My question that he still hasn't answered.

"What is it, Azar?" I lean closer and grip his back ridge. "What are you hiding?"

Hyperion didn't want to broadcast it when he landed, because he didn't want to undermine my authority with the others, but our father told Hyperion that if I don't go back to see him in the next week to provide an accounting, he's coming here to retrieve me.

Hyperion and Azar's much larger, much scarier, and much less reasonable father is coming here, to earth? That threat's a good reason to be in a bad mood.

"But that's an easy fix, right?" I ask. "Just go see him. You've done nothing wrong."

My bond flares bright red. *I'd have to take you with me, and I don't trust my father not to kill you. He's not a fan of humans.*

Which makes him angry, or nervous, or worried. . .but it shouldn't really be a big deal to him. If I die, then what? He'll be sick for a few days. It would be an inconvenience. But for me, his protection's the only thing that would stand between his father's wrath and my life.

It also seems like he's not very confident he can keep me safe.

The stakes we're playing for are very different, and this

puts things into perspective. I've been an idiot, getting jealous about Asteria and worrying about our future together. We aren't partners. We aren't even on the same side. It's not news to me, but somehow, I've let myself get lost, living with the enemy.

It's time for me to find my way out of this mess, just like my mother, or like he suggested I do for my mother, I'll wind up dead.

Or worse, I'll become a monster myself.

❦ 2 ❦
AXEL

As a hatchling, I was alternately adored and despised, depending on the color of my scales. When they were red, everyone was kind, solicitous, and polite. When they were gold, half the blessed looked at me like they wanted to eat me, and half looked like they wanted to kick me.

It was confusing and frustrating and unfair—I was the same either way.

But I always had Euphrasia by my side. Sometimes I caught her staring longingly at the waves on the shore, so I know it was hard for her to stay with me for so many years, but she did. Without her, the other blessed would surely have known what an abomination I truly was and tried to destroy me from the start. She kept me safe until I was large enough and smart enough to keep my secret on my own.

Had I not been raised by Euphrasia, I'd never have understood the way that Liz feels about her mother, her brother, and her sisters. She's practically trembling when I land, after explaining that in a week, we'll either need to visit my father, or risk him coming to Earth. I'm not sure which would be worse, but I worry that either way, Liz will be in danger.

Hyperion inexplicably likes Liz, and he even appears to be on my side with regard to protecting my bonded human. He thinks we might be able to put Dad off, but only if he goes in my place and has some good news to report. Without tangible progress on locating the heart, we don't have a lot of options. It took us days to subdue the local population here and make any real efforts at locating the heart once we arrived, so I'm not sure that forging ahead quickly with our move will be enough.

Hyperion had another suggestion, but it put me in a bad mood.

Liz slides off my back the very second I land and stomps her way down to the main area we use when I'm Azar. Once she's in the living area, she starts pacing, taking big, bold steps from one side of the entryway all the way to the dining room and back.

When she's agitated, she always paces.

I decide to shift—she's more accustomed to talking than using mental energy to convey her thoughts. It's the same reason we mostly speak in English when we're alone, even though she can speak and comprehend our tongue thanks to the magic of the bond.

"Oh." She freezes, her eyes widening. "You're wearing jeans."

"Is that alright?" I ask.

She swallows, her eyes still strained on my torso for some reason. "That shirt's pretty small."

"It's the size Gideon always wears. I thought maybe it was a current style."

Her lip twitches with what I've come to recognize as partially disguised mirth. "You're copying *Gideon* now?" Her eyes finally rise to meet mine, their greenish-golden flecks almost sparkling. She's happier than I expect her to be, in light of the recent news.

"You're not distressed anymore?"

"About your dad?" She sinks onto a large leather wing chair she dragged from the corner into the edge of the family room yesterday, before my brother showed up with his pile of bad news.

"What else?"

She shrugs and slumps down into the chair. "Hm, let's see. Your fiancée couldn't manage to take my mom's bond, so my siblings still don't even know that she's even alive. Your fiancée, in spite of all my best efforts to hate her, seems lovely. And dragons are still occupying my city, while I'm essentially powerless to do anything." She shakes her head slowly. "I'd say I have plenty of things to be distressed about."

"I don't think I'd call you powerless," I say. "Although we should spend a little bit of time every day testing what exactly your powers are now."

"Testing—wait. Do you mean training me to do things? Magical things? Not, like, magically lobotomizing other humans, but fighting and stuff?" She stands up almost robotically, like she's a puppet and someone has yanked on her strings. Her eyes are bright, though. She's definitely excited about it.

I've also noticed she hasn't been wearing her visor. "I know you don't particularly enjoy having the power to control other humans, but the whole reason—"

"No." She shakes her head. "I don't like it."

"Your visor focuses all your abilities. It's not just to augment your powers of mind control."

"Even so," she says. "I don't like wearing it. It looks like I'm one of the pod people."

"It's tied to me," I say. "And wearing it will help you identify what strengths you've gained."

She glowers, but she pulls it out of a box at the edge of the room and slams it into place on her face, the metal wings snapping upward as they're engaged. "It still feels like a collar."

With the mood she's in, fighting may not be the best idea. "We do have a lot going on today. Maybe we start the training tomorrow."

But my bloodthirsty little lunatic has already drawn her swords. I can't help my smile. I've adored her feral nature since she stabbed me with that defunct umbrella the day we met.

"More than practicing with the swords, we need to see what you're able to—"

"What exactly can *you* do in this shape?" She eyes me intently, her gaze dropping slowly from my face, downward.

For some reason, her gaze sends a little tingle from the back of my neck all the way down my body. This humanoid form is strange and it irritates me more than anything else. I don't feel quite at ease in it, probably because I'm so vulnerable. How humans can walk around with a mushy-squishy exterior is beyond me. One puff of flame, one snap of teeth, and they're nothing more than goo.

Even their internal support system is so frail. Mine is much stronger, but it's still less substantial than my typical blessed frame.

"Can you. . .throw fireballs when you're pretending to be human?" She arches one eyebrow. "Or, I don't know. Dig a big hole?"

"I haven't ever tried to control fire as a human. Remember, in this form, I'm Axel."

She glances around the room like she just revealed my secret to the world, her mouth slightly parted, her breathing staccato.

"Liz, no one's here."

"I swear, Axel, this whole thing's going to turn my hair grey. I'm not good with secrets."

"Why would your hair—"

"Never mind." She huffs. "Alright, I'm going to try to replicate it. When you want to make a fireball, what do you do?"

I shrug, lift one hand and fling two fingers. A tiny fireball a few times the size of that little mongrel the kids love, Fluff Dog, materializes in front of me and flies through the air, crashing into an end table and incinerating it before I snuff it out.

"Axel, that table was so pretty!" I like how she looks when her cheeks are flushed and she's agitated. It makes the bond between us thrum.

"There are many nice tables in the world, Liz."

"But that was our table."

I like that word, our. She hardly ever uses it in reference to me, but every time she does, I feel warm inside. Like I'm lying on the hot clay ground in front of Canterfall Lake, soaking up the rays of the sun on a slow, lazy day.

Slow and lazy days were rare for me, which made me treasure them more. So I don't care about the table. I'd blow up a hundred more to make her fuss at me just like that again.

"You try it," I say.

"No way," she says. "There's only one more table, and—"

"Try to make a fireball." I roll my eyes. The blessed never do that, but we really should. It's quite gratifying when you want to show someone that you believe they said something idiotic. "I'll snuff it out before destroying the other dead tree arranged in a way that you so admire."

"You're being annoying today." But she holds out one hand, and she squints, and she grunts and flips two fingers. Nothing happens, so she shifts, and then she huffs, and she tries the fingers again.

"The fingers weren't the important part," I say. "You need to feel the magic build inside of you, and then release it in the direction and with the purpose you desire."

"That makes no sense," she says. "There's no magic inside me, and I can't release something that isn't there, much less direct it."

I grab a vase I know she likes—though for the life of me, I'm not sure why humans want to display dead vegetation all over the place. It's macabre—and toss it up into the air.

"Axel!" Her eyes fly wide and she flings her hands out in front of her, but nothing happens. The vase shatters when it hits the marble floor. "Why didn't you stop it?"

The bond's practically vibrating with her anger.

"That was jade. It cost more than I've made in my lifetime."

"I can't freeze things mid-air like you did with Gideon," I say. "I would have done it if I could."

"But—you—then why did you fling it up like that?"

"I thought you liked the vase," I say. "So I hoped you'd save it without thinking. What did you think we'd be doing?"

"I thought you'd be a better trainer," she mutters.

"What does that mean?"

"The summer after kindergarten—the first year of school for humans—every other kid was getting swim lessons. Not me. My mom said that was for spoiled little rich kids. She took us to the neighborhood pool and threw me in."

I don't understand. "You didn't know how to swim?"

She splutters. "I suppose dragons are like dogs—you're born swimming?"

I shrug. "Not all of us like it, but yes, those of us who are gifted just know how to do it naturally."

"Well, buster, humans aren't like that. We have to learn

how to swim, and it's a whole thing. But I figured it out that day. . .so I didn't drown."

"Then it worked."

"It was unnecessarily traumatic," Liz says. "All those other kids learned over a period of several weeks. They started by putting their faces in the water and blowing bubbles. And then slowly, surely, one paddle at a time, the instructor drew farther and farther away and they learned to move their bodies the right way to navigate through the water."

"But you learned what took them weeks and weeks in mere minutes."

"Yes," she says, "but I could have died doing it."

"Your mother would have pulled you out."

"Maybe," she says. "Maybe it would've been too late." She looks more annoyed than angry now, and the bond is much calmer. This closer bond, paired with watching her face and her words, is helping me a *lot* with understanding how to read humans.

"Alright, what kind of training did you have in mind?" I ask.

"I didn't think we'd be doing it around nice, breakable things, and I didn't expect that you'd have no idea what you were doing. Weren't you trained? Can't you do for me what they did for you?"

"I wasn't dropped into a pool, but that was a lot closer to how my training went."

"What does that mean?"

"When it was time for me to fly, I was shoved off a cliff."

Liz edges away from the window.

I laugh. "I'm hardly going to push you out the window. You don't even have wings."

"Euphrasia seems nice. I didn't expect that from her."

"She didn't do it," I say. "She can't fly herself. It was my father. He also encouraged my brothers to try and kill me. That's how I learned to fight."

"Your dad sounds lovely. I can't wait to meet him." She frowns. "Did he hear you're entwined? Is that why he's demanding that you go back?"

"Not exactly," I say. "I was supposed to be going back periodically for meetings, since flame blessed are the only ones who can teleport, but then I met you and I couldn't leave you here, so. . ."

She closes her eyes and the bond grows heavy. "Great."

"What?" I step closer. It used to amuse me, but now that we're entwined, I find that I hate when she's upset.

She shakes her head and opens her eyes. "It feels like every problem you have is my fault."

"I'm the one who broke the vase and incinerated the table."

She rolls her eyes.

"The other stuff isn't your fault either," I say. "You're not the cause of my huge secret, and it's not your fault your mother's bond can't be transferred but people think it probably can. Those things are my fault."

"The fact that your dad's all demanding and sending you a fabulous fiancée isn't my fault either." Her bottom lip's poking out now.

"I don't understand why you seem upset by the mere existence of Asteria. You looked like you were getting along earlier."

She huffs and then starts pacing again, so something about Asteria's definitely agitating Liz. It's a good thing I haven't yet shared Hyperion's plan.

I've learned Liz usually does this, the huffing and the pacing, right before she explodes with a lot of angry words. Sometimes she just needs a little nudge to spit them out. "Do you like her or hate her? And why?"

She stops, pivots on her heel, and faces me head on.

Here it comes.

"She's *fine*." Then she goes back to pacing.

Now I have no idea what's happening. Poking at and pushing her like that has never not worked.

"Alright, well, until you want to tell me why you like her and hate her, maybe we should keep trying to—"

"I want to see my family, and I want to see Fluff Dog." She heads for the elevator bay.

"We have a lot of things—"

"Sometimes you don't have to attack things head-on in order to fix them, you know. Sometimes the solution just comes to you when you're doing something else."

What's she talking about? "Solutions never just—"

She holds up a finger and shakes her head. "Don't."

Don't *what*? I swear, humans are the finickiest creatures I have ever encountered.

She gets in the elevator and closes the doors before I can get on. Running down the stairs to reach the elevator bay before she can disappear doesn't put me in a wonderful state of mind. Even that amount of distance between us is a little uncomfortable, but maybe it's a good thing for us to practice having some space. The records say that entwined can only comfortably be apart once their bond is healthy and strong, but maybe that's not right. Maybe it gets stronger in the same way humans apparently develop muscles.

Through practice.

When Liz steps off the elevator and sees me, her eyes spark. "Of all the—"

"I think it's a good idea for you to spend some time with your family, without me," I say. "In fact, maybe I should fly as far away as I can. We can give that a try and see how you do."

"How I do?" Her brow furrows.

"If we can get used to being apart, I could go to see my dad without you." That would solve a lot of problems.

"Oh." She nods. "Okay."

"Okay?"

"Sure," she says. "Try and fly away." But then she frowns. "How will you know whether it's working?"

I tap my head. "Pretty sure the bond will let me know."

"Duh." She smiles. "Yes, I think we both need just a little bit of space."

I hate the sound of that, but I like her smile, so I swallow my irritation and watch as she disappears into her family's floor of rooms.

But I'm a little worried this may be my worst idea yet.

3

LIZ

Just before the dragons came, Gideon told me he was quitting—retiring from the world of mixed martial arts. He was joining special forces.

I had complicated emotions about it, but mostly I was excited.

For ten years or more, I've wondered whether Gideon and I might. . .when I doodled my name on my notebook in school, the only name other than Chadwick that I ever tacked onto the end of Elizabeth was his.

Elizabeth *Evans*.

It even looked nice. Cheesy, but nice.

Because Gideon and I have always been a perfect match. He's tall, and so am I. He's a natural fighter with a gift for pulling off wins no one expects—same. He's dedicated and disciplined and driven in the exact same ways as me. We even lived close, and sometimes, at night, he'd ride his bike over, climb through the window into my room, and lie on the floor next to my bed. He knew about my nightmares, and he wanted to help slay the imaginary demons that plagued me.

I didn't get nightmares as often as I grew older, but I never got them when Gideon was asleep on my floor.

He and I might have been an epic disaster in a relationship, or maybe not. Either way, we never got the chance, so there's no awkward interchanges or sordid past to contend with. There's nothing but my own memory of the possibility.

Of course, there's still a chance that the dragons might locate this heart thing and leave.

But now that I'm entwined, there's not much hope that I'll be left unless I can somehow work out how to be separated from Azar for more than ten minutes. For about a day, I was kind of freaking out that he now has a dragon fiancée, which was completely insane.

I mean, he's a *dragon*. Who cares whether they matched him up with someone equally scaly? I'm a human. My future can't be with a dragon-man-dragon who has loads of secrets and a lot of questions I never want to answer.

Oh, and by the way. . . He now wants to drag me to the place in Iceland that stars in every single one of my nightmares so that I can help him find something that's probably in the middle of a volcano. The last thing I want to do is star in my very own version of *Lord of the Rings*. I'm definitely no Frodo.

I zipped through the front entry of the apartment my siblings and Gideon are sharing, but I've been standing in the foyer alone for. . .at least a minute now. No one has even noticed I'm here. "Your security sucks," I shout.

"Our security?" Gideon walks out of his room, a towel around his waist, running one hand through his clearly wet hair. "What do you mean, security?"

"What—where—my—" I was not expecting to see this much of him. In fact, I can't remember the last time I saw him without a shirt on. At the gym, we train together a lot, but we don't share a locker room, obviously, and this is just so much *more* than I'm equipped to handle right now.

He's not as bulky as Axel—why am I thinking about Axel? I'm supposed to be practicing staying away from him. I'm probably just thinking about him because he's the last man I saw shirtless.

Not that he's a man.

I know he's not.

"Sammy, Coral, and Jade went downstairs."

"Downstairs?"

"They've been begging Rufus and Gordon to let them race for a while, and—"

"Race?"

Gideon's suppressing a smile. "Sammy's positive that Gordon's faster than Rufus, but I can't imagine, with his tiny legs, that—"

"You're letting them *race* on dragons?"

"They can't go outside or the other dragons will realize they're brights, or future-brights?" He shrugs. "I'm unclear. But either way, they've been stuck inside for weeks now, at the house before here, obviously, and they couldn't—"

"Race?"

He shrugs. "Kids love racing. They all do."

And there aren't any other kids for them to race in a normal way—on foot or bikes.

The dragons, in a surprising show of decency, transported all the children to the border of the city and dumped them over a period of several weeks after first arriving. My brother and sisters would stand out like sore thumbs if they were to go outside. But the scariest thing of all would be the others discovering their connection to me. Brights—humans capable of being bonded by dragons and controlling other humans—run in families, and in an attempt to curry favor, there's no way to know how many of the other dragons might try to bond them. Axel says they're super safe here, but the last thing I need is for him to be wrong.

I can't even imagine another Ocharta-adjacent situation.

Actually, keeping their existence a secret is one of the main reasons Mom hasn't seen them yet. That, and Mom's incessant requests that I mercy-kill her. The last thing the kiddos need is to see their mom begging to die.

In any case, earth dragons are relatively safe around the kids, since they can't bond humans, and Axel seems to trust Gordon and Rufus. Plus, I feel like the snake and lizard-looking dragons genuinely like Coral, Jade, and Sammy. I'm just not sure quite what that's worth in the dragons' world. Are they the kind of critters that are often fond of their food? Like, humans having a lobster tank and naming one of them Spotty and one of them Speckles?

I almost rip Gideon a new one for cavalierly letting them go down there, but I realize it's kind of pointless. It's not like he would stand much of a chance in an argument with two dragons.

"What are *you* doing here?" he asks. "I never get to see you without one of *them* tagging along."

Axel or Azar. He has no idea they're the same person, of course. He can't know. He thinks that Axel actually likes me—as if he even knows how to care about someone properly—and that the two of them are forcing me to like them back.

"Azar told me that we can only handle being apart once we've spent enough time together to be in sync or something."

Azar launches from the apartment upstairs into the sky and begins to move away from me. I grunt and wrap one arm around my stomach, not that it helps in any way.

"Are you alright?" Gideon's eyes scan me head to toe, looking for some kind of malady.

"Fine," I say. "We've decided that, just in case that's not quite right, maybe we should try getting a little bit of time and distance from one another. See if we can—" I freeze as a pulse of pain pounds through me.

"He's really. . .what? Just flying away?"

I nod.

"That's—can he hear me right now? Through the bond?"

"I'm not sure," I say. "I can't hear him, but I don't know whether he's communicating with anyone else." I don't bother explaining that most dragons communicate exclusively telepathically, and that isn't as easy to monitor through the bond anyway.

He sighs. "It seems like you should know more about this by now."

"You know, I accidentally threw the *How to Manage Your Conquering Dragon* manual away." I snap my fingers. "What was I thinking?"

His smile's wry. "Well, listen. This may end with me being roasted over a spit, but I've learned never to miss my window." He steps closer.

"Um, you're wearing a towel." I can't help my eyes tracking down his torso to where the towel meets the bare, gleaming skin of his waist.

"Right." He nods. "But there may not be time—listen to me for a second, okay?"

I shrug, another pulse of discomfort rolling over me. Now that I know it's coming, I can take it better. Maybe we can do this. Maybe by practicing dealing with—another wave hits, and I grit my teeth.

Gideon clears his throat and looks around. And then he starts to whisper. "I know they're forcing you to do and say things now. Azar's stronger or more demanding than Axel, but even with him at the helm, you're still you. I know you're in there."

"Gideon," I say. "I *am* still me. All the time." Another wave hits, and my nostrils flare.

He notices. "It hurts you for him to leave, like, physically hurts you."

I shrug.

"But while he's gone, we should come up with a plan. I have a way to get a message out, I think. Or, an idea, anyway. I'm not going to share that for obvious reasons, but listen. How terrible do the dragons feel if their Ensnared humans are killed?"

I don't love where he's going with this. "Not good," I say. "I'm not sure how long they're down, but I got the distinct impression it would incapacitate them. Or at least, they all thought that killing me would make Axel easy to defeat."

"The red nightmares are the two beasts that no one can destroy. Without them, the others are much more vulnerable." He lowers his voice to a mutter. "If you consider the humans needing to use blunt force trauma to rip off their heads 'vulnerable.'"

Part of me agrees with him. Part of me is horrified at the idea that if they could only remove the two red ones. . . "Are you suggesting. . .that I kill myself?"

His entire face falls. "Liz."

"It's a decent plan, but Gideon." I have to freeze for a moment, while I ride the worst wave of pain yet. My hands are shaking when I finally start talking again. "There are two fire dragons now, and Hyperion doesn't have a bonded human."

"But if ripping you away from the other one stuns him," Gideon says, avoiding Azar's name like using it might summon him, "and killing the other humans incapacitates the other dragons. . ." He shrugs. "We might have a chance."

When did I stop thinking about ways to take the

dragons down? When did I become complicit in their plans here, to subjugate whatever humans they need to in order to find this heart? I start pacing a little, walking all the way into the living room and back to the foyer, pausing only when another pulse of misery threatens to drown me.

I'm getting better at ignoring the pain waves, and they don't seem to be worsening. They're more consistent, but not more incapacitating. "What do you want me to do?"

"Nothing," Gideon says. "It's too dangerous to have you thinking about this at all. But when you see us making our move, get as far from the red one as you can."

Can I do that? I mean, I *am* trying right now. But increasing the latitude I'll have to operate apart from or against Azar may not be enough. Plus, we're not making a lot of progress. "You're wasting your time if you're focused on a plan with the US Military. It was delayed, but we really are leaving for Iceland soon."

Gideon frowns. "Are you worried about it?"

"You mean because of my kidnapping when I was little?" I'm whispering the words, and I hate that the memory still has the power to upset me. I shake my head. "Of course not. I have a massive dragon at my back this time."

"A dragon that's its own kind of nightmare."

I can't argue with that.

"What I can't understand is *why* are we going to Iceland?"

"You mean, why Iceland, instead of, say, Louisiana?"

He nods.

"The thing is, you know I have a strange birthmark." He's seen it, so without even gesturing, his eyes drop to my chest. "It's—"

"In the shape of a heart."

"Well, anyway, Azar saw the memory of what happened when I got kidnapped, and how the people in Iceland kept chanting hjartanu, which apparently means heart, and now he thinks we need to check there for some connection to what the dragons are looking for."

"What are they looking for?"

Duh. He has no idea, of course. "They want something that's called the heart, and that's as much as I know. It may be all they know, or maybe it's all they've been willing to share. Either way." I shrug. And then I double over, bracing my hand against the windowsill overlooking the courtyard far down below as I recalibrate from yet another miserable wave of pain.

The crash followed by a shuddering feeling down below us takes us both by surprise.

"What was that?" I'm asking at the same time as we see the windows below us explode outward, and a dragon goes flying through—a large brown, snake-like dragon.

With a tiny little boy on his back.

Without thinking, I throw my hand outward, and scream, "No!"

Sammy's tiny body freezes mid-air.

I feel it then, as a terrible, rippling tidal wave of pain crashes over me. "I can't let go," I shout. "But I can't hold on much longer." I can sense it now, like a massive ball of churning energy in my head, right between my eyes. I'm pulling energy from it and I'm directing it at my brother and it's working.

He's floating in the air, wobbling only slightly in the breeze.

Gideon vaults over the sofa in front of him and flings the balcony open. He's leaning against the railing, his hands reaching for Sammy, but Sammy's several floors below, and Gideon's way too small to come close to reaching him.

Down below, I sense other dragons gathering, and through the window, I see silver ones whipping through the air, but I can't trust any of them to help.

Until a wall of air slams into me, billowing aggressively through the patio door, and my monstrous red dragon snatches Sammy with his claws, banking and flying upward.

I finally let go, and then I hear the shout, but not in time to help.

I rush to the edge of the railing in time to watch Gordon slam into the ground with a wet-sounding thwack.

"You were holding him too," Gideon says. "You were suspending that huge beast in the air."

I didn't even realize it.

Azar flies back by, this time much slower, and I reach out and take Sammy from his extended talons. At least the waves of pain are gone, and it looks like Sammy's just fine.

"I'm so sorry I dropped Gordon," I wheeze. "I didn't realize I had him too."

Gordon's fine now, Azar says. *A little flattened, but fine. Wait until I'm done with him.*

I can't help feeling pleased that he's upset with his friend for endangering my little brother. I know he's probably just upset that his orders weren't followed, but I can't help hoping that there's some small affection there.

The fact that you suspended him in air at all is astonishing. Our training must not have been a total failure. But Azar's massive wings are flapping consistently to hold him aloft, and apparently it's one flap too many. . . for Gideon's towel.

When it flies off, fluttering over the edge of the balcony and disappearing, leaving Gideon entirely naked, I gasp, and then I spin around in the other direction. I hate the heat I feel rising in my cheeks.

I thought you were going to see your family. What exactly were you two doing in here before Gordon destroyed the side of my tower?

I really shouldn't tell him we were planning to kill all the dragons, but based on the flashing of his eyes, he might prefer the truth to his guess.

4

AXEL

Elizabeth insists that her friend passes as a warrior with the humans, but looking at him without his cloth coverings, I can't see how. Human forms are all inherently weak—no armor over their soft parts at all—but Gideon looks exactly the same as all the others.

The strike blessed flying past me is as unimpressed with Gideon as I am, but she's definitely eyeing the small boy clutched in my bonded's arms with great interest.

Who is that? Does it belong to the Elizabeth Chadwick?

It's not the *Elizabeth Chadwick,* I snap. *Her name* is *Elizabeth Chadwick.*

And that child belongs to her? Memna whips around to get another look, until I blow a stream of fire that sends them all careening away.

It's too late, though. Our days of hiding the existence of Sammy, Coral, and Jade and their relationship to my bonded are over.

But worse than the other blessed learning about Elizabeth's siblings are those milling about below who are murmuring about the other oddity they witnessed—a human holding a blessed suspended in air for more than sixty seconds. As far as I know, nothing like that has ever been recorded.

Only sixty or so strike blessed have bonded humans. Another sixty or eighty of the water blessed bonded a partner as well. All told, there are less than two hundred Ensnared, but that's likely to change. Now they'll all want one—and they've just discovered there are miniature versions of Liz, or at least one, and there's no way we'll keep their relationship a secret now that the blessed are looking for them. We hid them in plain sight as regular humans before easily enough, but Liz wouldn't cradle a tiny regular human in her arms.

It's really not the best time for this, either, what with the other problems already circling.

Liz and I both dealt with rolling waves of pain when I tried to separate from her, and I only flew a few miles away. I can't even contemplate teleporting home without her. I know Dad hates this planet and humans, or he'd be here leading the hunt for the heart himself. But bringing her back home with me is. . .inadvisable.

Forcing Dad to come here would likely be worse.

I drop down and check on Gordon, ensuring that he'll recover, and then I send the gathered blessed away. I also fly to the floor below Liz, where Gordon exploded through the wall. I make a red energy bubble to keep anyone else from bursting through, and then I vault upward to the top floor and shift into my human shape. I didn't like the look of shock on Liz's face, and I really disliked the strange sensation coming from the bond when that white flag whipped off, leaving all of Gideon bare.

Was she with that *Gideon* the whole time I was gone?

Where were her siblings and Gordon and Rufus? How did poor Sammy wind up blowing through the side of the building? What was Gordon doing, exactly? He's recovering down on the ground, but he wasn't in shape for an interrogation. Besides, as Azar, I have only the slightest connection to Gordon. I couldn't really linger, asking lots of questions, without drawing far too much interest.

And yet, there are many questions to which I still require answers. I shift into jeans and a t-shirt because that seems to be the clothing Liz favors most. Not that I need to look like her or dress as she desires, but sometimes it feels easier.

Stomping downstairs in human form is slow, and that's irritating in the extreme. It gives me plenty of time to wonder what to do about my dad, what to do about Gordon, why Gideon was with Liz alone, and what to do with him. It's irritating that he shows up so often. If only he were intelligent enough to be a bright, someone could bond him, but no such luck.

By the time I finally reach the right floor, Gideon's stepping out of his room, this time with pants on. He's buttoning up his shirt.

"So you do have clothing."

"Are you jealous of me?" Gideon's smiling. "I suppose dragons aren't very well endowed?"

Endowed? What's he talking about?

"Axel!" Liz practically jogs my direction, and I can feel the same thing as I imagine she can, an easing of the bond as she draws near.

"How are you two still so weird, now that she's bonded to Azar?" Gideon asks.

"I'm bonded to them both," Liz says.

Gideon blinks.

"That's not—" I hiss. "You can't just—"

"It's never happened before," she says. "And it's a little complicated, passing a bond."

"So, wait," Gideon says. "You're bonded to him?" He points at me. "But you're like, entwined with his best friend?"

Her eyes light up. "Yes, that's it. I'm bonded to him, but I'm more connected to Azar." She bobs her head.

"Are your siblings all safe?" I ask, scanning the apartment.

"Sammy was a little freaked out." She sighs heavily. "But he's fine now, I think. It was Coral's brilliant idea to *race* Rufus and Gordon, even though they couldn't go outside to do it, but then Rufus said the apartment below them had a really long hallway, and—" She cuts off and sighs again. "They're fine, and after the tongue-lashing I gave them, they won't be doing anything that stupid again any time soon."

"Good." I grab her arm. "Then we need to talk."

"But—" Gideon tries to grab her other arm.

A growl forms deep inside my chest, like the rumble of an angry blessed. It sounds strange coming from this small human shape.

Liz's arm twists and suddenly my arm's behind my back, and it hurts. "What's that? What are you doing?"

Instead of answering me, she kicks Gideon, and then she drops my arm. "Let's go."

"What was all that for?" I shift my shoulder up, working out the discomfort.

At the same moment, Gideon says, "Hey, why'd you kick me?"

"Neither of you should be grabbing people and bossing them around." But she marches to the elevator with me, chin held high. "I'll be back later, Gideon. Make sure the munchkins are fine."

He blinks.

"We do have some things to talk about."

Gideon's scowling as I shut the door on his irritating face. I planned to shout at Liz the second I could—she really can't go around telling people things without talking them through with me first. I'd already told Gideon we were romantically involved. But now that we're alone, I realize that her story does make more sense.

Also, she has both an earth and a flame brand on her shoulder blades. If anyone ever sees them. . .

Her explanation addresses their existence.

"He didn't believe it." She shrugs. "He kept asking why you were still coming around. He thought you were mind controlling me."

"It's fine," I say. "But you should check in before you just say things."

"Sorry." Her lips compress, and a little ripple runs through the bond. Is that what it feels like when she really is apologetic?

The elevator bings and the doors open before I ask, "What does *endowed* mean?"

Liz is frowning as she steps off. "Endowed? Like, from on high?"

Now I'm frowning too. "Maybe. I'm not sure."

"I think it means, like, a gift. But it might depend how it's being used. When did you hear the word?"

"Gideon asked if I was jealous." I can't help my snort. How could I possibly be jealous of him? "And then he said dragons aren't well endowed."

Her eyes dart down toward my pants and back up at my eyes.

And now I'm even more confused. "What did you mean, from on high? Does endowed have to do with being in the mountains or up in the sky? Because it felt like he was saying he was better at it than me, but I know he can't fly at all."

She claps a hand over my mouth without any warning, and suddenly, I'm staring into her eyes.

Her big, green, intent eyes.

"What's going on?" I try to ask, but it comes out like *whuningnon?*

But she shakes her head. "I forbid you to ask me about that." Thankfully, she drops her hand.

Or maybe not thankfully. I kind of liked having her pressed up against me, her hand pressed against my mouth. "I can't ask about dragons being endowed?" My eyebrows shoot up. "Why not?"

She swallows, her eyes shooting upward to look at the ceiling.

I follow her line of vision. "Is it something to do with the ceiling?"

"No asking about any of that again." Liz's voice is squeaky. "And no more asking me for lessons on kissing either, while we're making rules."

"Fine." I fold my arms. "I won't train you to use your powers any more, then."

She glares. "You suck at doing it anyway."

"I don't," I say. "You're just bad at learning."

"Whatever." She spins on her heel and starts to stomp away.

I reach for her wrist, then remember that made her mad downstairs, so I follow her instead. "Hey, we still have to talk, remember?"

She pivots and I nearly slam into her. "About what?" She lifts her eyebrows. "I told you I'll check in before making up any more lies that aren't lies."

"What?"

"I *am* bonded to you both," she says. "I just realized that owning up to that part made more sense."

"You should still check with me first."

"Noted." One eyebrow's still raised, and I realize she's annoyed with me. But why?

"Did something happen while I was gone?"

Some emotion flies through the bond and across her face so quickly that I can't figure out what it is. "Where did you go?"

"Go?" There are so few things I understand about humans that most of what she says makes no sense to me. "I didn't go—"

"When you left to test the bonds, you went somewhere. Was it to see someone? Asteria, maybe?"

But then, something she said earlier catches up to me. "Why do we need a rule that we can't do more kissing lessons?" I narrow my eyes. "Does it have to do with you and Gideon being alone together?" I'm not sure why it bothers me, but for some reason I have to ask. "Were you. . . mating?"

"Were we—" she splutters.

"Were you?" For some reason, a bolt of pure rage shoots through me, and I have an overwhelming desire to fly out the window, crash through the balcony and incinerate Gideon into a pile of soot.

"You said that I can't even kiss him." Her nostrils flare. "So how would we *mate*?"

"What does kissing have to do with—"

Elizabeth starts laughing then. Usually I like it when she laughs, but this is different somehow. It doesn't feel like she's happy. It feels like she's happy *at my expense*.

"What is so funny?" I ask when she finally stops.

"Nothing."

"Your reaction implies that kissing is somehow tied to mating for humans."

"Somehow tied?" Now she's laughing again. "You watched human movies," she says. "You must know they're tied."

"I didn't watch them myself." I shrug. "I said some of the blessed did, and they assimilated the information and then shared what they learned."

"Assimilated..." She shakes her head. "I don't understand."

"It took a lot of data collection to understand the basics

of your languages and culture. We assigned two strike, two earth, and two water blessed to assimilate information before we came, and they then shared that with me. I distributed it to the others."

She's blinking quickly as she looks at me. Then she sits on a chair, her lip shaking a little. "And your assimilated information hasn't given you any information on the connection between kissing and mating?"

"Mating is the creation of offspring—for us, the reproduction cycle begins with the laying of eggs. For you, it's squalling miniature humans. Yes?" Now I start pacing. She's clearly a bad influence on me. "We gained that information, that your young take a similar time to grow as one of our eggs, and that there are no eggs involved. The details surrounding that weren't something we cared to study further."

"What exactly did you study, then?"

"Human patterns and behavior when scared. Human methods of hiding and concealing information. Successful human interrogation techniques."

"You studied our pop culture to figure out how to interrogate us?" Her lip's twitching again. She's amused. "And you discovered what exactly?"

"Humans are selfish, cruel, and fear motivated."

She snorts. "You may not have gone about it the best way, but I can't argue with any of that." She steps out in front of me, interrupting my pacing, and I have to pull up short to avoid running her over. "But Axel, more even than fear, humans are inspired by love."

Something weird happens inside my chest when she says 'inspired by love,' like someone's pulling on my insides or something. I feel twisted up and dizzy and like I'm falling at the same time. "What does that mean exactly, inspired by love?"

"You said we're motivated by fear, and that's true.

When we're afraid of something, we'll do all sorts of things to avoid it and to keep ourselves safe."

"Right." I nod.

"But." She places one hand, palm flat, against my chest. I have that same, strange, wrenching kind of twisting feeling again, only stronger now that she's touching me. "Humans do their best work, their most inspired work, their truly *heroic* work when they want to help someone they love."

"Love." I nod. "Fine. If you won't teach me to kiss, then teach me to love instead."

She almost looks sad, for some reason.

"What? Is that forbidden too?"

"It's a bad idea." Her lips twist, and I want to press mine against them again. I know that kissing was somehow a part of our synchronization when we entwined, and that probably makes it a risk. The last thing we need is to mutate our bond further.

But that thought gives me an idea. Maybe the kissing—even tied to mating though it is for humans in some inexplicable way—will bring us closer, and therefore allow us more space, not less?

Why didn't I think of that before?

Ignoring her earlier prohibition entirely, I move toward her as quickly as I can, and I press my lips to hers. The first few times, I had no idea what to expect. This time, I have a lot of expectations.

Her mouth is just as soft as I knew it would be, her little sigh even more satisfying. I'm reaching my hands out for her hips to draw her closer when something unexpected hits me.

Literally.

Her hand, palm still flat, strikes the center of my chest with enough force to knock me backward, my chin lifting as my head falls back.

It frigging hurts, which it really shouldn't. Any blow she can inflict is nothing to me, but for some reason, this causes pain. Something deep inside of me roars to life, and I advance, ready to conquer this rebellious creature in front of me. I smell her small spike of perspiration, and I'm drawn even more inexorably forward.

She ducks away, racing around corners and around door-frames until she shoots behind a bedroom door and closes it.

"Elizabeth," I whisper. "You were the one who started the violence. Come out and talk to me." Why do I enjoy stalking her so much? Why is this so entertaining?

"No," she whispers. "Stay away."

"We're not done. . .talking." I can't help my smile. Closing in on her at last is always the best part.

"Yes, we are. We're done talking. We're done kissing. We're just done."

"No." I tap on the door one more time, but remaining polite isn't easy. "Open up."

"Not by the hair of my chinny-chin-chin," she says.

"What?"

"Axel, just go away for a little bit, calm down, and then you can come back."

"You struck me."

"You kissed me." She bangs on the other side of the door. "I told you that kissing is against the rules now. That strike was a reminder."

"I think that kissing may be the only way to repair our bond," I say. "And if so, that may be the only way I can go to see my father and still keep you safe."

She ignores me.

"Open. The. Door." I bang politely one more time.

"Axel, Flame and Earth Blessed, go away."

I consider slamming the door hard enough to dislodge the hinges, but that might hurt her. Instead, I shift my fingers just a little bit into talons and grab the frame, sinking them into the wood, and then I flex, ripping the door away from its frame, and flinging it across the floor behind me.

"Axel!" Liz is standing in the doorway, her eyes wide, her breathing shallow.

It's like she's begging me to never look away with all her prey-behavior. I can't help my small smile. "You called?"

"No." She holds out a finger and shakes it. "I didn't call. I yelled. Now go away."

"That's the same thing as calling me." I start toward her again, slowly.

She draws her swords.

And my smile widens. "Yes."

We dance, then. She strikes and parries, attempting to hit me with the swords she stole from me, and I don't hold back, blocking and dodging and striking with small controlled movements that match hers. I don't try to harm her, but I do try to disarm and contain her as well as I can, as fast as I can, and as intently as I can manage.

My tiny little human keeps up remarkably well.

It's impressive.

At least, she does for a while. As she tires, I see my opening. I drop my hands, ball them into fists, and then bring them up underneath hers, dislodging the sword hilts from her grasp and flinging them upward where they slam into the ceiling, sinking into the plaster.

"Gotcha." I move toward her again, slowly and methodically, never looking away.

She backs up until she's pressed against a large gouge mark in the wall. I brace my hands on either side of her face again, and I move in for my prize. "No."

"Why can't I kiss you?" I ask. "Am I really bad at it? Is it painful to you?" Is that why she whimpers? It doesn't feel that way through the bond, but clearly I don't understand humans very well.

"Painful?" Her breath is almost ragged. "Not exactly."

"Then why are you so against it?" I'm leaning toward her as if I'm being towed there, my mouth needing to press against hers again.

"You can't mate with me," she whispers. "You have to mate with that electro dragon. Right?"

I freeze. "If I learn to kiss you better. . .then we have to mate?"

She swallows.

"Elizabeth."

"Not exactly," she says. "But if you're at all like a human, if we. . ." She clears her throat. "If we get good at the kissing, then yes, we'll *want* to mate." Her eyes drop, looking away from me intentionally, as if she's trying to escape, and that hurts.

Like a venomous bite.

Like being flayed open.

For some reason, my entwined looking away from me, shying away in what closely resembles fear, it pains me badly.

"You'll. . .want to mate?" I ask. "With me?"

She shakes her head. "No. Never."

That stings too, a little. "Because I'm blessed."

"Because you're a dragon, and that makes you the enemy."

Without thinking about it, I slide one hand under her chin and tilt her eyes back to mine. "You really think I'm the enemy?" I look into her large, grass-green eyes. "You still do?"

She's scared.

What's she scared of? *Me?*

"You don't even know what love is," she says. "You're not human, so you'll never understand. But for us, kissing, mating, and love, they're all related. And the bond is confusing for me, okay?" Her hand rises and gently curves around my jaw. "You *look* like us, so sometimes it's hard for me to remember that you're *not* like us. You can't love me. You can't be what I, as a human, need."

"What do you need?" Some strange feeling surges inside of me, and I want to be able to do it, whatever that is. It's probably the bond. It's probably that we're entwined, so I want to protect her. That's what she said love is, right? When you want to keep the other person safe? "Maybe I already love you."

"Tell me this," she whispers. "When you find the heart and the dragons finally leave, what happens to me? What happens to all the Ensnared?"

Now I don't want to meet her eyes.

"When you all go home, what happens then to the human girl who can't bear to be very far away from you?" The pulse in the bond tells me that she already knows.

When we find the heart, and I leave, the quandary we face right now with my father will only worsen. "You'll have to come with us, back to our home, and if you refuse. . .you'll die when I leave."

I expect another slap, but this time, she just looks sad as she ducks underneath my arm and walks away.

I don't stop her, not this time. It feels like I've already done enough. For someone I want to protect, I appear to have doomed her.

5

LIZ

It's not like this is some big shock. The second he bonded me, I started thinking endgame. I knew that threatening my life would be a mere inconvenience for him, but my only bargaining chip was my own death even then.

This is hardly new.

But for some reason, after we entwined, I don't know. I thought some things were different.

And they are.

I'm totally screwed, now. No matter what, this bond spells the end of the line for me. I sit in the corner, alone, thinking, for a while. At the end of the day, this is a long-term problem, and it's not really a new one. The dragons are the bad guys, the conquerors, and we're their victims. That's always been true. They can't fall in love. They can't be anything to us but a plague.

So why do I keep forgetting it?

I'm the idiot who was jealous of an electro dragon mating with my captor. I take all of that remaining emotion —complicated by that big jerk trying to kiss me again—and

I shove it away. I wrap it up in bubble wrap, then tie it off in duct tape, and I hide it in the corner.

Never again will I care about Azar. Axel. Whatever.

To make sure that happens, I need to focus more on how much I care about Gideon. I'm actually ashamed that I've been *crushing* or whatever on Axel. Ugh.

Focusing on what matters may also help. Our looming problem has two main prongs. First, we have to figure out a solution to Axel seeing his dad that doesn't kill me, and second, we need to locate that heart and get the dragons out of here ASAP, whether it kills me or not. We can try and figure out how to un-entwine me then. If we can't, well, the loss of a few humans like me is acceptable collateral damage for keeping the world safe.

Finding the heart is the key to all the rest.

I can't help glancing down at my chest—does my weird birthmark and that Icelandic volcano really have anything to do with this heart they're searching for?

Once I'm suitably prepared to face the problem at hand, I march into the family room where Axel's been pacing. "Okay. I have an idea."

"What?" He stops, turning toward me slowly. His golden eyes are reserved, and his entire frame is. . .coiled, almost, like a snake prepared to strike. I hate how gorgeous he is, as if being deadly in every way and magical on top of that wasn't already enough.

"I have a few ideas, actually." I point at the massive dining table that's been swept against the far wall. "Maybe we can sit and talk about them."

He shrugs, following me over to a seat. Once he sits, I stand and move to a different chair. It's better for me to sit across from him than right next to him. I need to remember that we're not on the same team.

"We have one main goal that's the same for both our people—acquiring the heart so you can leave."

He frowns.

"Your brother's arrival has sort of delayed that, since we put off our departure to update him and accommodate the new arrivals."

"We're lucky my father sent him. My other brothers would have attacked me immediately and tried to take control of the Recovery."

Okay, that's news I didn't have. "So, wait, Hyperion's the good brother?"

Axel shrugs. "None of my brothers are really good, but he's better than the others."

"He says you have to report back to your dad quickly," I say. "Right?"

Axel nods.

"But could Hyperion go back to report in your place if he had good news to share?"

"What does that mean?" He narrows his eyes.

"You should mate with Asteria," I say. "Then Hyperion can go back and tell your dad that you're *busy*, and that you did as he asked. He can tell him that we have a, well, sort of a lead on the heart, too. Those people chanting in Iceland were all saying 'the heart,' 'the heart,' 'the heart.' Combined with my birthmark. . ." My hand rises to the spot where I know it's hiding under my shirt, the perfectly shaped reddish heart.

"My father doesn't need to know about the birthmark or your involvement," Axel says. "Just that we have word of a group of humans gathered in front of a volcano, chanting hjartanu over and over."

"Sure," I say. "Okay." But it sounds like he's trying to protect me, and while I like that, I also don't, because it confuses me. "But we need to focus here."

"Focus?" His eyebrows rise.

"You and I?" I stand up, bracing my hands on the tabletop and lean toward him. "We can't kiss. We can't even talk about mating. I wish we'd never entwined."

He looks wounded, like I slapped him, and the bond is a stormy gray.

"Think about it," I say. "Before we entwined, you could've left and I'd have been fine. Now, when you leave, I'll die." I sigh. "I wish we'd left things as they were. I'll help you, but we should try to undo as much of our connection as we possibly can."

"Undo?"

"Maybe if you mate with Asteria, and I spend more time with Gideon, we can—"

Axel explodes to his feet, shoving the solid wood table several inches toward me. "No."

"Oh, come on." I shake my head. "It makes sense. I know you're possessive, and I know a dragon's natural instinct is to *own* things, but—"

In the blink of an eye, he's vaulted over the table. "You can't—with Gideon, I forbid it." He's standing inches away, his chest rising and falling quickly.

"But you're mating with Asteria." I lift my chin, ignoring the surge of anger that makes me feel. "This only works if what you do, I do."

His hand grips the side of the table until his knuckles go white. "Liz, no."

I shove him. "So you can do it, but I can't?"

"*Do it?*" Axel crushes the edge of the table, wood splintering with a crack. "You *belong to me*."

I punch him in the stomach, wishing my swords weren't dangling from a ceiling. Stabbing him would be far more satisfying. "Wrong. No one owns me."

"I do," Axel insists, totally unfazed by being punched. "You're *mine*." This growling thing he's started doing really irritates me—because it's making something deep inside me want to purr, and I will *not* do that. Ever. Especially over some domineering barbarian trying to claim me like a side of beef.

"No." I shake my head. "And if you really do want to protect me like you say, you'll try this with me. Only being apart can really keep the other person safe." I look him right in his determined eyes. "If you want to save me, you have to release me." It sounds a little corny to me, like an inspirational speaker, but the dragons don't have those, right? He won't think it's cheesy.

His shoulders droop, and his brow furrows. Because he's considering it.

I didn't think he would, not really.

"What does human mating involve?" he asks. "Specifically."

"What does dragon mating involve?" I counter.

"For the flame and strike blessed, we fly," he says, "dancing as we do so. Once we reach a great enough height, we twist together, and then we fall in tandem, until we're able to fly as one."

I arch one eyebrow. "You make an egg by flying together?"

"Well, once we're twined in such a way—"

I hold up my arm. "That's enough, actually."

He closes his mouth with a click. But then he frowns. "What is human mating, exactly?"

Heat floods into my face. "It's—well." I swallow.

"Are you naked when you do it?" he asks. "Because when the cloth wrappings flew away from Gideon before, you both reacted."

"You don't technically have to be," I say. "But usually two humans would be. The things humans do. . .our clothing gets in the way."

Axel looks as disgusted as I feel.

"Listen, I think because of the bond, neither of us really

wants this to happen, and neither of us feels great about it. But I also think it's important."

Axel reaches for my hand, his fingers softly brushing against mine. "Are you sure? Because earlier, I felt like we might grow closer through kissing—and the records say that growing closer is how the entwined can gain both control and space."

"I suppose we'll find out, won't we?" I don't grind my teeth, but it's a near miss.

"If you insist." He drops his hand and steps back. "I should inform Asteria."

"And I should tell Gideon." As if lightning has just struck my brain, I realize what I'm saying. I'm telling him that I should inform Gideon. . .that we're *supposed to sleep together*. I doubt he'll object. I mean, guys tend to. . . I clear my throat. "I'll just head downstairs, then."

Axel's breathing picks up. "Right. I should check on Rufus. I'll come."

"You're coming *with me* to go tell Gideon?"

"Your siblings are there this time, presumably." Axel arches one eyebrow. "Is mating something humans do all together?"

I shake my head so hard it makes my brain hurt. "No. Absolutely not."

Axel swallows. "Well then, I'll just come down with you, and you can talk to Gideon about our plan. I'll check in with Rufus. And then we can tell Asteria."

Together?

He's coming with me to tell Gideon about our plan. . .to both *mate* with someone else? This can't be happening. And yet, somehow, it is. "We're making plans for it today, but we'll *do it* tomorrow?"

"Sure, yes, that sounds right."

I've had a lot of strange conversations with Axel in the last few weeks, but this is definitely the strangest of all.

By a wide margin.

"Let's go."

He nods woodenly and follows me down.

Only, as the elevator door opens onto the little ante-room on the kids' floor, another elevator on the opposite side opens too.

And my mom walks out.

"They're alive?" Her eyes are wide, her lips parted in what looks a lot like hope. "The rumors circling say that you have siblings here with you. The ensnared I spoke with said that Azar's protecting them."

Right now, as I'm about to go inside and tell Gideon that I'm supposed to. . . my mom shows up. I thought this couldn't get more awkward, but apparently I was wrong.

"When he bonded me, Axel and I made a deal," I say. "He said he'd keep them safe as long as I did as I was told."

Mom scowls and for a split second, it feels like the old Mom's back. "You made a *deal?*" Her eyes swing to Axel. "Why would you do that?"

Axel shrugs. "Your daughter's persuasive."

Mom's still staring. "But you could have just forced her to do what you wanted. Why would you make a deal to secure the same behavior you already owned?"

"Let's say that Liz intrigued me."

Mom frowns.

"Do you want to see them?" I ask.

"They're really fine?" Judging from the look on her face, Mom can't take another big disappointment. I don't blame her.

"They're fine."

Mom steps toward me, her hand outstretched. "Did you really save Sammy from falling off the tower today? Or was that Azar?"

"Azar wasn't here," Axel says. "Neither was I. That was Liz."

Sammy didn't *fall* so much as careen through the wall on the back of a dragon he was racing, but I don't figure Mom needs all the details. She doesn't look like she'll ever approve of the idea of Coral, Jade, and Sammy, having dragon guards turned babysitters turned friends. "It was me." I can't help smirking a bit. "Being entwined has a few perks, I guess."

"What else can you do?" But Mom looks decidedly uneasy.

"I'm still figuring that out," I say. "But for now, let's go inside. They've been asking about you." Which isn't strictly true, but they did when we first joined the dragons with Axel.

Before I can push through the door, Mom grabs my wrist. "Don't talk to them about Ocharta."

"Mom, they saw you get bonded before we left. They know."

She shakes her head, her eyes on her feet. "Not that—don't tell them how bad it is. Or what happens if. . ."

If Ocharta dies.

"We're still working on a solution for that," I say.

For both of us.

She bobs her head, which I take as some kind of acknowledgement. As I reach for the door, I barely hear her words. "Any word from your father?"

I wonder what it cost her to ask me that, and how much hope she's been shoving down, along with all the other things she wants and can't bring herself to dream about anymore. I may hate the dragons for this more than anything else.

The powerlessness.

The decimation of our future plans.

The ruin of my own, force-of-nature mother.

"No word yet," I say. "But I imagine he's alright, wherever he is." Or at least, I really, really hope he is.

It strengthens my resolve to follow through on our plan to drive some space between Axel and me. The last thing I need is to be obsessing over a dragon and always needing to be near him. Blech. Getting close to him to discover information is one thing, but believing that I was actually getting close to him was delusion.

When we walk through the door, Coral's the first to notice us, and when she does, she smiles and stands. The second she realizes it's Mom, her entire face freezes, and then she's sprinting this way.

I hadn't given it a lot of thought, how my siblings would be doing without knowing much about Mom's fate. I thought I was helping them by not telling them about the ugly reality of the bond with Ocharta. I've been doing my utmost to keep them safe in any way I can, but maybe I was wrong.

They're younger than I am, and they need her in a way I don't any more. That's clear from the moment they're in the same room.

Ocharta must not be paying much attention to her right now or something, because Mom almost seems like herself. She doesn't look nearly as broken in this moment as she has every single time I've seen her since the dragons came.

Unless.

"Did Asteria—are you—"

Mom turns abruptly, my siblings freezing. Her head shake's small, but it's firm.

Nothing has changed.

But how can she be here, now that Ocharta's free?

"What's going on?" Coral asks, intuiting the same questions as me. "Why are you here now? Have you been with the other dragons all along?" She glances between Mom and me. "That silver dragon—she bonded you, right?"

Mom nods slowly.

"Then why didn't you visit before?" Jade's voice is trembling.

"Ocharta bonded me." Mom's voice is small. "The strike blessed who fried most of your friends at the Boo Bash."

Axel's feeling uneasy about this conversation—the bond's a tumultuous yellow. Gideon's leaning against the wall, and he looks just as unhappy as Axel. Maybe more.

"Until now, Ocharta's been monitoring me closely, and lately, she's been trapped in a bubble by Azar, which left her. . .irritable. Angry." Mom shudders. "But earlier today, her sister came to visit." Mom swallows. "And a moment ago, she came back again. In fact, they're busy right now."

"Doing what?" Axel's voice is deceptively mild. Mom's explanation of her freedom worries him for some reason.

Mom shrugs. "They don't appear to like one another very well."

"They've never gotten along very well," Axel says. "But I heard Asteria tried to take your bond earlier."

"Tried and failed," Mom mutters.

"Asteria's presence here throws Ocharta's leadership of the strike blessed into question," Axel says.

Gideon launches for the wall, heading toward me. "Who's stronger?" His eyes are flashing. "Will Asteria kill Ocharta?"

Axel shrugs. "I'm not sure. At home, their parents never let it come to that. They're one of the rare families that didn't encourage such in-fighting."

"Fabulous," I mutter. "That means Ocharta could kill Asteria, too."

"Good riddance," Gideon says. "One less dragon's always a good thing."

"I like Asteria," I say. "But if she could die, that means Ocharta could as well." I glare at Mom. For someone who didn't want to talk about this, she sure is chatty.

"If either of them dies, it's a blessing," Mom insists.

Some of the old Mom's still in there, still fighting.

But she crouches down now, dropping one knee to the ground. "But kids, listen. That's not for you to worry about, okay? You listen to your sister, and you stay safe here with her."

Sammy wraps his arms around Mom again, tightly, but then his little voice fills the entire room. "But I like Gordon, Mom. Is that bad?"

"Who's Gordon?" Mom asks.

"That's me." Gordon and Rufus were clearly hiding from Axel—pretty sure they'd be in trouble when he found out how they were playing. But they're never far, not anymore.

When they step forward from around the wall into the hallway, Mom's eyes widen. "And you are?" Her eyes cut toward mine.

"Gordon's my best friend, Mom," Sammy says. "He's really bad at Uno, but he always beats me at Candy Land. Usually he'll play anything I want, and he brings me treats all the time. Plus, I can ride on his back—like he's my own dragon car. Even though he kinda looks like a snake, he's really fast, and we were totally beating Rufus and Coral before—"

Gordon's shaking his head, his eyes wide.

Axel's laughter surprises all of us.

"You're saying that your best friend," Mom says, "is—" She chokes.

"A dragon," I say. "Yes. He's an earth dragon."

Mom closes her eyes. She stands up, shifting Sammy's hands from around her waist to her hands. When she finally opens her eyes, she looks broken again.

Shattered.

She's staring right at me. "I can't say that I understand or approve of you pairing your brother up with a blessed." Her eyes drop to her feet, as if speaking out against them either scares her. . .or she's been ordered not to do it. "But does it have to be the weakest variety?"

"The earth blessed can't bond him," Axel says. "It makes them uniquely situated to care for a child who's sure to be a bright."

Mom's head snaps back up, her expression pained.

"They're young, but all three of them will be highly sought after," Axel says, "both for their connection to Azar, and because finding brights has now become more difficult."

"Are you implying that you care about their welfare?" Mom's eyes flash.

"I care about it because Liz cares about it." Axel arches one eyebrow imperiously. "Would you like me to find a stronger blessed to protect them?" His tone isn't mocking.

He seems utterly serious.

"You're the Prince of the Earth Blessed," Mom says. "So you'll know that I mean nothing but respect when I say this, but do you believe your earth blessed are capable of protecting my children, knowing their position within the society of the blessed?"

I frown. "They're at the bottom, sure, but—"

Axel steps toward Mom. "I think they're the best of our options, and Rufus and Gordon are my strongest lieutenants." He sighs. "Beyond that, everyone knows they're my two closest companions, so their presence is like my own."

Mom nods slowly. Then she turns to me. "I should head back before Ocharta notices I'm gone. Thanks for welcoming me, Entwined."

I roll my eyes. "Stop."

She shakes her head. "I can't stop. Besides, you should know that I'm grateful. You've done everything you can to keep them safe." A single tear forms at the corner of her eye and rolls down her cheek. "You've done what I couldn't—what I was too weak to do." Mom takes my hand then.

The hand that wiped away my tears.

The arm that wrapped around me every time I was afraid.

She squeezes. "Thank you."

Then she turns around and heads for the door.

"He's right." Gordon's voice is a surprise to me. He doesn't talk a lot when I'm around. Or, not to me, anyway.

"What?" Mom's hand is on the door handle, but she turns back, looking at us over her shoulder.

"Sammy's right." Gordon looks as sincere as I've ever seen a dragon look. "Other than Rufus, he is my best friend. I'll do anything I can to keep him safe."

"Thank you," Mom says, like she believes him.

Strangely, I do too.

Not that it's super comforting, given that he has no electricity powers or water powers or flame blowing capabilities. At least he could. . .burrow underground with Sammy? Or shoot dirt at any attackers?

Sheesh.

But when Mom leaves, I'm reminded of my real purpose in coming down here. All three kids and all three dragons are staring at me. I'm not about to talk to Gideon out here.

I point at him. "You."

"Me?" Gideon's smile rolls slowly over his face.

I nod.

"What about me?"

I point at his room. "We need to talk."

"I'll come," Axel says.

I shake my head. "Nope. No way. You're staying out here. Or, you know what? Maybe go check on your girlfriend."

"My—what?"

Shoot. Sometimes I forget that I'm the only one who

knows he's Azar. "Your boss's girlfriend, I mean," I say. "Didn't Azar tell you to go make sure Asteria's alright?"

Axel frowns.

"I have to talk to Gideon, remember?"

Now he's scowling. The bond is a dark amber color I've never seen.

"Or stay here if you want. I don't care." I grab Gideon's wrist and drag him through the doorway to his own bedroom door. I'm sure everyone's staring at us, but this whole situation is like a stinky, sticky old band-aid, and I'm about to rip it off.

Only, now that we're inside his room, Gideon's staring at me, and I'm starting to lose a little bit of steam.

"What's going on?" His eyes study me intently. "Did you. . .break through their control?" He looks absurdly hopeful.

"I think—" I swallow, and I try again. "I think that part of my problem is that I need a connection to humanity again. I'm disappearing," I whisper. "I think I'm disappearing into the dragons."

As I say it, I realize it's true.

The bond shifting was awesome and insane and terrifying, and I have no idea what it means. I know I feel less myself than I ever have before.

"I have these powers." I shiver, and my hands wrap around my own body, rubbing up and down my opposite arms. "I don't even want them, but they're—I don't know what to make of them. And they come with strings I don't want either. So Azar and I had this idea that maybe we could get a little space if only we each tried to connect with someone else." I lift my eyes slowly until I meet his.

They're practically burning.

Gideon's lips curl up into a smile. "Are you saying what I think you're saying?"

"Do you even want me anymore?" My voice is small when I ask, "Am I a monster?"

Gideon's jaw drops, and then he closes the space between us, his large hands covering mine. As he squeezes, he says, "No."

Unequivocal.

Sure.

Absolute.

It's exactly what I needed to hear, but I'm not sure I can believe him. "I'm entwined with Azar," I whisper. "And I'm bonded to Axel, too." It feels cathartic to say that, to at least acknowledge a connection to both of them. "That alone makes me feel split in two, but Gideon, I have to tell you something else."

He's still staring right at me.

"Neither of them has ever forced me to do a single thing, ever."

He blinks.

"They've never forced me in the way that Mom has been forced. Not once."

He frowns. "But—Axel did predicate your siblings' safety on your behaving as he wanted."

"Well, yes, and—"

"He never offered to free you."

"He couldn't—he did search for a way. And his offer to release the kids was genuine."

"You're still his slave," Gideon says, his hands tightening further. "He's still your master."

I nod slowly. "I suppose."

"There's no suppose about it," he hisses. "And if you think that I can help you find some distance from him, I'm all in." He releases my left arm and lifts his hand. Two of his fingertips brush against my mouth. "Tell me what to do, and I'll do it. Always."

"Are you saying I'm your master?" I can't help smiling.

"Liz, you always have been, since we were kids." His head lowers toward mine. "You always will be. No matter what." His mouth is almost touching mine. "I told you. I love you, Liz. Heart and soul, and I'm going to save you from all this, as soon as I figure out how."

The bond flares bright red. It's pulsing.

I should stop him. I have no idea what Axel might do out there when he's this angry. I remember him telling me that I can *never* kiss Gideon. He has repeated over and over that he owns me.

As much as I hate the truth, he does own me. I know it. He knows it.

Everyone knows it.

But I can't acknowledge it openly. I'm *me*. I'm not his possession. No one can own me or anyone else. So I snap my hands up, grabbing either side of Gideon's face and dragging his mouth the last inch and a half until our lips meet.

6
AXEL

When I was barely old enough to fly, Dad introduced me to Asteria and told me that, one day, we would mate. I didn't even know what mating was then, but I knew it was true.

What Dad said was always true.

When I grew old enough to understand more about what he'd said, I asked more questions. He told me that if I was truly opposed, I had options. Her sister Ocharta was viable, as well as dozens of others. But based on our temperament, he felt that Asteria would make a good partner for me.

"Choosing your mate is critical to the blessed in many ways," he said. "Your mate will guard and protect you when you're vulnerable. They'll guide and direct you when you're lost. But most of all, one day, you'll restore the strength of the blessed, and she'll make a strong mother to your future children."

"How do you know?" I had asked. Even then, I knew that no new eggs had been laid since we left Earth. He didn't tell me the answer. He didn't tell me for a very long time, in fact.

But he did prepare me for his latest edict from the start.

When Liz tells me she thinks we should each move ahead with mating. . .with someone else, of course she's right. I know she's right. I can't mate with her.

She's a human.

I'm blessed.

But beyond the most obvious, if I were to mate with Liz, and insanely, if it *worked*, instead of being delighted about the first blessed egg in millennia, her creation of any sort of egg would out me.

Or at least, if it was a flame blessed egg, it would.

Because only Axel could mate with Liz, who is a human. Unless everyone knew that Axel and Azar are the same, Axel's mating with Liz wouldn't free Azar from his need to mate with Asteria. Anything else would make public the secret I've dedicated my life to concealing.

So when Liz grabs Gideon's wrist, I want to incinerate someone more than I ever have in my entire life, someone I could easily reduce to ash in any form. But instead, I grit my teeth and bear it.

When she walks inside his room and closes the door, it doesn't create any sort of privacy from me. I can still hear every single word, every single sigh, and every beat of Gideon's wretched, unworthy heart.

Like someone who enjoys misery, I can't even distract myself. I listen to every last word.

"Am I a monster?"

Liz's words sear their way into my very soul. I've always known she sees the blessed whom she insists on calling dragons as enemies, as *other*. But the word she uses, monster, is infused with such hatred, such animosity, and such repulsion that I realize something.

She feels that same hatred. . .for herself.

Because of her connection to me.

I didn't understand the depth of her pain, or that it's inextricably connected to me. I didn't really comprehend how much she hated *me*. Not until this moment. And then stupid Gideon comforts her, and she lets him, in a way she has never allowed me to even try.

When he says, "Tell me what to do, and I'll do it. Always," her body relaxes. She softens. Her heart rate slows.

"Are you saying I'm your master?" I can tell by the light way she asks the question that she's smiling. She's happy.

Relaxed.

Free.

"Liz, you always have been, since we were kids. You always will be. No matter what," he says, and I wish, desperately, that I could see them. I'm sure he's touching her.

I'm sure *she's* touching *him*.

But I'm stuck, ignoring the things Rufus and Gordon are saying to me, standing in the family room like a statue, listening through the bond to the words he shares that can help her in a way I never can.

"I told you," Gideon says. "I love you, Liz. Heart and soul."

The bond burns then, and something inside of me catches fire. I'm doing my best to contain it, but I'm a creature of fire, flame, and heat already, and knowing that she's walked away from me and toward *him*, it's supercharging the lava that always simmers down inside of me.

And then I feel it.

When she kisses him.

I feel the heat growing inside of me. If I release it, it'll melt the entire building to the ground. "I have to go," I manage to mutter. And then I'm sprinting out the door.

Rufus tries to stop me. "Wait, are you alright?"

But I ignore him—not really capable of coherent

thought right now. The second I clear the apartment and reach the small room outside the elevator bay, I drop into a dead run and leap through the window, shifting into Azar as soon as I'm clear of the building, between one breath and the next, and then I'm flying.

Space.

I need to put space between Liz and me or I might kill her when I explode. The only thing I can think as I fly as high and as fast as I can is that there's no way I'm going to survive tomorrow if mating for humans is more than that kiss just was.

Not without murdering a *lot* of other creatures in a terrible deluge of fire and flame.

Where are we going? Hyperion drops into the airspace alongside me. *This looks like fun.*

Go away.

You're not being very friendly, he says. *I've been helpful and accommodating, you know. I didn't have to volunteer when Dad said someone had to follow you.*

He's right, and that just pisses me off more. Any other brother of mine would have forced a fight for dominance. Dad's actually trying to encourage me, and if I hadn't bonded Liz that day. . . But as it is, it doesn't matter whom he sent. We're headed for a confrontation either way.

The futility of our attempts, the collision course I've been flying down, Liz *kissing* Gideon, all of it has me so angry that an explosion is imminent. In that very second, I realize that finally, there's a target in front of me that can take the heat.

All of it.

So I inhale deeply, and I release a pillar of flame that would decimate Houston's city line if we weren't clinging to the edge of the atmosphere. Up here, there's barely enough oxygen to sustain the flame as long as I'm releasing it.

Even so, the force of it slams into Hyperion, hitting

him right in the center of his chest and blowing him far, far off my trajectory. It would make me laugh if I weren't so upset.

Easy there, brother. We've never quarreled.

In spite of everyone's attempts to force us to it. I should apologize, but I'm still too angry. The person who's making me the most angry can't withstand the heat, so I throw even more at Hyperion.

This time, he comes back at me, eyes sparking. *Remember. You started this.* As the fire erupts from his mouth, arcing through the space between us, I remember the first lesson my father ever gave me.

You're flame blessed, Azar, he had said. *Fire's a chemical reaction between oxygen and fuel. It's a powerful force that destroys, across the whole of the known universe.*

I had blinked up at him, my entire body smaller than his front foot.

For everything, except for our kind. *We're different than everyone and everything else. We're creatures of flame, made to destroy and remake anything in the world that defies us.*

I had looked around his chamber—a large stone cavern, devoid of anything comforting or comfortable, and I asked what only a hatchling would ask. *What if I don't want to destroy things?*

I can still hear the bitterness in his laugh. *You don't have a choice, son. You are what you are—death and flame will follow you all your life.*

As the vibrant blue flame spewing from Hyperion's mouth punches into me, I can't help remembering what I am.

Death.

And flame.

What I am not is comfort. Protection. Happiness. Fulfillment. I'm none of the things Liz needs. I am none of the things she wants. I can never be those things, because at my most basic, I'm a destroyer. I'm everything she hates and everything she fears.

So finally, I do what I do best.

I attack.

I incinerate.

I destroy.

And as Hyperion and I claw at, blast, and attempt to disembowel one another, my rage starts to ebb. The fire inside of me that has been boiling over since Hyperion brought the news that I must go to Dad or that he will come for me begins to recede.

Not all the way.

I'm a long way from calm or peaceful. But it's no longer threatening to explode and destroy everyone around me.

There you are. Hyperion ducks my latest, half-hearted eruption, and plants one taloned paw right in the center of my chest and shoves, hard, his massive wings flapping with gale force.

I careen backward, my wings pumping frantically to right myself and avoid slamming backward into the ground below. It's a near miss, but just before I'm about to collide with a small office complex, I flip over. The wind from my wings uproots two trees, but I don't destroy any more of Liz's precious human buildings.

When did I start caring about whether I destroyed her little human shelters? Why do I care at all? Liz isn't even here. She'd never even know.

Except when I wing my way upward, closing the space between Hyperion and me, I sense her. She's moving toward me. Quickly.

You've put on quite the show. Hyperion's looping in a lazy circle overhead. *Care to tell me why?*

To remind the blessed who leads them. What flame blessed truly means.

Smoke billows from Hyperion's nostrils when he snorts. *Try again.*

I have to mate with Asteria, I finally admit. *And I—I don't want to.*

Do I even want to know why not? Hyperion arches one scaly eyebrow.

I shake my head, picking up my speed, flying in a circle after him—chasing him.

You know what would buy you some more time? Hyperion wheels and pivots abruptly, dropping like a rock.

I bank and drop too, landing next to him on the ground. We're not too far from my tower, but I can't help wondering how Liz is approaching so quickly.

You're distracted by that human again? Hyperion sighs. *I need to get myself one. I hear she has some little whelps. Maybe one of them—*

I forbid it.

My brother very seldom looks shocked, but he does right now. *Why? You plan to bond them all? You can barely handle the one you have.*

It would upset her, I say. *And they're too young to bond anyone yet.*

If you really don't want to be forced to mate, then do the other thing—the thing Dad wants most of all. Find the heart, brother. Follow the lead you found before I came, and instead of flipping out about the chosen one mating, Dad will be delighted that we've made another kind of progress. Do that, and you can tell Dad to find Asteria another mate.

He's right about that. Dad micromanages only when he feels we aren't getting results on our own.

You're suggesting I accelerate our departure again—you're the reason it was delayed.

We can find everything we need once we're there—there are humans to do our bidding in Iceland as well.

I suppose you're right. Though Liz won't like it. She's

having the humans we've organized and trained here gather up a month's worth of supplies because she's insisting we leave them all behind.

But why *don't you want to mate all of a sudden? I thought you liked Asteria. She's attractive, smart, and not pushy.*

She is all those things, and I did like her well enough. Much more than her sister. But. . .

It upsets Liz.

It's a stupid reason that I can't even articulate without Hyperion scoffing. But it's still the truth. I don't want to do anything that upsets her, and for some reason, the prospect of me mating with Asteria does. Even more frustrating, the thought of her mating with a perfectly appropriate human —a union that might yield even more brights, which is a good thing if we wind up being on Earth for a long time— upsets me just as much.

Nothing could prevail upon me to confess any of that to my brother.

"Azar!" Liz bursts into the clearing.

On Euphrasia's back.

At least two dozen other blessed are flanking them, mostly other water blessed, but earth blessed begin arriving in waves afterward.

Why are you here? I ask, on a private channel to Liz alone.

She hops off Euphrasia's back and runs down the street toward me. "What were you fighting over?" She draws a sword she must have found somewhere—it's far too large for her—and turns, placing herself between Hyperion and me. "And why did he finally stop attacking?"

Once it becomes obvious she's trying to protect me, Hyperion laughs. *You think to protect him from* me, *little one?*

Her lip curls. "I protect him from anyone who threatens harm."

She's cute, Hyperion says. *Are you sure the others are too young? I'm intrigued.*

"What's he talking about?" Liz asks. "And why were you fighting? Is he in love with Asteria? Did he freak out when you told her?"

Told me what? Asteria lands beside Hyperion.

Liz spins around, the tip of her sword dipping slightly as her shoulders droop. But then her brows furrow, and it's clear it takes effort, but she talks to me on a private channel. *What are you doing out here? What's going on? You haven't even told her?*

I suppose I have no one to blame for the blessed being gathered around but myself. My fight with Hyperion freaked everyone out.

We've decided to move ahead more quickly with our relocation to Iceland, I say, as loudly as I can broadcast. *We'll be leaving tomorrow morning.*

"We can't leave tomorrow," a tiny voice says from the very edge of the gathering. When I follow the sound, my eyes recognize Sammy just as he slides off Gordon's back. What's he thinking, bringing a child all the way out here? I'm going to kill Gordon. Two major blunders in one day?

"Why not?" Liz sheaths her sword in some kind of bizarre, clearly improvised sling on her back, possibly ascertaining that I'm not in any clear or present danger from my brother. "Come here, Sam."

The murmurs around us rise up like steam from a warm lake on a cool morning. Wispy and insubstantial, but growing.

Who is that?

—Entwined with Azar's—

—younger siblings are always also bright.

Might be more likely to entwine too, if they're part of the same family.

—awfully small, though.

The connection to Azar alone—

Enough, I shout. Then I crouch down a little so I hope-fully won't scare Sammy. *Why can't we leave tomorrow?*

He doesn't look the least bit afraid. "Because I found a calendar, and guess what?"

No one guesses—not even his sister.

He finally sighs, clearly frustrated. "Tomorrow's *Thanks-giving Day*," he says, like that explains it.

"Oh, sweetie," Liz says. "Are you sure?"

He nods earnestly.

She pulls him against her and hugs him tightly. It's like she's trying to prepare him for bad news. "Even if it is," she whispers, "we can't ask the dragons to stick around for that. Besides, our departure on Thanksgiving would make the humans who have been cast out of their homes happy, right?"

"They're going to be celebrating wherever they are already," Sammy says. "And the first Thanksgiving was when the Native Americans helped the people who came to their land. I think we should do the same thing."

"The thing is," Liz says, "I don't think—"

Sammy frowns. "Well, it's not really up to you, is it? Their boss is him." He points at me, and looks at my face expectantly.

Bizarrely, I have this strange compulsion to give him what he wants. I want to make him smile. It's probably because, no matter how much she may argue with him, I know that Liz wants to make her brother happy. Just as she insisted he leave all his toys behind at the first building I stuck them in, while she really wanted him to be able to bring them, she's just saying that we have to go because. . . I'm not sure quite why, actually. Humans still confuse me with their bizarre motivations.

I do accept that I like to please Liz, even if I don't quite understand why the bond has created that desire in me.

Another twelve hours probably won't make a huge difference.

We will do this human Thanksgiving tomorrow, early in the day, and then we'll depart for Iceland tomorrow afternoon. Make preparations again, both for our departure and for tomorrow's fête.

Liz's jaw drops in a very satisfying manner. "But you said that tomorrow—" Her eyes cut downward at Gordon.

Gordon. I don't bother bellowing on a private channel.

My good friend slinks toward me, showing at least twice as much respect for me as he does when he thinks I'm Axel. That irritates me more.

Axel tells me you were tasked with caring for the small human.

Gordon drops his head to the ground, pressing his belly flat too.

And yet, this is the second time I have seen him endangered today. Were you entrusted with a task that is beyond your skill?

I will care for him instead. Euphrasia steps forward. *I'm quite good with errant hatchlings.*

"No!" Sammy shouts and flings his arms around Gordon's neck. His arms barely span a fraction of the width, but prostrate on the ground as Gordon is, Sammy's close enough to rest his face against Gordon's cheek. "He's my best friend."

Your friendship, *odd though it may be, is not in question,* Euphrasia says. *It's his capacity to keep you safe that we doubt, little one.*

"He can keep me safe," Sammy says. "In fact, last week, when one of the water dragons—"

Gordon's eyes widen and he shakes his head. It's small, but it's there.

Sammy frowns. "What I mean is, Gordon's really big and scary and he keeps me safe."

A much larger water blessed—Pilion—shoulders past Euphrasia. *I request the honor of guarding and protecting the Recovery Leader's bonded's small kin.*

Nice try. Callioch, strike blessed, flies over Pilion's head to wedge himself between me and the water blessed. *I demand that a strike blessed be chosen for the honor of protecting—*

"What's going on?" Liz asks. "Why are they—"

The earlier murmurs are nothing to the cacophony of demands that begin in that moment, all of them demanding the honor of protecting Sammy—and also of escorting him to Iceland when we do finally leave.

"None of you will escort or protect him," Liz shouts. She turns toward me, meeting my eye to make sure I'm not upset. She really needs to learn to trust the bond more. "My brother's already very fond of Gordon, and as Prince Axel's closest confidante, we have total confidence in Gordon's ability to protect him. I'm very grateful to hear that all of you will be eager to step in and help, should anything dangerous or threatening occur."

That shuts them up impressively.

Come, I say. *Let's head back.*

If I may ask, Euphrasia says. *What's this 'Thanksgiving' the hatchling is talking about?*

"It's a day for humans to celebrate all the things in our lives we're grateful for." Liz walks toward me. "So, for instance, I would give thanks that Azar and I have bonded and that now we're entwined. I might also give thanks that Sammy wasn't harmed today when he crashed through the side of the building."

"Or," Coral shouts from the edge of the gathered blessed. "We might celebrate that we're all about to leave Houston and return the city to the humans."

Every blessed in the area turns to look at her.

Liz closes her eyes. "Are they all here?" she mutters.

"Or I would give thanks that we were able to see our mother and that our whole family's alive," Jade says, from behind Coral.

"I might give thanks for those things, after I murder Rufus and Gordon," Liz says.

You just refused to let another blessed take over for Gordon, I remind her.

"That was before I realized how stupid they both are." She helps Sammy swing back up on Gordon's back, and then she turns toward me.

Of course, the murmurs about the two girls have already begun, and I'm sure that just as many blessed will now obnoxiously demand the chance to protect and escort them. Before all that nonsense can begin again, I decide to disperse the gathered crowd.

You may all return to your duties. I'll distribute more details about Thanksgiving and our upcoming departure through your leaders soon.

Once Liz is satisfied that her siblings are on their way back to the tower, Euphrasia following the soon-to-be-berated Gordon and Rufus, I launch into the sky, this time with my bonded safely on my back and a lot less anger simmering.

"Why didn't you tell Asteria?" Liz asks. "And why were you and Hyperion fighting?"

I've noticed that Liz changes the subject when she doesn't want to talk about something I've asked. I decide to try it myself. *What exactly do you do at this Thanksgiving?*

"Nice try, buddy. I invented that. Why didn't you tell Asteria that you two need to mate?"

I decided to move up the timeline instead.

"You *what?*" She leans down closer to my neck, her arms wrapping around me tightly. "But I already kissed Gideon."

And that did not help us find space. In fact, it resulted in me picking a fight with Hyperion and nearly burning the city down.

In an uncharacteristic move, Liz is quiet the rest of the way back to the tower, keeping her arms wrapped around me in a way that pleases me greatly. When we land, she slides off my back and walks toward the door.

Where are you going?

She freezes. Slowly, very slowly, she turns. "I have some cooking to do if tomorrow's Thanksgiving." She looks up at me slowly. "I—we can practice being apart for a little bit."

Nice try. I shift into Axel so fast, it makes her stumble back a step. "I'll come with you." I start to walk toward her.

She throws up a hand, which almost immediately intercepts the forward momentum of my chest.

I like the contact.

I lean further against her hand.

"Axel, you have to stay here."

"Why?" I ask, the heat rising in my body again, for some reason.

"I just told Gideon that tomorrow—" she chokes.

I wrap my hands around both her wrists. "No."

"We decided."

My hands tighten. "It didn't work. Undecide it."

"Axel, after I kissed Gideon, I told him—"

But I can't hear the words. Even the thought of her kissing him floods me with fury. I step closer. "If you kiss him again, instead of leaving, I'll raze your precious Houston to the ground. Every last building. Every single tree. Is that clear?"

Her breath catches.

"It was a bad idea for us to try to force a wedge between us. It didn't give us more space. It just caused misery for me."

Liz's heart is racing. Her breaths are coming fast and shallow. "Is that why you didn't tell Asteria?"

"Mating with Asteria shouldn't interfere with our bond. But until we get that worked out, I'm not willing to risk any more damage." Plus, for some reason, the idea of finally mating with her fills me with dread.

Instead of yelling or shoving me like I expect, Liz just nods. "Fine."

"Okay." I release her wrists, even though I don't want to. I'm not sure why I keep finding myself doing so many things I don't want to do right now, but I can't seem to help it.

"Tell me this, at least." She tilts her head. "Thanksgiving's all about giving thanks. . .and eating food. So to prepare for tomorrow, I need to know what you eat."

"I told you. I eat what you do."

"Not you, as in Axel," she says. "*You*, as in the blessed. The first Thanksgiving, the locals brought lots of new foods to the pilgrims that they'd never had before. They shared what they ate. So we'll make the things we always eat. Turkey. Mashed potatoes. Cranberry sauce, if we can find any. But what things do you usually eat?"

"It's not really—"

Liz frowns. "Please tell me it's not grubs. I know Gordon likes them, but there aren't enough grubs on earth to feed all of you."

"Liz."

"Or—what did I see Rufus eating last week? It looked an awful lot like a skunk, and it smelled, but I'm pretty sure that no one likes to eat skunks."

"Liz."

"No matter how weird it is, I promise we'll try to be understanding. But please, *please*, don't say it's humans." She scrunches up her nose.

"We don't usually choose to eat humans," I say, "but the earth blessed will eat a whole variety of things. Some love fish. Some eat cows. Some love fruits and vegetables. All of the blessed derive substances we need to survive from gases in Earth's atmosphere, mixed with our own magic, which is also plentiful in certain places here on Earth. But we all require some additional fuel, and. . ." I'm still worried about her reaction, given what I have discovered about human eating patterns.

"You know, come to think of it, I've asked you this before, more than once." She narrows her eyes. "Out with it. What weird thing do you eat, and why don't you want to tell me about it?"

"Shortly after we left Earth, the strike blessed, the water blessed, and the flame blessed began to develop special dietary needs."

Liz frowns. "What does that mean?"

"The earth blessed can tolerate most any organic material, and even some inorganic. But the rest of us can only consume one main thing, or we become quite ill."

"Just say it," Liz says. "Because I'm kind of freaking out now. It can't be worse than what I'm imagining."

"There's a reason we brought so many earth blessed with us," I say. "The water, strike, and flame blessed can *only* consume other blessed, and they mostly eat the earth blessed."

I've called Axel the Prince of the Rat Dragons. I've also said he was the Prince of the Mud Dragons. I've said lots of things in humor—poking fun at him. I did all that because I'd seen him. Sure, he didn't have wings, but he was a stunningly beautiful, powerful dragon prince who commanded *thousands* of gorgeous creatures who could destroy tanks. It never occurred to me that. . .

I was sort of dead-on with all my taunts.

He's literally the Prince of the Cow Dragons.

The other dragons *eat* the earth dragons.

They *EAT* them.

It's horrifying.

No wonder the strike blessed and the water blessed treat them so badly—they must feel pretty guilty to be eating other creatures just like themselves.

"Oh, no." I groan. "I stood up back there and told them that Sammy would continue to be protected by. . .Gordon? And he's, like. . . He's *fodder*." I feel sick.

"It's not quite like that." Axel starts to walk away, but I'm not done talking about this yet.

I leap toward him, grabbing at his hand to try and stop

him. My fingers catch his wrist, but the momentum pulls me into step beside him. As if the movement was the most natural thing ever, our fingers slide past one another, and our hands interlock.

My move would have made any teenage boy proud, that's for sure. It should come with a free soda and extra-large popcorn. Only, I'm not a teenage boy with sweaty palms and raging hormones. I'm an adult who should *not* be making heart eyes at the horrible Cow Dragon Prince beside me.

I snatch my hand back, and Axel stops walking. Then he does an about face to stare at me. "I have some things to explain, unless you're planning to yell at me again."

Do I yell at him too much? Is his sniping justified?

"No? Nothing more to say?" He tosses his head toward the sofas that were shoved against the side wall of the massive family room. They're made from a gorgeous, top grain leather, and the back cushions are beautifully embossed. Now that I realize what role the earth dragons play, I can't help thinking that we could spare some hides after tomorrow's feast and make a dragon scale sofa with them.

With powerful, intelligent creatures, some of whom I've met.

Ugh.

"I just can't believe you *eat* them. Aren't they your friends?" I shake my head. "I can't wrap my head around it. You're their prince, and you just let the other dragons eat them." What was it he said when Jade was ranting about the evils of eating meat?

Lions and dogs and other predators all consume the flesh of other animals. I suppose he's right about that, but they don't eat other lions.

Or do they?

I'm not a scientist. I suppose I really don't know

much about cannibalism, except that humans think it's wrong, and praying mantises get a lot of flack for doing it. I huff once or twice, but eventually I sit on one corner of the sofa. He sits next to me, but with a whole person's space between us, so he can shift sideways and look right at me.

"I'm not going to sit at a table across from any of the blessed tomorrow and watch as they eat a dragon leg. I just want to get that out there."

"I think it's time I tell you the reason we're here," he says.

"I already know. You came to recover the heart," I say. "Right?"

"Yes, but why do you think we need it?" He lifts both eyebrows, his shining golden eyes intent.

"I—" I shake my head. "I'm not sure, but knowing might help me do a better job of finding it."

Axel sighs, his broad shoulders drooping. "I said nearly that same thing to my father before we left, back when I was begging for more details. He didn't give me a very satisfactory answer, but I'll tell you what I know, starting with the most basic part, something that all blessed now know."

He's making this information seem much less valuable by telling me everyone knows it.

"There hasn't been a single new egg laid by any of the blessed since we left Earth. . .except among the earth blessed."

I blink. "Wait, so only they can reproduce?"

"That's correct, but before we left Earth, all of us could reproduce, and all of us could consume most anything. Local animals, flora, fauna, fish. Any of it. Once we left Earth, none of us could lay eggs anymore, and without consuming others of their own kind, the blessed began to waste away."

Waste away? "You mean they were starving?"

Axel shrugs. "I don't know, exactly. I wasn't there. I hadn't hatched yet."

"Wait—you don't remember anything, then?"

"I was actually the very last non-earth-blessed egg to hatch. Two others hatched the week before me, but. . ."

"But?"

"My egg was a brilliant color of crimson, Liz. And technically, according to the records, *three* eggs hatched in the hatchery the week before me."

Because he'd have been recorded as two separate hatchlings, by Euphrasia. He said she kept his secret. He's both Axel and Azar.

Wow.

"Your nanny's pretty considerate, and I think she must really care about you," I say. "When we started seeing blasts of flames in the sky, she came to check on me, first thing."

"I'm surprised you even knew what was going on." Axel folds his arms. "You seemed pretty. . .distracted."

I almost roll my eyes. "Please. One little kiss and you bolted like a trail horse who just saw a plastic bag rolling in the wind."

"Like—what?"

"My uncle had horses. Never mind," I say.

"I wasn't afraid—it took great effort for me to leave. What I wanted to do was eviscerate that guy and then incinerate his remains."

"Because of one little kiss? Really?"

Axel's frown is intense.

I can't help wondering whether it's just the dragon's natural possessiveness combined with our tighter bond. . .or whether he might actually care about me.

Which is stupid.

Delusional, really.

He's a *beast*.

I have to do a better job of remembering that fact.

"What are you going to do tomorrow when—"

Axel slides closer. "We aren't doing the mating with others thing now," he says. "We're going to Iceland so I'll have news to report about the heart."

"What if it's nothing? What if we get there and you still don't have anything to share?" I ask. "What then?"

He inhales.

"How bad would it be if your father came here?"

"For Earth?" he asks. "Or for me?"

"I didn't realize there was a difference."

Axel stands up and begins to pace. "My father assigned me to handle the return for a very particular reason, Liz."

"Which was?"

"There was a stupid prophecy surrounding the last egg to hatch."

"Wait, concerning *you*?" I ask. "Or about the last egg, whoever that happened to be?"

"The last egg." He stops and turns toward me. "Which happened to be me."

"Only, you were not one dragon," I say. "You were two, right?"

He shrugs. "I was one egg, and when I hatched out of the large, red egg, I wasn't a scarlet flame blessed."

He's clearly telling me something that matters to him, so I stand up too, and I approach him slowly. "You were gold?"

He nods slowly. "If it had been any blessed other than Euphrasia. . . But she believed in the prophecy that the last blessed to hatch would allow our successful return to Earth where we could recover the heart and heal our people."

"Wow, that's a lot of things they think you're going to do."

"But because I hatched out earth blessed," he says, "albeit with the royal golden scale color, Euphrasia fed me from the marine life of our new planet."

"And that's. . .bad?" I have no idea what that means.

"After eating for the first time, I shifted into something new. The flame blessed she expected."

"Oh." He's saying it like it really means something.

"I'm the only non-earth blessed among our people who can successfully process nutrition from the flesh of other things—not just my own kind."

I have to scrunch up my nose to ask this. "What happens when you *do* eat an earth dragon?"

He shrugs. "I never have."

"Whoa," I say. "Does Big Daddy know that?"

Axel goes back to pacing. "At first, he preferred me because of the prophecy. It made my siblings hate me. Euphrasia pushed me to share her food, worried that only eating marine life, I'd be slower, weaker, and smaller when it mattered."

"And?" He's not good at telling stories, clearly.

"The first time one of the other flame blessed tried to kill me, I defeated them."

"Wait, they try to kill you?"

"The magic from the creatures we consume sustains us," Axel says. "The strongest among us have defeated others of their kind. Eliminating your competition is a sort of side-bonus."

"You *kill and eat* your siblings, and that's encouraged?" When he said he didn't understand my protection of Coral and Jade and Sammy, I had no idea what he meant. I mean, I knew the dragons were different, but I didn't realize they *ate* each other.

"I'm not sure if we always did, but we do now."

"Let me get this straight." Now I'm pacing too. "You can't lay more eggs, so the blessed that exist are all that will exist." I stop long enough to wait for his answer.

He nods.

I go back to pacing. "But you also kill each other so you can have the strongest boss?"

"My people always have."

"But?"

"After I defeated my brother Rumsted, I refused to kill him."

I imagine that went over well. "And?"

"I thought my father might explode, but he didn't. He was impressed by my willingness to forgo my own desire for power for the good of our people."

"How did your siblings react?"

"Most of them thought I was an easy mark and tried harder to kill me."

"What about Hyperion?" I have to ask, since he's the only one I've met.

"He never attacked me of his own volition, and he stopped eating the others, too."

So his dad sent an ally, basically. "Maybe your dad coming won't be so bad. He could have sent someone worse, presumably."

"He could have," Axel says. "But he sent Hyperion with a threat."

That's true. "Okay, so about the heart, though." We've gotten sidetracked again.

"Dad wouldn't tell me exactly what it was, but he said the heart was a seal they put inside the earth to keep the humans on earth safe after their departure."

"A seal?"

"That's as close to a translation as I can come," Axel says. "It's something that blocks something else."

"And it was inside the earth?"

"It's why he wanted me to bring Axel along," he says, "which was a stroke of luck. But also, Axel controls the earth blessed quite well. They never revolt about the required sacrifices when he's around."

Sacrifices. So, the earth blessed that need to be eaten don't argue with their boss there, telling them to die?

Ugh.

"Okay, so you're here to unplug this seal, which will likely put the humans in danger, and then leave with whatever was protecting us?"

"Something like that."

"What if I say that I can't let you do that?" I stare right into his golden eyes, and I realize something.

He feels guilty.

"I don't want to leave you unprotected," he says, "but you seem to want us gone more than you want anything else."

"But I don't even know what the heart is or what it's protecting us from."

"I think we're about to find out," he says.

Helping them steal the heart and leave, which I thought was the patriotic thing to do, might actually be the worst thing I've ever done, for humanity, I mean.

And Axel doesn't even know.

"What happens if you don't get the heart?"

He shrugs. "I suppose we'll slowly die off until all that's left are earth dragons."

"And one flame blessed," I say. But the thought makes me sad.

Axel smiles.

"Is that funny for some reason?"

"You said blessed," he says.

"I—what?"

He steps closer, no longer pacing. "You always call us dragons, but you called me a flame blessed just now."

I hold out my hand, unprepared to deal with a kind Axel. "All I meant was—"

"You use dragon because you don't like us. But you

84

called me blessed." He steps closer still, his body pressing right up against my palm.

The hard ridges of his chest muscles are pronounced against my hand. "Axel."

"Yes." He smiles.

"You *are* my enemy—even more than I thought."

"But I'm not, not yours. Never yours." He shakes his head and steps closer still.

Unwilling to allow my arm to collapse, his forward movement shoves me backward. I splay my fingers, and they shift downward with the soft weave of his t-shirt. The small, square bulges of his abdominal muscles might be even more distracting than his pecs were. "You are."

"I'll never be your enemy, Liz. We're entwined."

For some reason, my stupid heart's beating faster, and my breaths are coming shorter, too. I need to start working out every morning again. I'm getting soft. "You're a dragon, and I'm a human, and you want to kill us, steal from us, and then abandon us."

"I won't abandon you," he says. "I've been thinking about it."

"You have."

He steps toward me again, but this time, when I shift back, the backs of my legs hit the seat cushions of the sofa, and I drop backward, my hand shifting down again. It's plunging awfully close to Axel's waistband, so I snatch it back.

But now there's nothing between him, where he's standing over me, and me.

He drops one hand on either side of my thighs, his head lowering slowly toward mine. "You, Liz, are *mine*, and I won't relinquish you. I won't free you, and I won't allow anyone to kill you. Not my brother. Not other humans. And not my father." His eyes study mine intently. "Are we clear?"

"You're saying you would fight your own father for me?"

His lip curls. "How do you think my father became the leader of the blessed?"

I blink.

"He killed his own father to assume control."

"You don't know that," I say. "You weren't even alive."

"I hear things," he says. "And if I have to, I'll do the same."

It's hot. I'm not going to lie.

I spent the better part of my life in a training gym, punching things and people. The fight for dominance is real, and in a fight or flight moment, there's nothing more attractive than watching someone destroy his opponent.

It's definitely part of why I always liked Gideon, if I'm being totally honest. And now I'm staring at an apex predator who's telling me he would kill *the* greatest predator ever to live.

For me.

It doesn't hurt that his hair is falling over his perfectly shaped brow just so, his eyes are shining like champagne in the moonlight, and his body is radiating the kind of heat that I should not crave.

It's the kind of heat that might boil a normal person.

But I want to rip his shirt off over his head and run my hands down every inch of his body. I want him to have a *reason* to kill someone for me.

I want to belong to him.

Which is so very messed up. I like the very person who poses the greatest threat to humanity. He just admitted that it's worse than I thought. I should be going for my swords.

But instead, I ask, "Would killing your dad make you a traitor? Or a patriot?" I can't help the corners of my lip turning up.

"All mourn the king. All hail the king." His lips purse.

I need to stop staring at them. It's not helping me.

"Would you kill someone for me, Liz?"

"I have," I say. "Several scaly someones, in fact."

"But would you kill a human for me?" He arches one perfect brow.

The devil tempts us in the worst ways. Ways that make it hard to turn him down. I never really understood that before, not fully, not until this very moment. Because the devil in front of me is. . .complex.

I don't know what to say, so I lean forward and act on another, less confusing instinct.

And I kiss him.

I just kissed Gideon. He was the man I thought I wanted to be with. He was the man I've liked for a very long time. In fact, when we kissed earlier, it was hot. My body still reacted.

I wanted him.

I've never been one who believed in soulmates, so I'm not suffering from some kind of crisis of faith or conscience for being attracted to two men. But comparing what I felt for Gideon to what my body is doing when I kiss Axel in this moment would be like comparing a gentle breeze to the gale force of a hurricane.

Axel's body flexes around me, his hands fisting against the leather of the sofa and his arms expanding. His neck cranes and his lips tilt me upward toward him as he takes control. But he does it slowly. He does it lazily, almost, like we have all the time in the world.

Which can't be true. Because I'm literally catching *fire*.

I know that human temperatures run at 98.6 degrees. Everyone knows that. But there's no way that I'm anywhere near that right now, and where our lips touch, heat sears its way through me, and I *love every second of it.*

My right hand slides up the side of his face and slips into his hair, while my left hand grabs the front of his shirt and pulls him down. Since he has no idea what he's doing, I wonder whether my yanking and pulling might confuse him. It might irritate him, even. But then he growls deep in his chest in a way a human never could, and my insides melt like steel in the center of a freaking furnace.

That's when I smell it—a roasting scent, almost like turkey legs being turned on a spit at the Houston Renaissance Festival. I pull back just long enough to see that where his fists are planted against the sofa, it's smoking.

"Axel," I whisper.

He shakes his head, and bites his bottom lip.

"We need to—"

"Don't say stop," he snaps. "If you say stop—"

I release my grip on his shirt and spread my hand out, moving it slightly, so slightly, so that I can feel the ridges of muscle underneath his shirt. "I wasn't going to say stop. I don't think I could say that."

His grin is wicked.

"But now that we have hit pause." I draw in a breath sharply. "I'd rather not burn this building down."

His laughter's high and bright. "I couldn't care less about that."

"I would," I say softly.

He frowns, as if he's not sure what I'm saying.

"I'd hate myself for it, but I would kill someone for you. I'm terribly worried that I would kill a great many someones, if it came to that."

Axel's eyes widen, and he stands, and something in our bond shifts, shuddering, shaking, and then dropping into place yet again.

At first, our bond was like shackles around my ankles, dragging me, weighing on me, pulling at me. I hated it and wanted it gone. Then after we entwined, my bond became like a climbing harness, keeping me from falling to the ground.

But now it's different in another way.

For the first time since that day on the playground by my house, the bond feels like a buoy, keeping me afloat in a storm-tossed ocean. I press my hand against my own chest, and I draw in a very full, very relaxed breath.

"What just happened?"

"I think our bond is settling in," he says. "I know it's late and you need to sleep, but tomorrow, I want to test flying farther away. I bet you'll manage a lot better alone."

I know he's hoping he can fly home to see his dad without me, and I should be grateful. The last thing I want to do is confront the leader of every single dragon on their own home planet. He's basically the destroyer of all things, as far as I can tell. But. . .

"I don't want you to leave me," I say. "Even if now you can."

And that's the real change. This morning, I was desperate for us to have a little space to exist independently, but now, I don't want it.

If anything in the world has the power to keep me away from Axel after that soul-consuming kiss, it's this truth: the more time I spend with him, the less able I seem to be to go without him. I may be the only person on earth who can save us from the fate that's hurtling our way, and when the time comes, I'm afraid I won't be able to do it.

❧ 8 ❧
AXEL

Liz is sleeping.

She fell asleep moments after her daily cleansing ritual, just after dropping onto a bed with wet hair. She used to insist on sleeping downstairs, near her siblings.

Now she doesn't even ask to leave.

It fills me with a sense of satisfaction, having her near me, in my lair, prone and vulnerable without fear. She knows I'll protect her. I immediately shift into my flame blessed form. I'm always the most comfortable in my strongest iteration, especially when Liz is around. She feels safe—I want to keep her that way.

Azar has a lot to do, and so does Axel for that matter. It was always hard enough playing two leadership roles, but it's harder still now that I must always be by Liz's side. I should be directing the blessed to prepare for our looming departure. I also have directions to give in order to prepare for tomorrow's Thanksgiving celebration.

But instead of sneaking out to work, I curl up beside Liz's sleeping form and watch her breathe. Just for a moment.

Her small chest rises and falls—in my shirt. She asked to wear it to sleep in, and it made me feel strange inside. Seeing her in it—the shirt she was just grabbing with her small, delicate hands—makes me want to curl all the way around her and roar.

Which is idiotic.

I'm not idiotic, so I don't do that.

But I am still here, watching.

The bond feels bright now, like a beacon in a dark night. I could always use it to locate her, but now she practically pulses with the same light from the bond.

My refusal to eat other blessed always felt like a deep, dark, embarrassing secret. Why have I always been so different? Why can't I do the things that others of my kind do? Why haven't I killed those who challenge me immediately?

It's not that I've never killed any blessed.

Of course I have.

We're a savage race, and when forced, I've dispatched my enemies whenever necessary. But to engage in a battle and instead of striving to incapacitate my opponent, plan to kill and consume them? It has never been something I could bring myself to do.

Perhaps because I'm earth blessed.

Or maybe because I'm weak.

That has always been my fear.

But Liz—the expression on her face when I told her. . . She's a warrior. I expected her disdain. But she looked relieved. She looked. . .impressed.

In all my life, I've only desired the admiration of two blessed: my father and Euphrasia. But now, I desire above all things to win the high regard of a tiny human woman.

Who hates me.

At least it's not personal. She hates us all. I can't even blame her. If my father's right, our removal of the heart may spell the humans' eventual doom. I shouldn't have told her my suspicions, but I couldn't keep it from her anymore. It was eating at me.

That's not a feeling I've experienced before, either.

Being bonded to a human is not for the faint of heart. They're like little tempests in bottles, walking around *feeling* things all day long. But after over an hour, I finally force myself to my feet. I project a bright red flame shield around her, and then I finally drag myself away.

Unlike the other times I've tried to leave, this time, it doesn't wake her. It could be that she's more exhausted, but I think it may be that the bond has actually relaxed. I'll test it more soon. For now, I'm just grateful I can fly far enough away not to bother her or allow others to see her themselves without causing her pain.

By dawn, I've met with the earth blessed, as Axel, and everyone else, as Azar, and plans are well under way for this Thanksgiving thing the humans do. Or at least, the humans are making plans for it. From the grumblings I heard, most of them are not keen on leaving all their subordinates they've trained here when we depart, but Liz is adamant that only the bonded humans will come with us.

I shift just after my arrival, so when Liz's eyes open, I'm sitting in a chair next to the bed with my feet propped on the small table beside her. I've learned that when I'm lying next to her, she becomes agitated. Maybe I should have done that for precisely that reason. An angry Liz is a fun Liz, but with the day we have ahead of us, it felt smart not to work her up right away.

When she meets my eyes, she smiles.

I made the right call.

Nothing I've ever seen, no sunset, no mountain peak, no chemical reaction in the sky or algae bloom underwater, has ever been as beautiful as her smile.

"Axel?"

I nod.

"We should get moving. We have a lot to do for Thanksgiving. I can't believe you let me sleep that long." She yawns and stretches, and for some reason, that makes me want to yawn. So I do.

I've never yawned before, and it's a strange feeling, like stretching my face.

"You know, when I was a kid, my friend told me that if you wanted to figure out whether a guy likes you, you can yawn. If he yawns too, it means he was watching you, and he does like you."

"Of course I like you," I say.

That makes her cheeks flush. Humans still confuse me sometimes.

"Don't you like me?" I tilt my head. "I mean, isn't that why you said you'd kill a human for me?"

She hops out of bed, all shaky and agitated. "I didn't say I'd kill a human for you. Don't say it like that, like you could just say, 'hey Liz, I need a human on the menu today,' and I'd just go fetch you a fresh one."

I can't help my frown. "That's not what I said at all."

"And you know what? While we're talking, I want my swords back." She crosses her arms and glares at me.

"Get them yourself." I stand up. Baiting Liz has become almost an art form, but I don't have a lot of time for it today. "And then get dressed. We need to head over to the banquet hall and—"

"The *what*?" Liz looks almost green.

"It's in the Convention Center. The strike blessed peeled the ceiling off one of the large rooms, and they've had the humans prepare—"

"Axel."

Usually hearing her say my name sends a little shiver up my spine, but not today. Today, she's annoyed. Today, she's about to yell at me for something. Actually, that's probably the more common way for her to say it. Last night was the real anomaly. Her breathy little sigh before saying my name made me shiver with pleasure. Last night, she said it like it was a prayer.

If she's praying today, it's not to me. I inhale slowly and brace myself for impact.

"It's sunrise," she says. "So if you have dragons peeling ceilings off buildings and destroying all the hard work of the humans who built it at *dawn*, where were you all night?"

That is not what I thought she'd say. I clear my throat. "I thought you'd be happy that I was out making plans. We have a lot to do before we can leave, and your brother wanted this Thanksgiving thing to be just right."

Her smile this time is twice as bright as the good morning smile, and it makes me want to grab her with both hands and squeeze her until she squeals. "I should have said this yesterday, but thank you for listening to him. Thanks for letting us celebrate."

She doesn't say that they haven't had anything to celebrate in a long time. She doesn't have to say that. I know. And it's our fault, so I just nod.

"But what kind of grotesque menu are your dragons putting together?"

"I think the humans are preparing the food," I say. "And just as the blessed don't need to sleep in the way that humans do, we do not have to eat as you do, either. We draw energy from the elements around us. The water blessed thrive in the ocean. The strike blessed thrive diving in the wind and sliding past the energy of the storms."

"Are you saying they're literally powered by lightning?"

"And the heat of the sun calls to me," I say. "The earth blessed derive nutrition from the earth itself and from burrowing into it. As much as we gain from those places, we are not often called upon to consume flesh."

"Thank goodness for small blessings," she says. "But

then, what should we prepare for the feast?" She frowns. "It's not like I can put a lightning bolt on a platter or mound up piles of dirt."

"Focus on feeding the earth blessed," I say. "They'll heartily eat anything you provide. The others will simply throng around the edges, happy to witness your tradition."

"Yeah, and they'll try to convince you to hand them my brother or sisters on a silver platter." She drops her hands on her hips. "If you think I'm going to let any of your dragons bond-rape them, you've lost your mind."

"Explain." The word literally has something to do with human mating, I believe, but it's not a word I really understand.

"Raping is forcing something on someone without their consent," she says. "And actually, every single human who is bonded to a dragon was raped, including me."

That accusation hurts me. "You still hate the bond?"

She shakes her head. "No, but I wasn't given a choice, Axel. No one should be forced into a position of control by someone else without a choice."

"A position of control?"

She ducks into the bathroom to change clothing, but she doesn't stop talking. "You haven't done it, but you could force me to do things. All the other dragons do."

"Do you really have to disappear to change your apparel?" I ask. "Can't you stay here, where I can see you?"

Her head pokes back out. "See? This is what I mean. Modesty is my right. I can choose what parts of my body people are able to see. You can't tell me what I can and can't share."

It's confusing. "We don't have this concept. From birth, every one of us is subject to the whims of my father. None of us are entitled to any rights. In fact, he's not either. If someone else is stronger, then they should take his power over us away."

Her head disappears, and this time, she keeps quiet. When she steps back out, she's wearing the clothing made from my skin that I gave her. She always looks beautiful, for a human, but in that, she looks stunning.

"Now you just need your swords."

"Can't you just shift and get them for me?" She bats her eyes, as if that will convince me.

"Get them for yourself," I repeat.

"Sometimes I think you're getting better, but then others, you're still a real jerk." She stomps on my foot as she walks past, and it actually hurts. I don't flinch, of course, because showing weakness is anathema to the blessed.

But it's an effort.

I follow her to the room where she lost her swords. They're still dangling from the ceiling. She flips her head back, staring at them with flaring nostrils. "And how, exactly, do you propose I get them? Did you see any ladders? Or perhaps a misplaced set of wings I can borrow?"

I can't help my smile. "You stopped Sammy from dropping to his death."

She huffs. "You know that I can't do that on command. It only works when the circumstances are dire."

"And when they're dire enough, maybe you'll get your swords back."

The words she says next are not words I've heard commonly used, but I make note of them for later. If I'm remembering correctly, one of them is a word she fussed at Coral for saying just last week.

"Now, if you're done—"

"I'm not done, you sack of scales. I'm not about to attend a big party full of both dragons and humans without any way to even poke them if they get out of line." She flings her hands upward and says, "I want my swords."

And they drop straight down and into her hand, amid a shower of drywall chunks and dust.

She's so shocked that she nearly misses catching them, and Liz has reflexes that would make any blessed proud, probably thanks to our bond increasing her capacity, but it's still impressive. "How did you—" She splutters. "You knew I'd get them down if you got me angry enough."

"It seems to be a surge of human emotion that allows you to use your powers for now." I shrug. "I had a hunch."

"So you weren't just being a jerk for no reason."

"I never attempt to be a bad person," I say. "It just seems to happen at times, at least, by your reckoning."

She rolls her eyes. "You offered to free my siblings," she says. "That's when I stopped hating you as much."

"I offered to fly them to the edge of our holdings," I say. "I didn't have any control over what happened to them beyond that point."

"You were using them to control me," she says. "And instead of holding on to that power, you offered to give it up. That's what made our bond better than rape."

"But you think that all the other bonds out there. . .?" I study her face. "You think they're toxic."

She nods. "I do."

"And that makes you hate us more."

"Not only me," she says. "No matter how stunning you are, no matter how powerful, no matter how much you may try to understand us—though I doubt most of you are trying very hard—as long as you're forcing us to serve you. . .as long as you are giving us no choice, you're evil. At least, by a human way of reckoning."

And as their leader, if I allow them to behave as they have been, I'm condoning it, and she blames me. It's something to think about. "But there's nothing I can do about the bonds now that they've been made."

"You can allow the humans to walk away," she says.

"Unlike entwined bonds, they won't have any ill effects from being separated."

"That we know of."

She shrugs.

"We need the humans to tend to the other humans, and they help expand the search for us as well."

"For the heart you'll steal, destroying Earth as we know it."

"What would you have me do?"

She frowns. "Can I think about it?"

"Could I stop you if I tried?"

She laughs then.

While I shift into Azar, and while we collect her siblings and travel to the center of the George R. Brown Convention Center—which truly has been flayed open in the center so that several hundred blessed will fit beside the gathered humans—she appears almost happy. The bond practically thrums with an effervescent sensation I quite enjoy.

It lightens my heart as well.

You look strong today, Asteria says. It's quite a compliment, coming from her. *She makes you strong.* Now she looks. . .well, blessed don't get jealous like humans do, but she appears to be irritated in some way.

Our bond makes us both stronger, I say. *It's new yet, but we're learning how to navigate it. Don't worry. It won't delay our mating much longer.*

Are you sure you still want to mate? She's looking at Liz with narrowed eyes and sparking talons. I don't like it. Before I can say a word, her head snaps back toward me. *Don't worry. I'm not my sister. I don't destroy what I fear.*

Where is Ocharta?

This Thanksgiving is a day of gratitude for them, Asteria says. *As a boon for your bonded, I brought her mother, but I ordered my sister to remain at the edge of the festivities.*

Ordered? I can't help the amused tone of my question.

While you deepened your bond, or whatever you do up in your tower with your human, Ocharta challenged me.

You didn't kill her?

Asteria's half-smile is attractive. Not many blessed are more beautiful. *My future mate doesn't kill when he defeats an opponent. I'm trying to make him proud.*

Well done. I don't tell her that the reason I don't want her dead is to keep Liz's mother alive. She probably already knows, but with the females, it's never wise to draw attention to anything that makes them irritable.

And I've been thinking. I'm sure you'd like someone more powerful than an earth blessed caring for your bonded's family. It didn't work for me to take her mother's bond, but I can bond one of the sisters when she's old enough and find strong but competent strike blessed for the others.

For some reason, the offer makes me vaguely uncomfortable.

In the meantime, I can transport all three to Iceland. It's not as if their weight is substantial.

Liz has stopped talking to the ensnared who are preparing the feast and has circled back around to where I'm standing. "My siblings really, really love Gordon and Rufus. I think riding on anyone else would stress them out, and I suspect the relocation will be stressful enough already, but if you could kind of watch over them, I would really appreciate it."

Asteria's lips compress, but I'm guessing it's imperceptible to a human. *Of course.*

But she's displeased. I'm going to watch that closely. I want the two of them to get along, but in my limited experience, two very strong, very powerful females often do not.

Did you see that your mother is here? Asteria asks. *I made sure that her bonded will not be.*

"Thank you," Liz says. "What a wonderful Thanksgiving gift."

Asteria's smiling when Liz's mother walks up.

"We need to talk," she says.

But she's not staring at Liz. She's looking at me.

LIZ

"Oh, no," I say. "I don't think so."

For the first time since the dragons came, my mother looks exactly like herself. She doesn't look broken, downtrodden, or conciliatory. Instead, she arches an imperious eyebrow, drops one hand on her hip, and pins me with a stare. "Your bonded, here, Azar, Flame Blessed Prince, is the one who decides where we're moving next. Isn't that right?"

I blink.

"Then I need to speak with him. He may refuse my request, but I'm making it, for the good of my own child."

You want to speak with me. . .for Liz? The set of Azar's head tells me that he's intrigued.

I know it better than anyone—his curiosity's the best way to get what you want with him. It kept my siblings safe, it kept him from killing me straight off, and I've used it countless times to convince him to give me my way.

But how did my *mom* figure out that's what would grab his attention?

Alright, Azar says. *Follow me.*

There's no way the two of them are going to march off

to talk about what's best for me in secret, even if I can hear everything she says through the bond, as long as I remain focused on it. "I'm coming, too."

"That's a bad idea," Mom says. "There are some things I need to explain to Prince Azar."

"Mom, I'll be able to hear everything you say. Walking off and talking to him around the corner won't change that."

"Nice try," Mom says. "But I'm bonded, too. I know you can't hear every word anyone says around him."

She can, Azar says. *Our bond is different.*

Mom frowns. "Oh."

"Let's all go together." I can't imagine what she might say to him that she wouldn't want me to hear, but it can't be anything good.

I start walking toward the alcove I'm pretty sure Azar was headed toward. There aren't many places big enough to allow for semi-privacy for a dragon of Azar's size, but the large conference room off to the side of this huge gathering space also lost its roof, and it should work just fine.

Mom looks annoyed, but when Azar follows my lead, she doesn't argue. I'm actually impressed that she's demanding audiences with Azar instead of dropping her eyes and begging me to kill her. We've come a long way. Asteria's assault on Ocharta and attempts to take her bond must've done more to raise Mom's morale than I realized. Or maybe it's just the renewal of hope that she might find a way out. I wish I'd discovered anything even the least bit helpful in dissolving bonds.

So far, my bond only ever seems to choke down tighter and tighter. At least I'm bonded to a pretty decent dragon instead of a mouth-breathing bond-rapist.

Mom marches past me once she realizes where we're going and then pivots on her boot heel and turns to face us. "You're sure we can't have a short conversation without her hearing?" She's staring straight up at Azar's massive head, ignoring me yet again.

He snorts and smoke puffs out of his nostrils.

"I'll take that as a no." She sighs—acting for all the world like she's been stuck spearheading another PTO event. She hated those, but as a stay-at-home, crystal-reading hippy, she didn't have any real excuses not to help with them.

"Spit it out, Mom. What do you need to say? We're supposed to start the Thanksgiving dinner soon, and—"

"I overheard people preparing." She folds her arms. "We're going to Iceland."

Azar's eyes cut sideways and he meets my face, clearly confused.

"Yes, Mom. I don't think it's really a secret."

She purses her lips. "I also overheard Ocharta some time ago—she mentioned a heart. It's what you're here to find, is it not?" Her face is inscrutable now, and I wonder what she's put together.

Azar nods slowly.

"You're going to Iceland, because Liz was almost thrown into the volcano there, and she said that there were people there chanting *hjartanu*, aren't you?"

That's not the only reason. Azar's tail is swishing, like he's agitated. The bond is a deep yellow, and I can't decide if that's pensive or irritated. I'm sure he's not used to being interrogated by anyone other than maybe his father.

And me, I guess.

"Pardon my impertinence in asking all this," Mom says, "but are there any reasons that have nothing to do with Liz?" She arches her eyebrow, acting like I'm not even here.

"Mom, they've been here for a month, and they've been searching everywhere for this heart. They've found no evidence of it anywhere. But Azar can see my dreams, and he saw the whole thing himself."

Mom flinches, but she never turns my direction. Her eyes stay trained on Azar. A muscle in her jaw starts to pulse, and she says, "Then I think you should know something." She pulls a phone out of her pocket and sets it on the ground in front of her. "I charged up my phone. Liz can show you how to use it. I have a file in there labeled *Iceland*. It has the video footage, the police reports, everything from that miserable nightmare."

"Mom, what are you—"

"After being stolen by Slavic sex-traffickers—" Mom flinches, but keeps talking. "She was taken, along with half a dozen others, by a faction within the organization."

"Mom, you've never said—"

She ignores me and plows ahead. "They didn't mean to come to Iceland, but two of the people were from here, and they thought they could hide. They were running from their boss—they were about to sell her when they realized they'd been found."

"They were taking me to the volcano," I say.

"When we found her, she had shoved one of them—the woman—into the volcano where they had hoped to hide and stabbed the other. She had freed herself and was running down the mountain, her feet run ragged. The police located the third member of the group of people who took her, badly injured on the side of the mountain, near the entrance to the volcanic ledge. When we arrived, we'd marshaled the local police and our own support team, and we had already located the five other girls they'd left when they were trying to complete the sale of Elizabeth. What we didn't find were any groups of people in or around the volcano. No one was chanting. No one was watching." My mom clears her throat. "No one else was there at all, not even the buyer they had been messaging. We believe he had already sold them out to their boss for a hefty fee."

"Mom, there were dozens and dozens of people, all

gathered there. They were all saying the same strange thing over and over."

She still won't meet my eye. She's staring up at Azar. "Trust me when I tell you that if there really were any other people there during her ordeal, we'd have found some evidence of it."

"Evidence?" I have no idea what she's saying. "Like, what? Glass slippers they left behind?"

"On the day we located Elizabeth, other than the people who dragged her up that hill, there were no humans present. There was nowhere for a hundred other people to hide. We'd have seen them, or some evidence of their presence. When the local police were finally able to interrogate the survivor, almost a week later, he would only say one phrase, over and over. In Icelandic, it was *hinn bölvaði*, which in English translates as 'the cursed.'"

"Are you saying I made those people up? That they didn't exist?"

I saw them in her dreams. Bless Azar for backing me up.

"Her father believes that her mind created them as silent witnesses to her story. The psychologist we hired said she probably feels tremendous guilt for killing those people, and that she needed an explanation. She needed there to be others there who saw what she went through and could testify that she had no other choice. She had to believe she was in mortal peril."

"Mom, I'm right here. Stop saying she."

But she doesn't turn around. She won't even meet my eye.

"Elizabeth was very afraid after that event, and she spent most nights sobbing. Her father insisted that we put her in training to defend herself, but as soon as we did, she manifested a disturbing amount of zeal for it." Mom drops her voice. "She was a natural fighter—vicious, talented, and almost preternaturally fast. All her teachers said so. She surpassed their skill within months, and we had to locate someone more talented to train her. I wanted to put a stop to it, but her psychologist insisted it was a healthy outlet."

"Mom, I'm right behind you. Please stop talking about me like I'm not even here."

"I disagreed with them," Mom continues as if I never said a word. "I thought it was bad for her. Those three people forced her to do something no child should ever have done—murdering another human. But her father listened to the experts and he kept agreeing to advance her more and more, training the violent streak that had manifested into something much stronger, an almost homicidal glee in fighting."

Her words are like daggers in my heart. Is that why she never came to any of my matches? I thought it was her fear for my safety. I had friends whose loved ones couldn't watch.

But my mom—was she afraid *of* me?

"If you're relocating all the blessed to Iceland on the basis of her experience, I believe you to be making a significant mistake. Respectfully, I suggest that you take additional steps to make a plan before relying on her story."

She wanted to talk to Azar to tell him that. . .I'm crazy? That I made up silent witnesses to justify murdering my kidnappers?

Something inside of me breaks in that moment.

"You left me to protect the children." My words are barely a whisper.

"She seems genuinely fond of her sisters and brother," Mom says, still not talking to me. "And who better to protect children from monsters than—" She cuts off.

But I know what she meant to say.

Who better to protect them from a monster than another monster? A monster who's fond of the ones who need protection. My own mother thinks I'm damaged in ways that can't be easily repaired. She thinks I'm not reliable, and that I'm not quite human.

My shoulders fall. My eyes drop to the ground, and my mind casts backward to that memory. It's vivid. It's seared into my brain.

I can see them—the hundred plus people crowded into the space between the small entry into the cavern and the ledge they tried to shove me down. They were there—all adults. Male and female. They were chanting. I couldn't have made that up.

Could I?

What about her birthmark? Azar's voice is skeptical. He's not a human, and his feelings don't always track the way I would expect, but it sounds like he disbelieves my mom's story.

"It's true that she has a heart-shaped birthmark," Mom says. "But I have a birthmark on my back. Her father has one on his knee. We thought that was why she made up the story she did."

"All these years, you thought I made it up? And where would I have gotten the word *hjartanu*? I don't speak Icelandic."

"You might have heard it from one of the attackers. Or perhaps you heard a police officer say the word." Mom finally turns toward me slowly. "You have no idea how much worse things could have been for you. Those three who stole you, they were in trouble with their boss—the leader of the ring. Your memories could have been far worse, and we couldn't even correct you without talking about a lot of things we didn't want to expose you to, not after what you'd already endured."

"You think being sold to perverts would be worse than people who wanted to throw me into a volcano?"

Mom's face is sad. "But they weren't throwing you into a volcano. That was merely the liaison spot."

Rage bubbles up inside of me. My mother thinks I *made up* my memory. She thinks her own daughter's crazy. "No way." I shake my head. "They took me because of my tattoo, and they were about to shove me over the ledge. How else would I have dragged that woman there?"

She turns back to Azar. "Even as a child, when questioned, she doubled down on her story like this." She looks weary. "There wasn't anything we could do to help her, then or now."

"You think I made it all up? The people telling me they took me for my tattoo—my birthmark? The people at the volcano, and the ones who were going to throw me in?"

Her face falls. "It was an awful thing you endured, but I don't think it has anything to do with the blessed or their search."

I stare at her, and I wish I'd listened. I wish I'd never followed them here and heard that my mother thinks I'm a homicidal, broken monster. A crazy, delusional one at that.

Azar takes a ponderous step forward, and he drops his head down low so it's right next to me. *I believe Liz.*

My heart swells. I know my mom's not trying to hurt me, but. . .

"I thought you might." Mom bows, doubling over entirely, and then slowly stands. "I mean no disrespect to you or to your bonded, and I certainly have never wanted to hurt my daughter. But look at the phone." She straightens and turns to leave, her shoulders square and her head held high.

As she walks through the doorway, she freezes. "Oh."

I spin around, catching sight of the toes of a pair of boots—Gideon's. He must have been listening in. How very Gideon of him, trying to protect me even now.

But I can't go find him right now. I have a phone file to inspect. My hand's trembling as I pick it up.

Liz.

I shake my head. "Let me just look at this." But I can't open it. I just keep staring at it. I have to remind myself that one thing no one has ever accused me of is being a coward. I ball my hand into a fist, and I crouch down, and I force my fingers to pick it up.

But by the time I straighten, Azar has transformed into Axel's human form. His hand takes me by the wrist. "Liz."

My eyes widen. "You can't do that here. Anyone could have seen you."

His arms wrap around me, pulling me against his chest.

Tears well up in my eyes. "No. You can't do this here. We can't. What if someone saw you come in here? I'm sure lots of dragons did. You're the size of a Boeing 747."

"Liz." His voice is deep, solid, and calm.

"She says I—" My voice breaks on *I*. "She says I made it all up. She says I'm a murderer. She says that's who I am deep down, that I'm messed up."

"I believe you."

But I don't even believe myself anymore. I tap away until I'm opening the file. I'm practically frantic to prove that my mom's wrong. I'm not a monster who murdered two people and maimed another when they were merely dragging me to meet up with someone else. There were people gathered there. They were going to shove me into the volcano—they told me as much.

The file's there, just like Mom said. It's marked *Iceland*.

A lot of it isn't in English, but there are photos. And there's a translation of the interrogation of the man who didn't die. I didn't even realize I killed the other man—I called him Driver. "I didn't think I even hurt Beer Can," I say.

His name's apparently Gunnar Jónsson.

The record shows that he was badly burned, and that a dagger struck him in his foot.

"Maybe the other people did that—not me. I ran after I

stabbed. . ." I hear myself. I sound as crazy as Mom said I am.

I close my eyes.

But when I open them, the files are the same. No record of any other people in the area. And Beer Can would never say anything except 'the cursed,' over and over.

My free hand tightens into a fist at my side, and I do the only thing I know to do to keep tears at bay. I prepare for a fight.

"Liz," Axel says.

"I am crazy," I say. "I guess I must be. I can't believe Mom knew it all along."

"You're not," he says. "A terrible thing happened to you, and all she has are images of papers. You were there."

I blink. "You—you still believe me?"

Axel nods, his eyes entirely sincere.

"But these papers—they're our human records. They're proof that what I said took place didn't happen."

His hands rise slowly, his fingers brushing the sides of my face. "I saw your memory. So if you're crazy, then so am I. Memories don't lie."

"Human memories do lie sometimes," I say. "We can change our memories if we tell them in a different way enough times."

"I believe you," he says. "We will go to Iceland."

"But what if my mom's right? What if there's nothing there but a volcano?"

Axel shrugs. "We've found nothing here, either. We'll be no worse off than we currently are."

And Houston will be free again.

A noise behind us, a rustling, has me spinning around and glancing overhead. "Someone could see you any moment. You have to shift back now."

His finger brushes across my mouth. "Are you alright? The bond's still. . .trembling."

Trembling. "You don't see colors?"

He shakes his head. "You do?"

I laugh. "We can talk about that later."

He nods. "Later."

"Now it's time for us to start the first dragon-human Thanksgiving. So get your red scales on, mister."

Axel leans a bit closer, pressing his fingers against my lip even harder. "I will, but before we start, I want to tell you something."

I want to bite his finger. I want to drag his head down toward mine. I want to *kiss* the dragon overlord I'm bonded to. Maybe Mom is right. Maybe I am a monster.

"Today, I'm only thankful for one thing." He releases me, dropping his hands to his side. "In all my life, I'd only had one blessed I cared about, and that was Euphrasia. I still care for her in a way very few blessed do. But now, I'm even more grateful that I bonded you. You brighten my life, Elizabeth Chadwick."

Before I can even respond, my horrible beast smiles a wry smile and shifts back into his large red form—the bigger, more terrifying beast, and also still the same. For a moment, as I stare up at his gleaming scarlet scales, at the power and majesty of the massive beast in front of me, I wonder whether it's really even that bad to be a monster.

Or maybe I'm just too far gone to care what I've become.

That may be the scariest thought of all.

‹❦ 10 ❦›

LIZ

Come, my monster.

I startle at the word, surprised both that Azar's making a joke, and also that he knew what I was thinking. But then it makes me laugh.

We have a party to start together.

I suppose we do.

I begin walking out the enormous, ceiling-less doors, but Azar grunts.

When I turn around, I realize that there's a saddle on his back. *You're riding with me. Flame blessed don't* walk *into rooms.*

As I scramble up his back, thankful he still drops his shoulder for me, I can't help thinking about Iceland again. "Do you really think it's a good idea to go?"

He doesn't mistake my question as being one about Thanksgiving. He knows what I'm asking. That's comforting in and of itself—having someone who always understands me. *I do. The heart's not near Houston.*

The heart. The object that, if they extricate it, might plunge Earth into sheer misery. And it would be my fault for assisting them.

If our removing the heart harms humans, we'll do anything we can to mitigate that before leaving.

"Do you swear?"

Azar's giant neck swivels so he's looking me right in the eye. His are bright golden, even in this form. The same, whether he's the Cow Dragon Prince, in his human form, or this massive, terrifying creature.

He's always the Azar I know and care about.

Liz, I'm a terrible monster, which I understand is something bad when you say it. But it means that there's very little for me to fear. The one thing that scares me right now is losing your goodwill. If I can do anything to stop that while still ensuring the future of the blessed, I'll do it.

My heart swells again.

It may be us against them—humans versus dragons—and without the heart, something namelessly bad might happen to humanity. But without the heart, they're dying slowly. They're forced to eat their own kind or disappear. I don't blame them for coming here. I'm not sure humans would have waited as long as they have to do it.

Azar's head straightens, and I realize he's preparing to launch.

I need to figure out this saddle first—it'll make it much easier for me to stay on. It isn't much like any horse saddle I've ever seen. There aren't stirrups, but there is a cushioned seat, as well as handholds. That's when I notice the strange straps that are dangling. "Do these go around my waist?"

Azar snorts.

I buckle them quickly, feeling much more secure. "This will make a quick dismount hard."

There's a latch.

I realize that he's right. If I want to hop off quickly, there's a simple lever I can flip and the straps will slide open. "Smart."

I run one hand gently over the bright red scales on one side of his body, and the bond slides into bright green. "You like that, huh?"

I like you.

A shiver runs through me. It's a strange feeling, affection for a horrible beast, but it's there nonetheless. Maybe my mother was right. Maybe I've been broken all along. What normal human could *like* a dragon like him right back?

I crouch forward, pressing my body flat against the saddle, and then I slide my hands into the grips. Without even checking in, Azar's muscles bunch, and he shoots straight up into the sky.

Once, at Universal Studios, I rode the Doctor Doom ride. It shot straight up before dropping like a rock. This ascent makes that one look like a kiddie bungee. But we finally reach a height Azar deems to be high enough—probably still visible, but impressively high. And then he circles in lazy swooping motions, slowly descending to the main hall.

I told each group to send twenty blessed.

"Even the earth blessed?" I ask. "How will you explain the lack of their prince?"

He's preparing last-minute departure details for me.

No one ever wonders about that?

It's an impossibility for us to take two shapes or possess two affinities, so no one questions it.

He's lucky about that, but it makes me wonder. We're getting close enough to the enormous meeting hall that I ask on a private telepathic channel. It's harder for me, but I need to learn. *Are you sure it would be bad for people to find out? Maybe they'd all be in awe.*

The bond darkens to a near-blood red color. *The blessed*

do not welcome new things. And even worse than new things are weaknesses. As it is, my friendship with Axel is seen as a bizarre quirk. If people knew I was Axel, they would see it as a weakness that needed to be expunged from the royal line.

Expunged.

That's not good.

I suppose he knows the dragons better than I do.

As we land, the bond color doesn't lighten, so I release one of the grips and stroke one hand down his side again. It works. Blood-red becomes grey. It's not green, but at least it's better.

Welcome, blessed and bonded. In a few hours, we'll leave Houston, but this celebration, a human gathering in which they express gratitude for what they have, will also serve as a celebration of our successful return to Earth. We will soon be moving forward into the next step of our recovery attempt, but we will do it confident that nothing the humans can send our way will endanger our mission.

As if they all got some memo that I missed, every single dragon in the gathering looks straight up at the sky and screams, a bizarre bugling sound that differs for each creature. Some are clear and quite lovely. Some sound more like the grinding of gears. But all of them are expressing their support of their leader, and I suppose that's good enough.

Even Hyperion adds his roar to the cacophony.

Only Azar remains silent.

I sit up straight and pat Azar's neck. I'm not sure how he'll feel about this, but I feel like, as his entwined, I ought to say something as well. "Today, humans often express the things they're most grateful for, so I'll take this chance to express how grateful I am for the safety and health of my mother, my sisters, and my brother. I appreciate all of your support in keeping them safe."

"I'm grateful for Gordon," Sammy says without missing

a beat. "At school, the other kids used to make fun of me because I talk different. But Gordon never does, and he always plays any games I want to play."

When I glance sideways, I notice that Gordon's in his snake-brown shape, coiled up next to Sammy. Even surrounded by all these other dragons, my little brother doesn't seem the least bit nervous. I'm sure that's because his guard is here. I wish I felt more confident that Gordon could keep him safe if it came down to a fight.

"I heard that when we leave, the humans who aren't bonded will be allowed to remain," my mother says. "Is that true?"

Yes, we've decided— Azar turns to look back at me. *—that it would be for the best if the Houston humans were left here. We'll find new humans in Iceland to serve you as needed.*

"We put a lot of effort into training these," an electro dragon bonded I've met but can't name grumbles at the end of the long table.

I slide off Azar's back and drop to the ground. As I walk toward the table, all the bonded bow their heads.

They bow every time they see me, and it makes me nuts.

"Stop that nonsense."

But other than Sammy, Coral, and Jade, they keep their heads down as if they're saying grace.

"Knock it off, I said."

They all lift their head at the same time, like marionettes, and I realize that I forced them. Only one of them meets my eyes when they pop up—my mom.

Her words come back to me then. *Who better to protect children from monsters than. . .*another monster?

Only, she's not the only one who is scared of me. She's not the only one whom I forced to obey. They all see me the same way—monstrous.

I reach the empty chair in the center of the table, and I realize that Azar's walking right behind me, hovering. He wants to make sure no one's rude, I imagine. He's worried about me, which I appreciate. But it's not necessary.

Monsters don't have feelings that can be bruised. Right?

"What are all of you grateful for?" I look up and down the table at the hundred and eighteen bonded humans. They're young. Old. White. Black. Hispanic. Indian. Asian. Male. Female. There's no unifying theme or consistency, though I heard there's a father and a daughter among them. I haven't spent enough time getting to know them, but I've had a lot going on, what with my bond, Azar's demands, and my siblings.

Penelope stands at the far end, her silver hair shining. "I'm grateful for an entwined leader who cares about us, who cares about the rest of the humans serving us, and who cares about doing the right thing."

Azar's roar surprises me, but the other blessed join him right away.

A cerulean-haired woman stands next, her dark brown eyes shining. "I'm grateful for my bond to Jericho. I know most of you here wish you hadn't been bonded, but I don't. I love swimming with him, and I love seeing things I'd never have seen in a million years."

A terribly large and long blue dragon, shaped a bit like a blue version of Gordon, is standing just behind her. He tosses his head, and I know it must be Jericho. It's the first evidence I've found that Azar and I aren't the only pair who aren't totally miserable with our bonds.

"I'm also grateful for my blessed." An older man with bright silver hair stands—but honestly, it looks from the lines in his face like the color might not have shifted much when he was bonded. "I know most of you were terrified when you were bonded, but Helvetica asked me whether I'd mind before bonding me." His smile's shy. "My wife passed six months ago, and this has been the first happy thing that has happened to me since."

"You can't really expect most of us to be grateful for being made slaves." Mom's eyes are flashing. I know her dragon's not here, but I'm worried that she can still feel what Mom's saying.

How many of you regret being bonded? Azar asks. *And how many of you were bonded against your will?*

I expect most of the humans to stand, or raise their hand, or something, but no one says a word. No one even moves.

"They won't be willing to risk the ire of their blessed or of you, my lord." Mom stands. "But it's no secret that I regret it. I hate my bond. It was done entirely against my will."

Mom's back with a vengeance, and what she said to me this morning—it was hard, but I'm glad she's acting like herself. It feels like something vital that was lost has returned. Even if that vital thing despises me, I wouldn't wish it gone.

Choices aren't something the blessed value overmuch, Azar says. *In fact, it's not even encouraged, for the blessed to make their own decisions. Certainly not when they defy the will of their rulers.*

Azar, Prince of Flames. Axel, Prince of the Earth Blessed. They like their rulers and their orders. They maintain a pecking order—even among the blessed.

"Humans have leaders, and we're expected to obey laws, but we also value individual choice," I say. "And I'm grateful that you've allowed me to make most of mine."

Without fear of reprisal from your blessed, how many of you bonded humans would dissolve your bond if given the chance? Azar seems to be in earnest, but I fear that he's in for a real shock if they believe his offer of protection and speak honestly.

Mom stands.

So do a dozen other humans.

And then another dozen.

"Azar doesn't ask empty questions," I say. "If you really wish you could dissolve your bond, stand. Your blessed won't punish you for it."

They will not. Not unless they want me to incinerate them against their will.

A dozen more stand.

Coral's counting, too. "Forty-one," she says.

"That can't be all of you," I say. "Almost eighty of you would *choose* to be bonded to your blessed?"

"What about you?" I notice that Penelope isn't standing. She is, however, staring at me with clear eyes. "You're entwined, but would you walk away if given that chance?"

I open my mouth to say that if I had a choice, I'd never be bonded to a dragon. But is that true? If Azar gave me that choice today, what would I do?

It's complicated.

Flying with him, fighting with him, they're exhilarating. They're different than anything else I've ever experienced. I think about how, without thought, he shifted and hugged me. He doesn't have emotions like we do, or at least, he didn't. But he's learning, and he cares. Part of me thinks that I can do more good for humanity right here, bonded to him, than I could anywhere else.

Is that an excuse?

Maybe.

But it's a plain truth that. . . "If I were given the chance to walk away right now, I don't think I'd take it." I turn around and face Azar. "Maybe that's the key to the reason we entwined. My blessed, he listens to me. We're not a partnership, maybe, and I wasn't given a choice at the start, but he never forces me to do anything now. He asks. And I believe that, if we knew how, he'd give me the choice today.

He'd let me choose to be bonded to him." I inhale slowly, and then I say, "That's the reason, I suppose, that I would choose to bond him today. Because I firmly believe he would give me the chance to say no."

❧ II ☙

AXEL

The blessed don't feel love. We don't feel longing. We don't care about things that humans care desperately about, but maybe Liz has infected me, because in this moment, I do care.

I wish I had the capacity to offer her a choice. I wish I could undo our bond. . .and let her choose it.

I was never given a choice, not for anything important in my life, and I haven't given much thought to it. Blessed *take* what they need. They force their will on the world around them, if they're powerful enough to do it, and if they aren't, well, the world forces on them.

It's the way things are.

It's how they'll always be.

But watching her, asking the tiny humans what they would *choose*, I long to give her that choice. I want to make a different kind of world for her—the one she deserves instead of the one we have.

Hearing that she would choose me if she could, well. It's a sharp plunge toward the ocean on a crisp, cool day. It's the windiest lift under my wings, sending me soaring. It's the bright rays of light from the ball of fire that powers this world suffusing all my limbs with a warm and steady strength. It's *everything* to me, and I burn to give her a gift even half as good as telling me that she would *choose* me if she had the chance.

Hyperion has been watching the proceedings with a curious look. Asteria, beside him, looks almost angry. The other blessed are watching with curious looks on their faces, mostly, but some of them look agitated.

And, of course, a few are furious.

I'm guessing their humans are standing in front of the table right now. I made those soft little creatures a promise, a promise that Liz expects me to keep.

Two more humans stand, their eyes downcast, clearly still afraid of a reprisal.

Liz sees it too. "I was, frankly, surprised to hear that a few of you would, like me, choose to stay with your blessed. I'm not very shocked to see that many of you would not make that choice."

"I think the behavior and temperament of my blessed has improved," Penelope says, standing, "but not by enough. I too, if given the chance, would leave."

Sixty-eight humans, in the end, stand. It's a small thing, standing up, but it's an impressive act of defiance in and of itself. Even though they chose differently than she, they may actually be the humans who are most like my Liz. They've chosen to hurl their broken, discarded umbrellas at their blesseds' throat, consequences bedamned. Like Liz, they're brave enough to fight in spite of overwhelming odds stacked against them.

In light of my promise, I say loudly, so that all the gathered blessed can hear, *the sixty-eight humans who have stood will remain here when we leave. They are hereby freed.*

The murmurs among the blessed are explosive and immediate.

You can't dissolve their bond, Asteria says. *You'll leave the bonded blessed at risk. They can't keep their bonded in line or safe.*

I shake my head. *They bonded humans without first gaining permission. They did it without thinking about the fact that the humans are living, sentient beings—they shouldn't have done it, nor should I. We can't fix what we did, but we can pay the penalty for our actions.* I spread my wings, and raise the force of my words. *No more humans will be bonded without first gaining their acquiescence.*

When we reach Iceland, the remaining bonded humans will be forced to manage the local population all alone. Hyperion looks even more amused. *I don't really care—they don't do much for me. But I imagine it won't make your followers very pleased.*

They shouldn't have acted as they did, I say. *And once they did bond another living being, they should have treated them with more respect and less force. They should have made the bonded humans like them, or at the very least, respect them.*

Why does the ability to force the humans' behaviors exist, if we're not supposed to use it? Asteria asks. *We're the dominant beings. Why must we earn their respect?*

My future mate's asking, but she's clearly asking because of the feelings and thoughts of the other strike blessed. If I want to keep things under control, which I must as Recovery Leader, I don't have a lot of options. I pull on my bond, drawing Liz to me.

Like it or not, this is the way of the blessed. If I want them to accept an authoritarian command, even one that forces them to rectify a prior misdeed, I must have the strength to back it up.

Miracle of miracles, Liz responds to my tug. *Get on.*

She does, without argument or complaint.

The second I sense her gripping the saddle, I burst upward, winging up as high and as fast as I can. And then I wheel around, the rage inside of me building. The blessed want to be ruled by force? They don't want to grant others' choices? Fine. I'll show them what that feels like.

Liz presses a hand against my side. "You can't kill them."

They're defying *me—questioning my authority.*

"But you just told them that they can't keep their bonded humans—I'm sure that stings. And you're telling them they just have to *agree* with you. That's exactly what you're telling them is wrong."

Someone has to lead.

"But if you lead with reason, you won't have to fear their actions when you aren't close."

She's such a brilliant, blinding light that sometimes I wonder how I lucked into bonding her. *What do you suggest I do instead of roasting them into submission?*

"Show them how you *could* behave, but how you choose *not* to behave and then ask them to do the right thing. Ask them to release their bonded of their own will, because the humans don't want to stay with them. Ask them to make the right decision."

Then I can incinerate anyone who doesn't choose correctly?

Liz's laughter is like a gorgeous sunrise, brightening even a dark and irritating day. "No, you mustn't do that. You must lead them and hope they follow."

This plan is doomed to failure.

"I thought the same thing about us, Azar." She pats my side, and with that one line, she wins, because she's implying that we aren't doomed. I want—very much—for that to be true.

Even so, I'm angry enough at the blessed for challenging me that I can't simply land again. Instead, I swoop overhead and release all the rage that's pent up inside. As ever, it comes out in the form of molten heat. It would hit the people below like a wave, probably killing most of the humans, so I use my power to negate it just before it does.

Even so, it makes a decent show of strength as I land.

I could incinerate anyone who disagrees. I could force you to heed my orders. But I'm not going to do that. Just because we can do something, that doesn't mean it's the right thing to do. So I'm going to apologize to my bonded.

Liz slides down my back.

I turn to face her. *I'm sorry. I should not have bonded you without asking. I should not have threatened you, or used your siblings' safety as a bargaining chip to secure the behavior I wanted.*

"A lot of the other bonded have asked me how we entwined, and I think the answer is mutual trust. In order to entwine, the bonded human and their blessed must begin to trust each other."

It's not lost on me that my bonded is trying to say blessed instead of her favored term—dragons. She's really trying not to be outrageous in this charged situation. They may not notice the small things, but the blessed are murmuring, and not in the same way as before. They sound less angry and more contemplative.

My job as your leader isn't just to order you to do something. It's to show you the better way to behave and trust you to do it. So today, I'm asking you all to do the very thing we should have done from the beginning. Ask your bonded if they will stay with you. Entreat them to work toward a partnership, instead of being your slaves. If they refuse, if they can't ever see a way to trust you, then let them stay. And in the future, should you want to bond a human, don't force them into it. You should be entering into the bond with a desire to entwine, not just ensnare.

"Will you bond me?" Sammy asks, loud and clear. "Please?"

When I turn, he's looking at Gordon, his hand outstretched. Even with my blessed heart of stone, I'm moved.

I'm sorry, Gordon says. *I would, but I can't. Earth blessed can't bond humans.*

Sammy's face falls. "I hate all your stupid rules."

You can't fly, Gordon says. *Neither can I. I hate that too, but I can't change it. This is like that. If it was a rule I could break, I'd do it for you.*

A tear rolls down Sammy's cheek as he nods. "Alright. If I find a four-leaf clover, I was going to wish you could bond me, but instead I'm wishing for you to have wings instead."

I'd give you the best rides through the clouds. Gordon and Rufus are the fiercest and the strongest of my earth blessed. Even the strike blessed wouldn't attack them without a large group. To see him being so gentle with a human. . .it's shocking.

I'm not the only one affected.

All around me, blessed begin to ask their bonded for their permission to work toward better bonds.

"Ocharta's not even here," Liz says. "Should we let her land?"

I notice her circling overhead. She could probably hear everything said, even watching as she was from afar.

Liz's mother shakes her head. "Nothing she says will change my decision."

She will not be allowed to disagree with me. I can give Liz and her mother that much. Liz may trust the others to follow my lead, but Ocharta would never voluntarily agree to relinquish her control over anything or anyone.

Liz doesn't argue, thankfully.

In the end, only forty-nine humans opt to stay in Houston. Their blessed agree that they may remain while we travel to Iceland. The other humans agree to go voluntarily with their blessed, many in the hopes that the bond may be improved.

Two of the pairs are at an impasse—one strike blessed, one water blessed. Neither blessed is willing to relinquish their human, but the humans are also not willing to voluntarily relocate.

You will both stay here in Houston, then, I say. *In a week or two, I'll send Hyperion to collect you, either with or without your humans.* I pause, looking at them both in turn. *You disappoint me.*

The humans could kill us when you leave. Trillius snorts, the tiny fins alongside his body rippling slightly. He's such a light blue that he could almost disappear if he flew instead of swimming.

Petrine tosses her head, her silver eyes flashing. *You're sentencing us to death.*

No more than you sentenced them to the same when you bonded them. You can choose to release them and come with us. Or you could try to convince them that you'll change, that you'll listen to them, and not simply force them to do things against their will.

Trillius gnashes his teeth. *The lion will never lie with the lamb. They have this analogy here on Earth. We will never be sheep, no matter how much you try to scare us into bleating.*

"Even lions follow the pack order," Liz says. "And your leader's asking you to make better choices. Every decision we make has consequences."

"Are we ever going to eat?" Coral asks. "The food's getting cold."

"Yes," Liz says. "Sit. Azar will work all of that out, but we should eat. Cold or not, this is quite the feast." I can tell she's trying not to think about all the humans they forced to make it for them. At least she's planning to free them soon.

"Why aren't the blessed eating?" Coral asks. "We made a lot of food."

"Here." Sammy hands a whole turkey leg to Gordon, who snaps it up without issue.

I don't tell them that most of the blessed are having a pre-departure feast behind the building from our gathering

—several earth blessed were sacrificed for it. I have trouble talking about it. I know it's our way. Either the earth blessed die or they all will, and at least the earth blessed are able to procreate, but it's not a very reassuring thought as their prince.

Coral and Jade are feeding Rufus, too, and he's eating, in spite of sideways glances from the gathered blessed. I wonder whether the other humans know what the water and strike blessed eat. Clearly Liz's mother does. She looks almost as sick as Liz looked when I told her. You'd think the humans who hate us would be fine with our winnowing down our own population.

Deciding there are unlikely to be many altercations from this point forward, Hyperion launches into the sky, heading for the blessed feast. It's exhausting to open up portals, even relatively short hops from here to Selfoss, Iceland, and he's offered to help me.

Once Liz finishes eating, she circles back around. Thankfully, the two remaining idiots, Trillius and Petrine, have decided to leave their humans here and travel with us to Selfoss. It's not ideal, but it's better than forcing them to stay, knowing they'll be attacked upon our departure. It was too much to hope that all the blessed would be able to convince the humans they'll change their ways.

Liz looks calmer now, which is probably the result of the progress we've made today with healing the bonds of the other human-blessed pairs. Maybe it really *is* a special day. Thanksgiving. It sounds special.

"Hey." Liz leans against my front leg. "How are we getting there, exactly? You said you can move us all, but what are you going to do? It's not like the earth blessed can fly there, and it's a long way to swim."

You've seen my red energy domes, I say. *I'll create a portal using the same energy, but instead of a dome to hold something in or keep things out, I rip the fabric of our current location, punching a hole through to the place we want to go.*

She blinks.

It's tiring to create and exhausting to hold.

"You need to eat too."

I'm careful to send a very private message, just to her. *I can't do that in front of anyone. Not as Azar, remember?*

She frowns, but doesn't argue.

Eventually, though, I do have to eat. *I'm leaving to check on preparations, and I'll return as Axel.* He can be seen eating anything. *I'll have him bring your belongings from the tower.*

Liz looks a bit uneasy when I leave, winging away from her as she grows smaller and smaller. It's notably easier for me to fly away than it was only yesterday. Talking things through with her has made things more comfortable between us, and today's progress helped even more.

I do wonder whether anyone else will entwine. Some of the blessed-human bonds don't seem so miserable. Maybe more of them will develop into something strong, healthy, and robust. After grabbing Liz's bags—two fairly large fabric-shelled boxes—I shift. Working out a way to carry them via clipping them together and slinging them across my back takes longer than I anticipate, but the bond's solid and bright, so I don't worry too much about being away.

When I finally reach the gathering again, Liz is talking to Gideon and they look pretty heated. Fluff Dog has even gotten involved, coming out of hiding behind Sammy's leg to bark and bark at them. I'd been intentionally not listening in on her conversations, trying to give her a little bit of privacy. I manage to have private conversations telepathically with other blessed. I figure she should have a bit of time without me peering over her figurative shoulder.

But now I regret it.

"—stay here with the other humans. It's the only smart move for you."

"I told you I won't be separated from you," Gideon insists.

"You were gone earlier," she says. "Don't think I didn't notice. You snuck out to try and get a message through."

"I'm still a human," he says. "I'm not going to apologize for trying to help my own kind. Even when some of them are confused."

I clear my throat.

"Oh, good. Your weaker, somewhat less tyrannical overlord has joined us. At least he's in his worm form, so he won't be wrapping his arm around your shoulders."

Blessed don't roll our eyes. Or at least, we didn't before we realized how great it feels. Now I find myself doing it in all the situations where I would formerly have flayed someone open.

"Gideon, I already told you—"

"You said we were going to. . ." He looks around, taking in the listening ears of Coral, Jade, and Sammy. "You said we were going to *be* together. You said it would help you get some distance from them."

I assume he's referring to our former plan of their mating. Even the thought of that makes me begin to shake. It's difficult, but I must stay calm. If I don't, I'll shift into Azar and reduce him to a pile of ash on the spot. *No.*

Gideon's eyes cut toward me. "I heard it was your idea, actually."

It was, I admit. *Sort of. But it was a bad one. We found a better way.*

"Oh, I don't know about that." Gideon reaches for Liz's hand.

He's lucky she backs up, yanking her hand away, or I might snap his off at the wrist. "Listen to me, Gideon. You're miserable here, and there's clearly nothing you can do to protect Sammy, Coral, or Jade. You should go home to where you can actually do some good. You'll be much happier there, too."

"What about your mother?" Gideon asks. "Are you sending her away?"

"No," Liz's mother says. "I'm going."

"No, you're not," Liz says, her face doggedly determined. "You're both staying here, far from the upheaval caused by the dragons."

"You can't force us to stay," Gideon says. "Especially not after that speech you made earlier about choices."

"You didn't even hear it," Liz snaps.

"I heard it was pretty extreme, with the dragons pretending to try harder not to be tyrannical." Gideon's lip is curled.

Liz turns to face her mother. "You're staying here." She lifts her chin. "You *have* to."

"No," Gideon says. "You can't force us—"

Liz's shoulders straighten, and her eyes flash. "I *can,* actually. Do you really think Azar will deny me?"

A muscle in Gideon's jaw pops.

"I need to stay with you," her mother says.

Liz turns to her mother. "You tasked me to care for Sammy, Coral, and Jade, and I'm doing it. You may not approve of how, but if you want me to continue to keep them safe, you'll stay here. Safe. Out of misery."

Her mother meets her eye, and some kind of interchange takes place between them that I can't follow.

Liz's nostrils flare. "If I have to, I'll force Azar to order your dragon to leave you here."

"You wouldn't kill her, but you'll order me to be left?" her mom asks.

"I'm just that awful." Liz is resolute, her eyes hard.

"I'm coming," Gideon says. "I won't let you leave me. If you do, I'll get a ride to Iceland and break through all over again."

Liz ignores him.

But an hour later, when we're forming the blessed into groups, her mother isn't present, but Gideon is.

I'm not giving him a ride, I say.

Liz laughs. "I wouldn't expect it."

I'll do it. Asteria's landing is light—always surprisingly light for a blessed of her size. She's been graceful since the first time I saw her. For a blessed, there isn't one that's more lovely, and yet, my admiration for her has diminished significantly. I can't really explain why.

"It would be funny if you bonded Gideon," Liz says. "Since he and I—and you and Azar. . ."

Where's she going with that? She and Gideon. . .are what? Were almost mated? Because she's *not* mating with him now. And Asteria and I. . .I can't even think about it anymore.

He's not a bright, Asteria says. *He can't be bonded, but he did say something interesting earlier today. He says you're bonded to both Axel and Azar.* Asteria tilts her head, clearly pressing for an explanation.

I didn't notice Asteria talking to Gideon, but it has been total chaos in preparation of our departure. I should have known that what Liz told him would eventually leak.

Liz nods slowly. "That's why I couldn't really tell you how to take my mother's bond. Azar took mine, but he didn't remove my connection to Axel in the process. It split my bond so that I'm now connected to both of them."

Are you now entwined with both? Asteria's gaze is not aggressive, but she knows something about it is strange. I worry she won't let this go.

"It's weird, right?" Liz shrugs. "The only thing worse for my mother than being bonded to Ocharta would be split-ting between two dragons." She's acting like it's almost a human jest, but I worry Asteria won't accept that.

But you aren't displeased, Asteria says. *You don't mind the change in the bond. Did you choose to bond also with Azar? Or was that forced upon you?*

I shouldn't be so desperate to hear her answer, but I can't help it. I know it's not what really happened, but I still want to know how she'll answer.

"Azar was. . .a surprise. I neither chose it nor fought against it. To be honest, I wasn't at all upset. I suppose you could say that he'd already won my trust by saving me several times before it happened."

The bond brightens and shivers. It makes me shiver, too.

I should bring Azar to make the portal. But I don't want to leave.

Will she ride with you? Asteria almost never speaks to me when I'm Axel, but maybe my real connection to both Liz and Azar has changed that. It's interesting that she appears to like Azar enough to tolerate all the baggage he now drags along with him.

Azar, I'm sure, I say.

Does it bother you? She's staring at me boldly.

I think about her question. If I were only Axel and not also Azar, would it bother me always to be left out? Probably. Is it fair that, in this form, without the firepower or wings, I'm always treated as lesser?

I've never considered any of those things before, and I doubt Asteria has either. In fact, the blessed tend not to think about the right and wrong of things—there's just the way things are. All these moral quandaries aren't something we contemplated. Liz and her radical ideas are changing us all.

I never worry about things that can't be changed. I want Liz safe, and Azar keeps her safe.

Would you be upset if her bond were stretched further? Asteria is intent—clearly thinking about something in particular.

"What do you mean?" Liz asks.

When I was trying to take your mother's bond, I could sense yours, Asteria says. *I'd like to bond you as well.*

She looks entirely serious, and I know it's irrational, but even more than I wanted to destroy Gideon, I want to *end* her. I want to shift forms and roast her for the other blessed to eat.

She can't have Liz.

Elizabeth Chadwick is *mine*.

12

AXEL

The snarl that comes from deep inside me is feral and very, very impolite. It wouldn't be outside of her rights for Asteria to challenge me over my behavior.

Liz, who has no idea how our interactions work really, intuitively pats my side, her hand gently stroking my scales. "It was hard for Axel to adjust to sharing with Azar, and that bond has barely settled. I'm not sure we should really talk about spreading me even thinner quite yet."

Her calm dismissal helps, but if I stay here, I'm going to start a fight I'm not sure I can win with Asteria. *I have blessed to direct. Excuse me.* I incline my head easily, and then I catch Liz's eye before ducking around the corner.

Where Gideon's waiting for me. "Can I ride with you? I feel like you can at least understand how I feel, being left by her all the time."

He has no idea. *I'm sorry—I have too many earth blessed to direct. I'll have Azar assign someone.*

"Never mind. I'll just ride with Azar's girlfriend." Gideon shakes his head. "At least you really seem to care about her. The big red one has a girlfriend and still won't let Liz go." He tsks. "That guy's disgusting."

A human bonded and a mate serve different purposes. A mate is for propagation. Liz is...

"What?" Gideon steps closer, both his eyebrows shooting upward. "What purpose does she serve for you and Azar, exactly? You can't mate with her—even if you could, she can't give birth to baby dragons, clearly. So what do you really want with her? What does the big red devil want?"

I think about his question, although I really don't have any time to spare. What do I want with Liz? I want to keep her safe. I want to hear her opinion. I want to please her. None of those are imperatives for the blessed. She might be the key to helping us locate the heart, or her birthmark may be a coincidence. It actually in no way resembles the shape of a real human heart. It may be nothing more than a random human skin mark that mimics the human symbol for a heart as her mother insists.

But if that's true, why do I think of her all day?

If our bond is unimportant, why can't I even imagine letting her go?

What has she changed in me? She feels as crucial to my future as my own self, and I can't even contemplate sharing her with anyone—not a human she's fond of like Gideon or another blessed that I'm fond of like Asteria. Without suitable answers to the questions he's asking, I settle for sharing the one truth I do know.

Liz is my world now.

"Mine too, scaly. Only, you're ruining everything about it, and you're turning Liz into someone I don't even know." He spits on the ground and stomps away.

Her mother called her a monster. Her erstwhile mate says he no longer knows her. Liz is under attack from all sides, but if I kill the people making her feel small, it'll upset her further. For a blessed who has been taught to destroy anything that threatens me and my future, it's a frustrating quandary.

I travel far enough away that I sense no other blessed, and then I shift and return to take her away from Houston. It's not a solution, but it's the only path forward I can see.

As I land, I hear the conversations around Liz. Her sisters are arguing, but the source of their contention is strange.

"—since only one of us could bond Rufus, I'll let you have him," Coral says.

"You just want a bigger dragon," Jade says.

"Is that wrong? You guys like Rufus and Gordon, and I do too, but I also like big dragons. And you know, prettier ones, too."

"Rufus is pretty," Jade says.

Coral laughs. "*Sure* he is."

"I like the little yellow blobs—"

"Do you even hear yourself?" Coral asks. "You like his blobs?"

"Fine, then who would you bond?" Jade is full of righteous indignation at her sister's attack on Rufus, but I can't really blame Coral.

Rufus is not attractive by blessed standards either. Impressively powerful and strong, yes. Attractive? No.

"I mean, I'd like a red one, but there aren't many, so I guess a big silver one would be fine."

"You would look horrible with silver hair," Jade says. "Do you really want to look like a granny?"

When I walk toward them, they stop talking. Luckily Rufus wasn't here to hear their evaluation. He returns just after I do, bringing a report about the preparations of the earth blessed.

Asteria will carry Gideon and Coral both. Liz's little sister deserves some discomfort for her disloyalty, even if she only spoke the truth.

"Wait," Coral says. "I want to ride with Rufus."

I walk away, unwilling to police Liz's small siblings—nothing ever seems to make them all happy. She can handle the details of that herself. I look around at the clean lines of blessed, all standing outside the convention center as discussed, many of them with their bonded humans.

Some notably without.

Interestingly, the blessed who are without their humans don't look angry or resigned. Most of them look almost relieved. I wonder whether controlling insubordinate humans all the time was taking a toll on them as well. I really wish my father had mentioned the nature of the bond and that it could be a real asset if we were willing to learn from the humans and trust them.

He almost made it sound like the humans were destined to be our enemies. I suppose there's some truth to that, when they understand what exactly will happen when we take the heart back. The earth blessed at least are in nice, clean lines. The strike blessed are milling around at the edge, clearly irritated that the earth blessed, as our shock troops, will be traveling first. The water blessed don't look much less annoyed, but they're mostly churning around in the nearby bay.

Liz walks up, dragging the bags I left with her. When I shifted this time, I fashioned straps to the saddle to which her rectangular bags can be attached. It only takes her a moment to attach them, which is good, because it has started to rain.

"That's the problem with ripping the roof off," Liz mutters. "You're stuck getting drenched at the whims of Mother Nature."

A little rain won't hurt you, I say.

But she rolls her eyes. "Tell that to my leather boots."

I can make you new boots the next time I shift. Dragon leather. It won't be harmed by something as inconsequential as rain.

"We definitely need to talk about this," she says as she climbs up my back. The rain causes her to slip—twice—and I see the point she's making.

Sammy doesn't seem to have any problems as he scampers onto Gordon's back like a squirrel sprinting up a tree. Liz must have helped them clip Fluff Dog's little box with holes on the sides to Gordon's saddle, which is probably for the best. Rufus becomes agitated and overreacts much more quickly than Gordon does, so keeping the tiny irritant with the calmer of the two is a good call.

"Have you considered that it's going to be really cold in Iceland? Because I'm going to need you to make me, like, a big wooly coat when we land."

I snort. *You won't need a coat to stay warm around me.*

"Right. You have that fire-blowing air-warming magic. I almost forgot. But what about them?" She looks over at where Sammy's reaching through the small box with his fingers and Fluff Dog's licking them furiously. They're wearing coats, but perhaps not coats designed for the temperatures of Iceland. Perhaps she's worried about the small, yappy dog.

The dog's fluffy. I'm sure she'll be fine.

"Not the dog, idiot. I'm worried about Sammy."

Idiot? The bond still thrums with affection, so I don't think she meant to insult me. Perhaps it's a strange human term of endearment. *I'm sure Gordon will make him something.*

"If a dragon's going to bond my little brother eventually, it sure would be nice if it could be Gordon."

Do you really think that?

"Why not? You mean, because he can't fly?"

He's earth blessed.

"I know," Liz says. "But he's still a dragon, and he's powerful and strong while also being kind."

They're the lowest caste among us. You wouldn't mind that?

"He's not slated to be eaten soon, is he?" She arches an eyebrow.

Only the very old are consumed— Her smirk tells me that she was jesting. *We need to get everyone through before we're all swimming our way there.*

As if he could hear our conversation, Hyperion lands next to me, his enormous shape sinking deep into the mud forming in front of the Convention Center. *I'm willing to make the portal for all the earth blessed, and you can—*

I'll handle theirs, I say.

But there are more of them. It'll take longer, and that will tire you.

I'm entwined now, I say. *I have more strength than I did before.*

More than me, Hyperion says. *That's what you mean.*

He's different from my other brothers, which is why he doesn't become upset by my comment. He has never grown angry easily, but he's especially tolerant with me. *I would greatly appreciate if you would open a portal for the water and strike blessed.*

You open yours first, he says. *Then I'll match it.*

We're going to land in the mountains, just North of Selfoss. I've promised Liz that we'll first petition the local humans for their assistance.

Why don't we just go straight to the volcano you want to investigate and see whether the heart's there? Father wants to hear from you soon—we can't mess around. We need results.

Hyperion has always tried to boss me around, and I usually don't mind much, but this time, I was placed in charge of the search. Not him.

I won't let him force me into acting rashly.

I refuse to rush this. Thorough and measured action is better. We'll go to Selfoss and establish a base of operations. Then we'll check things methodically, and once we have any evidence of where the heart may be, we'll take it to Father.

If he doesn't come looking for us first. Hyperion looks displeased, but he doesn't press it further.

"How do you do it?" Liz asks. "Opening the portal, I mean."

Carefully and with great concentration, Hyperion says. *Or he'll open a hole into the ground or a portal into the middle of the sky.*

Which is fine for me, I say.

But it would be very bad for the earth blessed your dear friend leads. His sneer when he mentions Axel's also expected. He may be my kindest brother, but that also means that he resents my friendship with Axel more than the others do. Hyperion vaults into the sky and shoots across to the other side of the courtyard, where the heads of the strike and water blessed have congregated.

One of the reasons Father chose me is that I'm very, very good with portals. I can open one faster and hold it longer than any of my brothers. Only this time, when I finally open one, it's large, even for me. It's easily twice as large as the one I opened on our journey here.

Showoff, Hyperion hisses.

But I have more blessed to transport than he does, so I ignore him. Once I've checked that it opens onto solid ground, the edges of the portal held open with a churning red energy—a shuddering expulsion of magic—I order the earth blessed through.

Rufus and Gordon surge forward as they normally do, but I stop them.

Hang back.

They exchange a strange glance—it's odd for the Prince of the Flame to be giving them direct orders.

"Axel said you could stay near me," Liz says. "I asked."

They nod and fall back, waiting until the first earth

blessed column has passed through. With more than eight thousand earth blessed to journey through, even moving two at a time, it takes quite some time for them to all pass.

By the time the last column finally ends, Liz and her siblings are all soaked to the bone. Asteria's waiting alongside Rufus and Gordon, and finally, I wave them through as well.

"It's weird you don't go through first," Liz says. "What if there's danger on the other side?"

We're traveling into the mountains to avoid harming any human settlements with our arrival, per your request. I'd have sent Hyperion first if I thought there might be any risk to the blessed, but from our research, Iceland is both peaceful and harmless.

"The humans could—"

Nothing they've been able to do in your precious United States has been able to hurt me. You confirmed that Iceland doesn't have a military at all, and it relies on its location and lack of natural resources to keep it safe.

"Still," she says. "I'm sure the other nations of the world are united in hating you."

Then we should go through quickly to make sure everyone's fine.

Liz looks around the now-empty convention center. "Now that we're leaving, I'm actually a little sad. Your tower was nice, and everything I own is completely soaked —probably ruined by now."

We'll find new things for you in Iceland. I step through the portal, and the wave of cold air slaps into my face like an icy fist. It's honestly a little refreshing to me. My whole world is always heat and light, but I can only imagine that for Liz it feels terribly cold.

It's quite dark when we arrive, which I understand it will be all but five hours a day, but the sky's painted with brilliant, shifting green lights. It's bright enough that I can easily make out the shapes of dwellings down to the south of our location. There are a few on our side of the winding river, but most of them are congregated to the south.

It must be Selfoss.

I don't know many words in Icelandic, but 'foss' is one of the few I do know. It means waterfall, so I expected there to be quite a few waterfalls near this area, with a town named Sel*foss*. So far, I don't see any. Everything's coated in a layer of white, which I understand is called snow. I haven't yet experienced it myself.

"It's so beautiful," Liz says with a sigh. "I've always wanted to see the northern lights." Then she shivers.

That, I can fix easily. I inhale the freezing cold air deeply and radiate some of my excess heat. The white snow, already trampled by thousands of large feet into tightly-packed heaps around us, melts and Liz leans down closer, patting my neck. "Thanks."

"Wow, what time is it?" Sammy asks, yawning from Gordon's back. "It looks really late." He's also shivering, so I radiate a bit more than usual.

"They're six hours ahead of us," Liz says. "So it's almost midnight here."

"That's why it's so dark." Jade's eyes are wide as she watches the shifting colors overhead. "But I'm not tired at all. Can we stay up all night?"

Liz laughs. "We should head into town and get the introductions over with." She's absolutely positive that, with her help, things will go very differently than they did for us when we landed in Houston. I have my doubts, but I haven't argued with her about it. She slides off my back and begins hiking toward the edge of the mountain shelf, like she thinks she'll be walking all the way down.

What are you doing? I use a tight communication channel, not keen on others hearing me ask a question that could be perceived as mocking her. An irritated Liz is adorable. An embarrassed one, not so much.

She doesn't slow down. "I'm going to introduce myself to the town."

It's miles away. You want us to wait here for three days while you slide down the frozen mountain and die of hypothermia?

She stops moving, and I can tell by the shaky timbre of the bond that she's really irritated. "I'm athletic. I'll make it just fine by tomorrow afternoon."

I can't help rolling my eyes, but at least she can't see it. *We'll go together.*

"Yes, riding in to talk on an enormous fire-breathing red dragon will set just the tone I'm going for."

I launch into the sky, swing around in a large arc to land squarely in front of her. *If you think you're going down there alone, you don't know me at all. I will never allow that risk to you.*

She jogs a few steps toward me and jabs me in the chest with her tiny index finger. "You don't know *me* if you think I'll allow you to fly over there and spark some kind of war here."

I lift my head. *Then we are at an impasse.*

"I'll go." Gideon slides down Asteria's back and strides toward us. "You can wait up here, and I'll go and make the introductions."

"They surely saw us all arrive." Liz looks around. "Nighttime or not, they would have noticed the arrival of more than ten thousand dragons." She sighs. "Fine. *Fine.*"

"You should send me with one of the earth dragons," Gideon says. "Axel should be fine. He's not quite as bad as all the others—more reasonable, usually. Then you can't be angry she's in danger, and it'll be faster than waiting on one of us."

Except there's no way for me to shift here in front of everyone.

"Where is he, anyway?" Gideon looks around. "I figured he'd be the first one through, but I never saw him."

Hyperion shoots up into the sky, swinging a large, relatively bright arc around the entire area. If anyone missed our arrival, they're surely aware of our presence now.

When he lands next to us, he bugles. It's a blessed courtesy, announcing our arrival. Any other blessed would also recognize that he's flame blessed from the sound, but to the humans I doubt it means anything at all.

Liz is glowering when she starts scaling my back. "Let's just go and get it over with." She drops her voice to a whisper. "Try to look nonthreatening."

I try my best to suppress my smile as I launch into the air. There are few things in life I like better than flying with Liz. The bond always shimmers, for one. But her little sighs and involuntary exhalations of air and the way she crouches down when I speed up never fail to entertain me.

Before landing, I accelerate, sailing past the river, over the town, and beyond. Once we reach the ocean, I turn back, looping around to Selfoss again.

"What's that for?" Liz asks.

I'm giving them time to prepare before we arrive in case Hyperion's announcement was their first notice that we're here, but I also like to get a feel for the surrounding geography before I land in a new place. Landing is the dangerous move—it allows them to send something over the top of us, which is where you're sitting.

As we reach Selfoss again, I fly lower and much slower. It's easier for me to regulate Liz's temperature this way, but also, we can see the town better when we're close.

Although many of the buildings have snow on top of them, you can make out that some of them have very brightly colored rooftops. It's quite different than the grays, browns, and blacks of Houston. The streets are also lined with brightly painted homes. Perhaps they like to decorate the buildings more because the surrounding land is blanketed in white. All in all, the town is tiny. Nothing at all like Houston.

"Where should we land?" Liz sounds. . .tentative. I

wonder whether she's nervous, now the time has finally come. It must be strange for her to be approaching her people on our behalf. She wants to smooth things over with the humans, as a human, but she also wants to make things easy for us.

It's not comfortable to have one foot on two sides of a line. I know that better than most anyone.

I notice a very large building just next to the river, with two rectangular structures on either side of a tall tower. It looks prominent. I circle and land in front of it.

We wait, but no one comes out.

"They're probably hiding inside," Liz mutters. "I would be."

She slides off, and although I want to stop her, I don't. I'll be behind her, ready to incinerate anyone who attacks.

It won't help if the humans use their irritating little projectiles, but. . . I project a magical shield around her, and she freezes and turns around. "What are you doing?" The frown on her face is precious.

Keeping you safe.

"I look like a crazy person. I can't walk in there with a red bubble floating around me."

Why not?

She rolls her eyes and tilts her head. "Get rid of it."

I shake my head.

"Azar, do it now."

I refuse.

"If you don't take this dumb thing off—"

You'll what? Draw your swords and strike me?

Her sigh's prolonged, but I ignore it, and eventually she turns around and walks toward the building. After banging on the door for quite a while, she finally draws a sword and uses the hilt to smash the handle. I move forward, shifting into my human form to follow her inside.

"Axel," she says. "What on earth are you—"

"The others can't see us from here," I say. "And I'm not letting you disappear from my sight."

"Humans have things like cameras. They could out you—have you thought of that?" She groans. "Why did you bring me to a church, anyway? I probably just smashed their door open for no reason—no one sleeps at a church."

"This is a church?" I look around.

She just ignores me, stomping through the doorway into the dark building loudly and unafraid.

I have to jog to keep up. "Humans worship their god here? How? Do they pray and chant?"

She continues to ignore me, bursting from one room into the next, all of them empty. After a few more moments of searching, she gives up. "Well, there's either no one here, or they're hiding."

A moment later, I've shifted back into Azar, and we're flying over the streets of the city. Not a single light is on, and not a single person appears to be awake. "Hey, you have dragon senses. Are they better than mine?"

What do you mean?

"Can you hear humans?"

I can sense their heat and hear their heartbeats if I try.

"Do it," she says. "Find me a human."

But there aren't any. *I fear they've all fled. There's not even any significant animal life. They took their horses, their cows, all of it, with them. There are a few stray dogs and cats, if that's of interest.*

"How can that be?" Liz is barely hanging on to the saddle. She flings her arms outward. "Where did you all go? And how did you know we were even coming?"

She screams, long and loud.

And that's when I feel it. *Wait. I found one.*

I swing wide and drop in line with the Ölfusá river, shifting slightly as it bends and winds, and then I feel the single heartbeat again. I hover momentarily, isolating the heat signature. There.

Just on the north side of the river, there's a tiny, red-roofed home sitting in a largish yard for a human, between two much larger homes. *I feel it there.*

I land in front of the home.

Liz slides down slowly, looking around. Her boots crunch in the snow as she lands, and I radiate slightly, melting the snow around us in a wave that moves outward from where we're standing. Liz draws one sword, preparing to smash the door handle again, more than likely, but as she approaches the door, it opens and a hunchbacked woman with white hair steps onto a small porch.

"Welcome," she says. "I've been waiting for you."

13

LIZ

Nothing has been normal in my life for a very long time, but today has been bizarre, even by my new standards. An old woman in Iceland welcoming me into her evacuated town in English is just. . .

"Who are you?" I ask. "The town oracle?"

"I am Margrét, and I'm not an oracle, but when they asked someone to stay, I volunteered." She smiles with a cackle, her teeth darkened, perhaps by coffee or perhaps just by age. She looks like she could easily be a hundred years old.

"How long ago did they evacuate Selfoss?"

"Two days?" She shrugs.

"But you speak English?" It may be a strange thing for me to ask when there's a dragon behind me, watching our interaction with interest, but I don't speak any Icelandic. It feels almost too lucky that the one woman who stayed speaks English.

"They told me that the humans who had bonded dragons would likely all speak English." She shrugs. "But almost everyone in Iceland speaks fluent English anyway."

And now I feel stupid. "Oh, okay."

"Would you mind if I. . ." She walks down the steps and toward Azar, her mouth gaping open. Tears roll freely down her cheeks. "He's so beautiful." Now she's sobbing in earnest, sobs wracking her hunched frame. She's trembling and also smiling broadly as she stares up at Azar.

"He's really amazing," I say. "But can you tell us why everyone evacuated and where they went?"

She shrugs, wiping at her eyes. "We were ordered to leave, so most people went to the city, or they left to stay with family." She's still staring at Azar, barely even looking my way.

I sheathe my sword, feeling a little stupid for drawing it at all. "But you stayed."

"I told you. They wanted someone to stay," she says. "I think they assumed you'd demand a sacrifice, and they were hoping I'd be sufficient." She laughs then, tears still streaming down her face. "And if you want to eat me, it's fine. I won't even fight." She drops to her knees in the mud, never lowering her face. "I've always wished that dragons existed in our world. I've lived a long life—feeding one of them isn't a bad way to go."

I can't help rolling my eyes. "Get up. Azar's not eating anyone."

She turns toward me slowly. "You're heith?"

"What?" I frown, starting to be annoyed by this woman. "I don't even know what you're saying."

"Have you read Sibyl's Prophecy?" She turns back toward Azar again. "The poet who told of Ragnarök—Sibyl." She shakes her head. "Of course you haven't. Americans are Christian—they don't study our Norse traditions."

"What are you talking about?"

She shakes her head. "Heith are the shining ones. You're heith, are you not?"

She means you're a bright.

"Wait, are you saying that to you, I'm shining in some

way?" I blink. "I don't—no one in America can tell—I can't see what the dragons see."

"There have always been shining ones among us. They're the ones chosen by the gods and giants."

"I have no idea what you're saying."

The old woman turns toward Azar. "If I can serve you, I'll do it, great master. It seems that I may be of some limited use as a teacher, if you'll allow it."

Azar inclines his head slightly.

"I assume you're not alone?"

He nods.

"All the homes here are empty. Their occupants fled, along with their most treasured belongings. Please, have your companions join us in Selfoss."

I wonder whether she's ready for ten thousand dragons to descend. "At least the river and the ocean are both close," I say. "That'll be good for the water blessed." I doubt Gordon's going to find many grubs in this frozen tundra, though. I hope he ate lots before we left.

"You should know that a storm's coming. It's early for us, but it's looking like it will be a large one." The old woman shivers. "If you'd been just a day later, you'd have been fighting your way through swirling piles of snow."

I climb back up on Azar's back, the woman watching in awe, and say, "Stay warm. We'll bring the others, and I'll be back to talk to you as soon as possible."

Azar takes off without a backward glance, winging his way toward the dragons waiting on the top of the mountains. *Axel will need to be present, running most of the details of settling the earth blessed.*

Which is a problem if everyone's watching me and Azar.

"What if you and I left to check out Eyjafjallajökull?"

What?

"We can say we're going to look at the volcano, then fly

over it at least, and then you can return as Axel to direct where people should go. Then you can come back and get me."

You think I'd even consider leaving you there, in the place of your nightmares, alone? When he snorts, tiny plumes of flame escape, as if to punctuate his refusal.

"Oh, please. I was a kid when that happened. Now I'm an adult, and it's not as if anyone will be there, waiting to try and shove me in."

A lot of eyes are on Azar right now. He knows it as well as I do.

"You don't have to put me down right next to the volcano. We can just say that's where we're going, and then you can book it back."

We land moments later, the dragons restlessly milling around in front of us. Those with humans appear to be the most agitated, probably because their ensnared humans aren't properly dressed for this weather. None of them can heat the air, so they may be dealing with a lot of complaining.

"The city of Selfoss has been abandoned," I shout. "We can enter the city and the humans can take up residence in the homes."

The humans have evacuated, Azar proclaims. *Selfoss is ours, but the homes are quite small. A storm is on its way, so those with bonded humans will have top pick of residences, with any other shelters open to any blessed who can fit inside.*

I'll help the others look for caverns, Asteria says. *None of us will enjoy being frozen to death.*

She's right about that.

I'm taking Elizabeth Chadwick to investigate the local volcano where we believe there may be clues to the location of the heart. Axel will be directing the settlement process, in conjunction with Asteria of the strike blessed, and Leviticus of the water blessed. Hyperion will remain with those settling in Selfoss to mitigate any disputes and ensure your safety. Things appear peaceful here, but remain vigilant. The humans are occasionally crafty.

In typical Azar fashion, he doesn't wait for any questions or commentary. He vaults straight up into the air—had I not been prepared for something like that, I might have fallen off and plunged to my death. As it is, the icy air feels like it's trying to turn my fingers to stone until Azar remembers to heat the air around us.

I expect him to go just far enough away to disappear—a bit hard in the area, given that other than the massive, flat-topped mountains north of Selfoss, there's not much around us other than miles and miles of snow-blanketed ground and small houses.

But, he doesn't slow down at all. His massive wings pump frantically, rocketing us toward the mountains rising in the west.

Toward Eyjafjallajökull.

As we approach, I watch in awe as we wing our way higher and higher, flying past snow-capped peaks on either side. The last time I was here, I was stuffed into the back of a van. I was ignored, shoved, and abused.

This time, I feel like the queen of the world.

But when we reach the side of Eyjafjallajökull, I begin to tremble. Everything else may be different, but somehow the feeling of approaching this volcano is the same. As if he can somehow tell I'm nervous, Azar banks sharply left, and dips quickly.

That's when I see what he must have seen much earlier.

A small hut.

It would barely qualify as a shed back in Houston. They sell buildings this large at hardware stores, and people plonk them down in their back yards to house their lawn mowers and golf carts. Rats and cockroaches love them, to be sure, but here it's the only shelter anywhere around, and I'm sure it looks better than dumping me on a pile of rock. Assuming I can open it, it'll provide some shelter while I wait for Azar to return. Even if it's not insulated and consequently it's no warmer than anywhere else, it should at least provide cover from prying eyes.

Azar plows into a snow bank as we land, the piles of snow melting immediately thanks to his radiation thing being ratcheted up to full blast. Of course, all his weight and all that water is a bizarre combination that results in mud splattering all over both of us. I'm groaning while I climb down his mud-slicked side when all the mud just. . .slides off.

"What the—"

Earth blessed, too, remember? Azar shifts right into his golden form—which is new. I don't think I've ever seen him go from red straight to gold. Instead of the usual car engine sounds, there's a high-pitched whining when he shifts from dragon to dragon—downsizing, really.

"That was cool."

Axel grins, his teeth all exposed in a way that would have terrified me a month before. *If you liked that, you'll love this.* The muddy mess on the ground shifts, and suddenly the area in front of me isn't wet and sloppy at all. In fact, it looks like a freshly plowed field. *Now, stay here, hidden, until I can return for you. I'll see to your siblings and your friend.*

Gideon.

I wonder what exactly he'll do for him. Hopefully nothing too terrible. "I should have at least said something to them before leaving. They'll be worrying about me."

Not for long. Axel takes off running before I can ask why he didn't just fly back. But now that I'm thinking about it, I realize that with so many flying dragons that have now been released, he'd have no way of knowing when he might be spotted. In some ways, Houston was an easier place to hide, with all the enormous buildings. This vast, open land, full of gorgeous views and strange lights, feels and looks so different that it's a bit terrifying.

I'm not sure how long I watch the northern lights before I start to get bored. They're stunning, and the shapes keep shifting slightly, from neon green to bluish, then to white, and back to green. It feels like I'm standing there for quite some time, awestruck, but it's probably not very long. Our brains have been trained in the modern age that constant stimulation is necessary.

I try meditating. We used to do it before I had a fight.

But it's freezing cold, so all I can think about is whether Sammy, Coral, and Jade are warm and safe. Then whether Gideon's picking a fight with Axel. Whether the weird old woman's alright. I can't decide whether I liked her or whether she gave me the heebie jeebies.

I should have come up with another way for Azar to switch to Axel. I need to be around when he's giving orders.

Then I worry about whether the other dragons will pick fights with Axel while Azar's not around to keep him safe. I'm basically running round and round in futile mental circles, and I don't love it. Although there aren't any dragons anywhere in sight that I need to hide from, I finally hobble over to the shed to see what's inside.

It takes about four strikes with the hilt of my heart-stone blades before I knock the lock open, and I find myself hoping that my difficulty means there's something great inside. No such luck.

It's carcasses.

Someone has strung meat carcasses up in the shed, possibly to cure? They don't smell spoiled, but the scent is overpowering all the same. I back out immediately, closing the door as best I can, which isn't very successful. Thanks to the lock I busted, the door swings open as soon as I close it. The wind isn't helping me, either.

That's when I first notice the howling.

It could have been going on before, certainly, but now I can definitely hear the faint howling of wolves in the distance. Is that why this shed was locked with such a nice lock? Was it to keep the wolves from eating the curing meat? Ugh. And now I've opened the door to invite them to come for dinner.

Axel told me to stay put, but I doubt he meant to leave me here as bait for the local arctic wolf pack. I have swords, and I know how to use them, but I don't know whether I can bring myself to kill cute, shaggy wolves who are just hungry. I'd probably just toss meat at them until they disappeared.

But what if they prefer fresh meat?

I start walking away from the howling, but that also happens to be toward the volcano. I stop myself once I realize my direction, but a moment later, I'm trudging along again, as if encouraged by some unseen arm. About three hundred yards along the path, I notice the gnarled form of a tree that's right next to a large boulder.

I've seen them both before.

On that night so long ago, I fell and face-planted right beside this exact tree. I remember thinking that it looked like my great-grandmother's fist, just before she died.

It still does, honestly.

I pick up the pace, something inside of me almost compelling me forward now. As I climb, the wind worsens, ripping at my dragon-scale clothing, which wasn't really made to keep me warm to begin with. My only solution to the now-constant shivering is to move faster—why didn't I insist that Axel craft me a thick cloak or something before he left?

Probably because we both assumed the shed would provide some shelter, at least from the pernicious wind. I suppose I could have held my nose and stayed there, so really, it's my own fault that I'm freezing out here.

But I can make fireballs. Right? Right.

I look up ahead at a dried-up bush protruding from a patch of ground where the snow layer is thin. I focus as hard as I can, and then I fling my hands outward.

Nothing happens.

At least no one's here to laugh at my failure.

I continue onward, moving as fast as I possibly can without slipping and falling flat on my face. It's hot where the volcano was—I remember that much. Plus, I'll get a sneak peek into the place my mom says I imagined. Who knows? Maybe I'll find evidence of this heart.

Or maybe I really am nuts, and I made it all up.

But as I climb higher and higher, I hear something even more disturbing than the howling of the wind.

Chanting.

I freeze in place, my booted feet no longer moving.

My mom's phone showed me the truth, the reality. There were no people present years ago when I came. No one was chanting. No one else was even *there*. I was alone with the woman with the artificial leg, Beer Can, and Driver. I murdered them and escaped down the mountain for no reason—Mom and Dad were already closing in on us.

But if all that is true, then who am I hearing now? The chanting sounds just like the voices I heard before.

I'm trembling all over, and I can't tell anymore whether it's from the temperature or from my own fear, which is now clawing its way up my body to lodge in my throat. I'm a strong, confident warrior, and yet, without my big dragon as backup, apparently, I'm a big fat coward. The problem is that, surrounded by all this dark, snowy wilderness, I'm not sure whether it's safer for me to head back to the wolf-bait shed, or continue climbing upward toward the volcano-of-crazy-chanting that I know is probably all in my head.

I want to sit down and sob.

Maybe Azar will sense my distress and come flying to the rescue.

But what if he can't tear himself away? Or worse, what if he winds up tipping his hand to someone, just because I'm a big, fat baby? I offered to be his cover story, so I can't chicken out now, because of some howling way off in the distance and a little residual childhood trauma. I decide to keep marching up. Then when Azar does return, I can at least explain myself as doing a little recon in their urgent search for the heart.

I do take a small moment to appreciate that as our bond has strengthened, we can manage being apart again. A week ago, I'd be writhing in agony on the ground because he was so far away. Now I'm just struggling with an existential crisis because I don't have my dragon-sized security blanket.

Buck up, Liz. Be worthy of the old lady's awe and admiration.

Stop being an anvil around Azar's neck.

I increase my speed to a jog, because somehow, a third of the way up the mountain, the snow from the base is now gone. The ground must be warmer here, closer to the opening to the volcano, or who knows why? I make great time, even wheezing for breath in an embarrassing way, as I climb up, up, up.

But that's when I balk again, because I can hear it.

The chanting's louder, and it's not wind-tossed, not anymore. It's clear. It's crisp. It's almost ominous—it feels like the disembodied voices just out of my line of sight are demanding something of me.

Hjartanu. Hjartanu. Hjartanu.

Over and over and over, the same as before. Like drums, the staccato rhythm repeats. Endlessly. Tirelessly. There must be hundreds of them. Thousands, even. Men. Women. *Creatures*. The voices are ragged and intense, and now that I'm drawing closer, it feels almost as if they're dragging me forward.

I slip and fall, my hands slamming into the ice-cold, snow-coated rock of the path. I right myself, and I keep on moving. I'm not sure I could stop if I tried, but I don't want to stop either. Something brought me here years ago, and something's calling to me now. We're connected, this volcano and I, and Azar needs me to find out how. The world needs me to find out, because until the dragons get what they want, they can't ever leave.

No matter how much progress we make, I know deep down that the dragons and the humans are at odds. Quintessentially, fundamentally, our two cultures are opposed. Until they get what they need, until they return to their home, we're all in danger. As I finally reach the summit, I see the wide opening to the tunnel. The top of the mountain's a large dome, sunken in the center, but covered in snow, but the tunnel they shoved me into before is still there, its maw gaping wide and dark.

I shove my fear down into a small ball and kick it into the corner of my mind. If I don't keep it under control, Azar will feel it, and I know he'll come. As I walk toward the tunnel entrance, I see something I either didn't notice before, or something that wasn't yet there. Above the arched entryway, there's a symbol carved into the rock.

A flame—and next to it, three crudely carved skulls. Fiery death? Is that what it means? That would be close enough to true. Certainly, traveling down the length of this tunnel leads to a place where flame can kill any number of people.

Did the people who lived near Eyjafjallajökull ever sacrifice humans in the hopes of staving off eruptions? Were they willing to kill others in order to preserve their own lives or their own safety? I suppose that's what I did, years ago, when I shoved the woman who I thought was trying to kill me into the pit of flame.

The real question is whether she actually was.

Because if she wasn't, then I'm the real villain.

As I enter the tunnel, something inside of my chest flares up, fiery heat flooding my entire body. My foot lands on the ground, the snow that has collected on my boots falling in chunks to the ground. Where it melts immediately.

Like it does around Azar.

Something strange is happening around me here, for sure. But what? I need to know, so I keep walking. Without even the aurora borealis overhead to light my path, I falter. It's pitch black, and anything at all could be beside me on this path. I turn and look backward, and a dozen paces away, I can still make out the entrance.

But the only thing up ahead is a deep and profound darkness filled only with the chanting voices, calling, calling, calling. I turn around, fear clawing its way up my spine. Creatures are in there. I can hear and feel them. I shouldn't be here.

Unless it's all in my head.

I'm frozen for a long moment, unsure whether to forge ahead and face my possible hallucinations, or turn back and wait for Azar to come with me. In the end, the only thing worse than being crazy would be leading Azar in with me too so he could see how insane I am.

So I move alone, deeper, deeper, deeper.

It's the chanting that's pulling me along, I know. It must be. And that reminds me of what I still have in my pouch at my side. My mother's recently charged phone, the one that shows that I'm nuts. The report is quite clear that no other people were present at the end of this tunnel. There are police reports, images, and trial statements that all back up what my mother told Azar.

I'm nuts.

There was no one here.

But in this moment, instead of looking at that report again, I use the phone for the flashlight. I fumble around until I finally free it from the pouch, and I turn it on. Now that I have a light, I shine it all around myself. Bats, startled by the sudden appearance of light in this dark place, explode down and out the entrance of the tunnel, several of them knocking me in the side of the head. I crouch down, nearly dropping the phone, but once the sound of beating wings and panicked bats has stopped, I stand back up. The chanting never slowed, and I stumble forward again, moving inexorably toward it.

The ground becomes hotter with nearly every step, and I move faster, too. The tunnel around me shifts from jagged rock to smooth, black, almost polished looking stone. I don't recall that change from before, but I was pretty agitated the last time I was here.

And finally, I see the end of the tunnel. It started out large, but it narrows and narrows, until near the end, it's barely large enough for me to walk through without bowing my head. I can see the very end, thanks to the brilliant red glow coming through the doorway.

I know what I'll see beyond, when I step through.

Or at least, I know what I think I saw the last time.

A large, cavernous room, with a huge, flat ledge. Hundreds of people will be there, chanting *hjartanu*. And then, just past where they're gathered, there will be a protrusion of rock that hangs out, protruding over the churning mass of lava below.

When I finally emerge from the edge of the tunnel, it's almost exactly as I remember it. The cavern is still there, smaller than I remember, but not by much, and the black ledge really does stick out over the boiling lava—even smoother and flatter and more ominous than I recalled.

Only, there aren't any people, not standing around, not on the ledge. No people anywhere.

But the chanting's loud, persistent, and clear.

It's not coming from the ledge, though. It's coming from. . .I step closer, stumbling forward without much control over my own actions. Heat rolls in almost debilitating waves upward, crashing over me from the lava pool. I crouch down, and I inch my way forward until I can peer over the edge of the rock.

That's when I see them.

Creatures are teeming through the lava, leaping and sinking, screaming and chanting. *Hjartanu. Hjartanu. Hjartanu.* They're humanoid in shape, but they have massive horns curving outward or protruding sharply from their skulls. All of them are charred and blackened, as if they're in the process of roasting and burning and peeling every single second of their miserable existence.

And when I straighten up to stare, they all look right back at me.

The chanting stops.

"Oh, shoot," I say, right before I run.

❧ 14 ❧

LIZ

have no idea what I saw when I was a child. In my memory, at least a hundred people, regular humans, were standing in white robes, all of them chanting the same thing. *Hjartanu. Hjartanu. Hjartanu.*

The woman who had dragged me into the volcano ripped my shirt open and exposed my birthmark, a perfectly shaped red heart, just over my left breast. The people who were gathered had gone wild then, and now that I think on it, their faces might have been a little deranged.

But the beasts that were teeming in front of me had *fangs*. They had *horns*. And when they saw me, they hissed, and began to churn their way closer.

Of course I ran.

Only, the second I hit the tunnel, I drop the phone and am plunged into the pitch-black dark of nothingness. I almost immediately stumble on who-knows-what and face plant, which hurts pretty badly. The palms of my hands are surely bleeding, and my knees sting just as badly. On top of that, all the air is knocked clean out of me.

When I turn back, panicked, toward the cavernous room, I realize that. . .

No one is chasing me. When I creep back, the people inside the lava are already watching for me, and when they see me again, they churn faster, but within seconds it becomes clear that they can't escape the limits of the lava. Somehow, they're stuck in there, perhaps paying penance for some horrific deed, locked in an eternally burning pit. I stand there for quite some time, watching them, before they become bored of me and resume their rhythmic chanting.

If the phrase, the heart, has some meaning to them, it apparently has nothing to do with me. In my memory, the people who were present chanted louder, almost in a frenzied manner when they saw me, but these demon-creatures don't even care that I'm here, once the initial surprise wears off.

It feels as if I was summoned, examined, and then dismissed. I should feel relieved—and of course I do. Who wouldn't be relieved that the demonic creatures aren't able to hop out of the volcano and attack them? I'd have to be insane not to be relieved.

But I'm also a little disappointed.

What exactly am I going to tell Azar? We traveled here, leaving Houston, releasing half the humans the dragons bonded and all the humans the ensnared had trained in their former home base, all so that we could make progress to report to his father in their search for the heart. Azar believes that somehow I'm connected to this place, but if I am, I have no idea how. At least, to the demons here, I'm boring.

I stand up, steeling myself against the fear of the disturbing sight in front of me. Maybe they just need a little more information to pique their interest. "I'm Elizabeth Chadwick, and I'm seeking an object or barrier or something that the blessed call the heart," I say.

They ignore me.

"Hjartanu," I shout.

If they understood my attempt to copy them, none of them lets on.

"Do any of you know anything about the heart?" I shout again, and I wave my arms wildly.

Still, nothing at all.

I do the only other thing I can think to do at that point, and I reach up and unbutton the top of my dragon-skin tunic, and then I tear it down, exposing the birthmark that, in my memory, sent the people who didn't exist into a frenzy.

"Do you see this?" I ask. "Hjartanu!"

First, one with forked horns notices the mark, and then the others notice it as well. They begin to surge toward me, which is alarming at first, but once I'm again reassured they can't seem to escape the lava, I calm down a bit.

That's when I notice that their chant has also changed.

In place of 'hjartanu,' they're now chanting another word, a word I don't know at all. Cutch-vwaith. I have no idea what it means, but I hope it'll mean something to the old lady in Selfoss. Satisfied that I have a new clue, and that maybe I am somehow connected to this place, I walk toward the exit. Between Azar and the old woman, hope-fully one of them will have an idea for our next step.

When I leave this time, there won't be a woman with a prosthetic leg and a dagger, bent on dragging me back toward the lava. But as I turn to leave, buttoning up my tunic, the demons do react.

They downright freak out.

Their chanting increases in intensity, and unless I'm badly mistaken, more of them show up. A lot more. There were probably only twenty or so at first, I'm guessing, but the horn patterns for some were quite distinctive, so I could kind of ballpark how many were milling around in the sizzling, bubbling lava. Now, there are much closer to a hundred. They're slamming into one other, shoving the others aside, and their eyes are all wide, frantic. They're now shouting *vera* and that same word, *cutch-vwaith*, over and over.

And dragons show up.

Now, amidst the horned demon-people, there are three —no, four—maybe even *five* dragons spinning, leaping, and twining past the gathered demons. They're hissing, spitting, and roaring amid the chants of the horned humanoids.

Their arrival makes me run even faster.

By the time I reach the tunnel entrance, lava starts to spray outward, splattering on the ground I was standing on moments before. *Vera, vera, vera, cutch-vwaith*, over and over and over, louder and louder. The churning and chanting and lava spray increase in frequency, and I can't stay and watch for another second.

Fearing another fall, I fumble around for Mom's phone for a moment until I remember that I already dropped it. Finally, I take off, lurching my way down the tunnel as quickly as I can manage without falling flat on my face.

When a blast of air—calling it hot would be a major understatement—slams into me from behind at almost the same moment I hear a loud cracking-popping sound, I'm genuinely worried that some of them managed to break through. So when I realize that Azar's drawing closer, finally, I'm relieved. I hope I'm not dragging him away from anything important, but I'm beginning to worry that *I* might be in real danger.

Who are those people and why do they have horns?

Why did the dragons turn up, too? Why are there dragons trapped in the lava, and what does it mean? Why are they so interested in my heart mark? What do they want with me?

And possibly most important of all, what would happen if they did manage to free themselves and come after me? Do they want to eat me? Roast me? Drag me into the volcano?

Or maybe they just have questions that need answers—too bad I have none to give.

My foot hits a rough spot and I sprawl forward, barely avoiding face planting against the rock. My already-scraped hands protest the abuse vociferously, but there's no time for even brushing them off. I shove myself back up to my feet and keep jogging forward.

The ground starts to get slick, and I slide and slam into the side wall, ripping a tear in my tunic that also shreds the skin along my elbow. On the way down, the tunnel felt insufferably long, but blessedly, I manage to escape quickly after just the one fall and then slam into the sidewall, bursting out of the utter darkness of the small tunnel into the stone clearing at the side of the mountain. The snow has all melted, probably from the heat those lunatics are generating in the volcano, and as I collapse on the wet ground, I can hear wings beating overhead. I'm initially relieved. . .until I realize that Azar isn't here.

Not yet.

He's moving this way, but he's not here.

It's a red dragon, but it's not *my* red dragon.

What are you doing here without my brother? Hyperion looks genuinely curious. *You appear distressed, Elizabeth Chadwick. May I lend you my assistance?*

Before I can breathe a word of response, an enormous creature—ten feet tall, at least, naked, black, and smoking, bursts through the exit from the tunnel. He's bearing down on me with a bare few feet to spare, and he's livid. He shouts *cutch-vwaith* loudly, his fangs bared, horns curving back away from his head, and then he leaps toward me, clawed hands outstretched.

The flame that erupts from Hyperion's open mouth incinerates the creature, punching him backward into the tunnel as he explodes, ash scattering like confetti from some kind of party grenade.

Whoa, Hyperion says. *What in the world was that?*

"Nothing good." I'm still puffing from my run, and my elbow and hands are all stinging pretty badly.

My brother dropped you off and left you to explore the volcano alone? Hyperion sounds incredulous. *You should really pass your bond to me. I would never do that.*

Neither would Azar, if he didn't have a secret to hide. "It's fine," I say. "He's almost here."

As if my words summoned him, Azar rockets through the sky overhead, crashing into the mountain next to me. *Are you alright?* He stomps his way down to the outcropping we're standing on.

She was almost eaten by some kind of horned nightmare, Hyperion says. *Next time you want to ditch her somewhere, let me know. I'll watch over her for you—I quite like her.*

"I'd have been fine." I unsheathe my swords.

She's lying, Hyperion says. *She was staring at him with her eyes all wide and shocked and her mouth was dangling open like this.* His jaw goes slack and his eyes widen dramatically.

I grab a rock and lob it at him. "I didn't look like that at all."

You so did. Hyperion's laughing. *It was the funniest thing I've seen all day, but only because I kept you from dying.*

"It was a good thing you were here," I say. "Thanks for saving me."

Hyperion smiles, and his teeth are much scarier than the demon beast's were—razor sharp and gleaming. *It was my pleasure.*

Go back now. Azar doesn't thank him. He doesn't even

look at him. He's too busy inspecting me, his giant head lifting and shifting to catalogue my every scratch and scrape. *I have many things to do before we can return to inspect the volcano.*

But this is the main reason we're here, Hyperion says. *And you said a storm's coming. We should look into the creatures before it hits.*

Later, Azar says.

"But I'm fine," I say again. "Hyperion reduced the creature to a pile of—"

Come with me. Azar's being awfully authoritarian.

"Now, look here," I say. "We can't just leave Hyperion sitting here, waiting for us to go back in there."

But before I can say anything else, he grabs me with his front claws and launches into the sky, leaving a very amused Hyperion to stare up at us from below, shrinking as we shoot upward.

What on earth *were you thinking, traipsing into that volcano alone?*

"I could hear them," I say. "The chanting—I don't think it was coming from humans when I was there last. Today, it was coming from creatures trapped in the volcano."

Azar flings me straight up into the air and flips around, sliding underneath me. And then he really starts to move. We're flying so fast that my vision blurs. The tears leaking from the corners of my eyes are freezing in place.

Do you know how many times in my life I've been truly afraid?

The bond's nearly black. I wonder whether he knows I can't possibly talk at this speed. He finally slows up, but the only thing underneath us is miles and miles of dark ocean in all directions, and the only thing above us is the susurration of the aurora borealis.

Never. In all my life, I've never known real fear, and today, I realized why. His head whips around so that he's looking at me as we zoom through the sky. His eyes are such a bright gold that they're shining in the dark like lanterns. *I've never cared enough about someone to really, truly care what happened to them. But today, I was terrified. Never, never, leave the place I put you and go off on your own, placing yourself in danger when I'm too far away to do anything about it.*

"I'm sorry." I could say more, but anything else feels. . .superficial compared to what he just confessed.

I couldn't leave when I realized you were in danger—good job masking, by the way—because I was surrounded by other earth blessed. So many of them. It took me far, far too long to come up with an excuse to leave. And then, I move so slowly in my earth blessed form that I couldn't get to you quickly enough.

I've never seen a car go as fast as Axel at his top speed, but I suppose it's all relative.

"Are you calm enough to talk about what happened yet?"

He whips his head back around and takes off. I barely grip the saddle handles in time to keep from flying head over heels backward. I guess that's my answer. I'm not sure how long we fly—I really need to find some kind of watch—before he slows. I wait for him to tell me that he's ready to talk, but I realize that's not going to happen.

After a few lazy circles close enough to the coast that I can make out land, I just start speaking. "The volcano was calling to me. I can see that now, with a little distance between us and what happened. At first, I was fleeing the wolves."

Iceland has no wolves.

"It does so," I say. "I could hear them howling."

You heard the wind, Azar says. *Our research says there are no wolves. I also haven't sensed any—domesticated dogs only.*

Now I feel a little stupid. "Well, I thought there were wolves. Or maybe I was just looking for an excuse." Is that true? Am I that stupid?

It's not stupid—you have a connection to that place—to whatever's trapped in that volcano. I shouldn't have left you so close.

"We're lucky Hyperion came when he did."

But why *did he come?* Concern runs through the bond. He doesn't like his brother taking an interest or saving me.

"He roasted the demon thing that came after me, which I'd like to think I might have been able to fight, but to be honest, I was pretty exhausted, and I might have been in shock."

What is it, and how did it get out?

"I have no idea," I say. "When I got through the tunnel and into the volcanic ante-chamber—actually, I'm not sure what to call that room, to be honest—I thought it was empty, even though I heard the chanting. I felt pretty crazy."

But you weren't.

"Well, Hyperion saw the demon too, so I'm going with not crazy, just. . .somehow attuned to a very strange. . .something."

And? We're headed back to Selfoss now—I can see it up ahead, set just below the mountains. Unlike before, some of the lights in the houses are on. That's encouraging.

"Well, when I got there, they were chanting, same as before. They were saying *hjartanu*, and there's something else that's strange." I pause. I'm not sure how he'll take this. "At first there were only those demons who were humanoid, but with lots of different sizes and shapes of horns. But then there were also. . .Azar, there were dragon shapes in there, teeming around in the lava."

Inside the volcano? Now he looks interested. *Flame blessed?*

I understand why he'd ask. I mean, they are basically swimming in fire. "I couldn't really tell. They were sort of writhing or, I don't know, like, dipping and ducking and then disappearing and reappearing in the lava."

Azar's shoulders droop a bit—was he that excited at the prospect of more of his kind? That bums me out a little.

"Anyway, the horned guys were the only ones there at first, and they saw me, which was weird, and they all looked for a moment, and then they just stopped caring. I should have been relieved, but it kind of bugged me. How many people really go into that volcano? Shouldn't my presence be a little exciting? So I pulled my tunic down and showed them my birthmark."

And?

"They flipped out. They started shouting some other words I can't remember."

Try.

"They said something as I was leaving—a girl's name. Vera, I think?"

And what else?

I shake my head. "It was weird. Like cutch vwaith or something. That's actually the one they said first. They only said the other one when I went to leave, and then when I left, one of the demon things managed to leave the lava and follow me."

We should ask the old woman about the words. They could be Icelandic.

"I thought you integrated everything from earth."

He shakes his head slowly back and forth. *I only learned a handful of languages that were flagged as the most common. English. Hindi. Mandarin. Spanish. Russian. Arabic. The others we merely learned the words for "the heart." In any case, information about specific nations, especially small ones like Iceland, wasn't considered critical. There may be a blessed here who knows more, but we should ask the woman first. She may also know local legends about the volcano.*

Before I even realize what we're doing, Azar's landing in front of the woman's tiny house. "She may be asleep," I say. "It's nearly morning here."

But she's not. She's sitting on her porch, her eyes wide, her face turned toward the sky, staring at the two strike blessed darting back and forth across the sky, silver flashes against the aurora borealis.

Until we land. Then her attention is fully returned to us.

"I wonder if she'll cry again," I whisper. "At your unbearable magnificence." I can't help teasing him.

Shut up.

At least his shaky, I'm-so-upset-I'll-either-incinerate-something-or-cry energy is gone. That was disturbing. "Sorry to bother you again," I say.

"You're his bonded. You'll never be a bother." The woman smiles. "It's my pleasure to serve."

This is super weird. "Okay. Well, the thing is, I went to a nearby volcano—Eyjafjallajökull—I know I'm pronouncing that all wrong, but anyway, I went, and something really strange happened."

She steps toward me, her eyes widening. "What? Tell me."

"I saw these, like, lava creatures swimming in the volcano." I wait for her to laugh. She doesn't. I wait for her to arch one eyebrow and tell me I'm insane. "And apparently that's not so weird to you."

"You're not the first to see the cursed."

"The—the what?"

We're the blessed. They're. . .the cursed?

The woman's eyes widen dramatically and her mouth drops open. "He spoke to me."

"I mean, I could hear him too, but yeah. He can talk."

She drops down on her knees and falls flat on her face, her hands extended up over her head, her palms also flat on the ground. She doesn't move, breathe, or talk.

She just lies there.

It's annoying.

"Alright, so yeah, Azar's pretty great. But the thing is, they were talking to me."

She sits up abruptly—pretty fast for such an old lady. "They could see you?"

"Wait, so people around here just know about the burning people and the dragons in the lava?"

She frowns. "Dragons?"

"Alright." I start from the beginning, and it turns out some people have reported hearing or even seeing the people who chant "the heart" in the lava, but no one has ever seen dragons in there.

"The legends have been passed down for some time. The humans who displeased god, through cowardice, betrayal, or treachery, were trapped in the volcano, doomed to burn until someone comes to restore their hearts to god's good grace."

It explains why they chant 'the heart' over and over. "But which god are they being held hostage for?" I ask. "Aren't there a bunch of them?"

"The Allfather, of course," she says.

"Right." I nod. "Odin."

What did you say? Azar asks.

"Odin—also called the Allfather sometimes—is a Viking god," I explain. "I think he's had a lot of names, but those are the two most common these days. He's just a myth, though. Don't worry."

He may be a myth, but my father's name is Odinn, Azar says. He's definitely very, very real, and that's a bizarre coincidence, don't you think?

15

AXEL

From almost the moment I was large enough to leave the hatching caverns, I've been surrounded by my siblings, but not at all in the same way that Liz watches over hers.

No, mine wanted to eat me.

All save Hyperion.

My father had read the prophecy about the last egg and believed it. He thought, as the last hatched, I would be the key to restoring the future of the blessed. Yet, even his decree pertaining to my safety didn't keep me safe. Had Hyperion not followed me around so dutifully, even Euphrasia could not have kept me alive. The blessed may not feel the same range of emotions as humans, but we know desire.

And when someone else is receiving attention or acclaim, we want it for ourselves.

The urge to destroy is almost overpowering, at least, it always has been for my brothers. At the time of my hatching, there were twenty-nine of them. Now, there are twelve left, and Hyperion's the oldest and the largest.

He's killed seven of the seventeen who have perished,

and all of those kills have been to protect me. I thought father was sending me a message when Hyperion came to Earth, that he was still on my side, and that he believed in me.

But now, hearing there are demon creatures trapped in a volcano, by all counts the volcano that's calling to my bonded, I wonder exactly what my father knows. . .and what he plans for me to do. My father sacrificed his eye when our people left Earth the first time, and he has been bitter about losing it ever since.

What information did he withhold about Earth and our reasons for leaving? What sacrifice will he demand of me to restore what was lost? When I left, I didn't have anything I would mind losing. My eye? Fine. A limb? Done. My future mate? Acceptable.

I'd have given anything, done anything, lost *everything* to ensure that we had a future. In fact, I couldn't even imagine something that I wouldn't sacrifice. But now I have something I won't consider losing.

Liz.

When she was in danger, I was almost ready to divulge my secret and brave the collateral damage—I nearly shifted on the spot in front of all the earth blessed and a few others—just to get to her faster. Only the fear that Hyperion might be forced to put me down because of it, dooming her in the process, restrained me. My weakness is hers as well. I have to remember that.

Hearing that this human god has the same name as my father—it's concerning.

"What else did you say the humans were chanting?" the crone asks. "You said they said two other words. Right?"

Liz nods. "After they saw my birthmark, they—"

"What mark?" The old woman straightens, her back still a bit stooped, but much less. "What did you show them?"

Liz swallows and looks around, clearly not keen on showing anyone else the thing that resulted in her being dragged toward that volcano in the first place. But finally, she unbuttons the top of her tunic and tugs it down, showing the bright red mark in the shape of a heart at the top of her breast.

The old woman's frown deepens. "And what did they say when they saw it?"

Liz shakes her head. "I don't speak whatever language they do—maybe Icelandic?"

"Probably Old Norse," she says. "But close enough. What did they say?"

"It sounded strange, like cutch-vwaith or something?" Liz frowns and coughs. When she speaks again, her voice is lower, and it sounds like she's trying to mimic a sound. "Cutch-veith?" She shrugs. "That's as close as I can get."

The old woman closes her eyes and stumbles backward, slamming into the steps of the porch and falling backward on her rear end. She shakes her head. "Can it be?" She tilts her head. Then she shakes it. "No." She opens her eyes. "They must be mistaken. You're human, are you not?"

Liz laughs. "No reason to fear me. I'm one hundred percent human, for sure."

The old woman blinks and nods. "Yes. Human. They must be mistaken. Or perhaps you're just part of the sacrifice."

I straighten. *The what?*

The woman turns toward me. "In the beginning, there were two different groups of gods, you understand. The Vanir, and the Aesir. The Vanir lived in Vanaheim, and the Aesir, in Asgard. One woman sparked the first war between the two realms of the gods, wreaking havoc on all the humans condemned to be collateral damage in their war."

"I've heard of Asgard," Liz says. "I mean, who doesn't like a little Thor eye candy?"

The old woman glares. "That movie was absurd. This is real." She shakes her head.

What's eye candy?

"It's ridiculous, when she has a dragon at her side, that's what." The woman sighs. "In the real story, the one Marvel butchered for that mess of a film franchise, the Vanir gods sent the Aesir a weapon that sparked the war—Gullveig. Some say she was the sister of Freya, queen to Odin. Some say she was Freya herself. Either way, she attacked the Aesir as they must have intended she would do, and they burned her for it."

"Could they have been calling for that Gullveig person to show up and talk to me? Maybe she's in there with them?"

"She's not in there with them." The woman laughs, and it's a harsh sound—not happy at all. "She was reborn after dying, not once, not even twice, but three times."

Liz pales. "At the entrance of the tunnel, there's a flame carved, and next to it, three skulls."

The woman nods. "I've been to that tunnel and didn't see that, but it could be a reference to Gullveig's deaths. They burned her three times, and each time she rose, stronger than before."

Liz is trembling.

She hasn't eaten, she hasn't rested, and she's been through quite an ordeal. *It's time to go. You need sleep.*

"I need to go back to that volcano," she says. "We should go right now. Your dad won't wait."

Absolutely not. You will sleep now. We can go tomorrow, with allies in attendance.

She wants to argue. I can see it in the set of her jaw and the flashing of her eyes, but she inhales, her nostrils flaring, and then she sighs. Her entire body deflates when she does. "I should check on Sammy, Coral, and Jade."

Yes, you should.

"I should like to come," the woman says. "When you go tomorrow."

"It won't be safe," Liz says.

"Do I look like I fear death?" The woman's smile is a little off. Even I can see that. "To witness the lava-burned, to be there when you approach Eyjafjallajökull, when the cursed are restored, it would be the highlight of my entire life."

"When the cursed are restored?" Liz asks. "What does that mean?"

"Those who were doomed to wait on redemption are all there, hoping for someone to release them."

"But then, where will they go?"

"I assume they'll go to an afterlife, but I don't know, girl. That's why I want to see it!"

I don't like her. The woman feels almost like a ghoul—desperate to experience something horrible. She may be in awe of the events happening before her, and she may be sharing what she's read, but it still makes me uneasy.

"The other word the cursed were saying," Liz says, "was Vera. Is that a girl's name here too?"

The woman shakes her head. "Nay, vera means *stay*. They were begging you for your help, and now, so am I. Those cursed souls have been punished long enough, and you may be the only one who can free them."

As Liz mounts my back, an idea occurs to me. *Could their calling her Gullveig be a message? What if the only way she can help them is to be burned and die, like Gullveig before her?*

The crone's laughter makes me want to incinerate her on the spot.

"But Gullveig didn't stay dead," Liz says.

"And you aren't Gullveig," the crone says. "All good deeds require sacrifice, and not everyone comes back stronger."

No. Absolutely not. I launch into the sky, swinging in wide arcs. *You are not going to sacrifice yourself to save a bunch of demons. I forbid it.*

Liz laughs. "You won't get any argument from me, but we do need to find the heart."

I'll go with you tomorrow, and we'll see what we can discover about the volcano.

"Where's my family?"

They're waiting on word of where to settle.

"So we need to pick a building to stay in, because that storm's coming, right?"

I've been searching as we made a sweep, but the buildings here are much more limited than in Houston. *None of these homes are large enough.*

"What about that?" Liz points at the sprawling building next to the large open fields.

That's some kind of athletic facility, and the strike blessed have already asked to use it and been granted permission. My understanding is that it didn't have adequate facilities for personal hygiene for a large number of humans. I'm on my second sweep, just passing near the home of the crone, when Liz points again.

"It's not a skyscraper, but for Selfoss, it kind of is. The sign says *Hotel Selfoss*, and it's a few stories high. Let's check that one out."

It takes her a while to convince me, but she's probably right that it's one of our best options. The building's a long rectangle, perched on the edge of the land near a bend in the river Ölfusá, and there are some wide, large rooms on the far end.

Most importantly, there aren't a lot of options in Selfoss. Once I've blown a hole in the far end on the top floor and patched it over with a red shield, I transform into my Axel form and help Liz shift furniture around. She understands the value of having a little space for the two of us, and I'm trying to be understanding of her desire to keep her siblings near.

If she feels for them anything close to what I feel when she's in danger. . . *Yes, I think they could easily occupy the western wing while we keep to this side of the building.*

Liz is delighted to get the power turned on, thanks to the whirring of a generator. Who knows how long that will last? But for now, there's a heater that has even turned on. We won't need it on our half of the building, but for the children, maintaining proper heat is a concern, especially with a storm coming.

When we find a storage room full of food, she's even more excited. "Can you bring them here?"

Do I look like a delivery service?

Liz tilts her head and examines me carefully. As her eyes study my face and fall lower, roving over my golden scales and more delicate shape, her lips part slightly.

What?

She smiles then. "You're absolutely gorgeous as an earth dragon. I might like you better this way."

Don't be ridiculous.

She steps toward me then, slowly, her eyes soft. "You know, you scared me at the beginning, in this exact form. You're enormous—larger than a small airplane. And your scales are exquisite." She reaches out a hand.

I inhale sharply, desperate for her to touch me of her own volition, but I'm afraid that if I move, she won't. I don't even breathe.

"Axel." She looks up, her hand frozen in the air between us. "Why did you say 'don't be ridiculous'?"

I can't help narrowing my eyes. *No one prefers Axel to Azar.*

"What if I do? Would you spend more time in this form?" The corners of her mouth turn up. "What if this form felt less terrifying to me?"

Does it?

She shrugs. "Not really. They're about the same. You're you, no matter what shape you're in."

I shift into my human form, taking the chance to make her a dragon-skin cloak, this time from Axel's skin.

She gasps and backs up three steps.

"And what about this shape?" I offer her the cloak. I should've made one before—it's cold here. But now I'm using it as a lure. She almost touched me, but then she backed up. I want her to come to me, so I'm baiting her as I've seen her do with Fluff Dog, holding a piece of bacon.

She swallows and lifts her chin. "I said you're the same in all of them."

"But this one's very small. Weak, even." I bite my lip. "Do you like this one just as well as the others?"

She shrugs. "Sure." But her breathing's strange. Her eyes are bright.

"Are you cold?" I jostle my hand, drawing her attention to the treat again. Come and get it, Liz.

"What is that?" She frowns. "A big chunk of cloth? Are you making me create my own clothing now, even though your magic allows you to fashion it entirely?"

I laugh. "Hardly. It's a cloak. You can wrap it around you." I lift it up and use my other hand to show her how it can be fastened to surround her body or left open to vent.

"Oh." She steps closer.

Good girl.

"It's gold."

"You said you liked those scales."

She swallows again. "I do." She reaches her hand out.

"Good." I drop my hand a bit, forcing her to come closer, still. What's with her being so skittish?

She lunges forward, her hand brushing past me to snatch at the cloak, and I yank my arm back even faster, my smile widening. "Come and take it."

"Oh, stop. We need to go get the kids."

"And we will," I say. "But you should be warm while doing it." She feints left and then leaps on me, her arms wrapping around my body in pursuit of the cloak.

Something inside of my chest lurches.

I *like* having her body clinging to mine. I like having her arms wrapped around me. I like her breath against my ear. I've never liked this bizarre human form. It's weak. It's small. It's *vulnerable*. But with her around, maybe vulnerable is, for the first time in my life, a good thing. Maybe being vulnerable means being accessible to Liz.

Maybe it makes her like me more, and maybe she'll want to touch me more as well.

I drop the cloak to the ground, and I bring both my hands up to cup her cheeks. "Liz."

Her eyes, when they find mine, are fearful. "Axel, I can't." She tries to escape, releasing her grasp, but I'm too fast.

My arms drop underneath her bottom and pull her closer. "You have to earn that cloak."

"What does that mean?" The fear multiplies.

"Why does that scare you?"

She shakes her head, her fair hair falling forward, across her brow. "It doesn't." Her breath fans out over my face, and there's another, smaller lurch inside my body.

"I think it does," I whisper. "Your eyes say that you're nervous at the very least, and so does the bond. It's quivery."

She rolls her eyes. "Stop with that nonsense." She wiggles, trying to force me to drop her, but something about the way her bottom's shifting in my hands makes my heart beat harder in my chest. There's probably some kind of problem with this human-physiology. It certainly doesn't seem very strong. And yet. . .

"I like when you do that." Now my smile's broad. "Do it again."

She freezes. "Do what?"

"Wiggle around. You can do it all you'd like." I lean closer, planning to sniff her neck, but she turns toward me.

And then she closes her eyes.

I sneak a little closer and breathe in deeply near her neck—pure, unadulterated pleasure. Her smell's a mixture of blood, sweat, and flowers. I've never smelled anything else like it—I could smell it all day and never have enough. But then I shift my face until it's right in front of her, and I blow on her nose. "Why'd you close your eyes?"

Her eyes fly open, and her hands shoot out, knocking herself free. She falls backward, landing hard on the sweet bottom I so enjoyed holding a moment ago. "Ouch." She says a few other strange words, and then scrambles to her feet, darting around me and snatching the cape off the floor. "We need to get my siblings. Let's go." She snaps. "Shift already."

"I did something wrong," I say. "It would help me if you could tell me what it was. I'd prefer not to make the same mistake again."

Her head whips around and her mouth dangles open.

"You looked almost pleased, and now you're irritated with me. What caused it?"

"You were groping my butt," she says. "And then you *blew on my nose*." She shakes her head. "What's wrong with you?"

I step closer, and her heart starts hammering in her chest. "What would Gideon have done in my place?" I can't help my snarl. I hate thinking about him, but not as much as I hate the fact that he would know just what to do. He wouldn't leave her glaring at him. He'd have her panting or grabbing or something equally horrible. "Also, what's groping? I was led to believe it meant feeling around for something, as in groping around in the dark, for instance, but you jumped on me."

Liz splutters, and that draws my attention to her mouth.

That gives me an idea. "Did you want me to kiss you? Is that why you closed your eyes?"

Inexplicably, Liz draws one of her swords as if she's preparing to fight me. "Why don't we do a training session before we go grab the kids? That would be good, since presumably we're going back to the volcano once we get them settled here."

"A—training?" Why does she pull out a weapon every time I change into my humanoid form?

"Come on." She slashes at me, and then she spins backward, almost crashing into a chair. Then she waves her arm at the offending chair and it flies away, collapsing as it clatters into the wall.

"Hey, you made it move without touching it. Nice work."

She brandishes the swords at me. "Yeah, yeah. Let's go."

"I don't understand why—" But she's slashing at me again, like she wants to remove a chunk of my body. I duck and hop and spin, but her sword manages to catch the front of my shirt, dragging downward, slicing my shirt open.

She freezes then, staring at my very normal human stomach. She did that last time, too, when I whipped my shirt off. I shrug out of the remains of my shirt, and her breath hitches in a very satisfying way.

I'm definitely on to something. For some reason, removing the clothing humans themselves put on to regulate their temperatures—only necessary because of a humanoid body design flaw—makes them act strangely. Liz stares at my chest and stomach, her eyes not rising to my face at all.

"Are we done training, now?"

Her head snaps up, her mouth parted slightly.

"Should I go and retrieve your brother and sisters?"

She blinks. "What do you want with me?"

"What?"

"Am I just a key to you?"

Now I'm the one blinking. "I don't understand."

"Your heart's locked up in a volcano, or it's trapped underneath the earth. Or maybe it's at the bottom of the lake. Maybe some kind of tortured demon people who made bad decisions in their lives are guarding it. We don't know, but it looks like I may be the key to unlocking whatever it is that's blocking you from retrieving it. Is that my only value to you?" She frowns.

"Where's this coming from?" I step toward her.

She flinches.

That makes me feel. . .*very* bad. "I would never hurt you."

"Unless you have to, say, fling me into a volcano to save all the dragons or something."

"I would never do that, not even to save them."

Her eyes flash as they challenge me. "What if it's the *only way* to retrieve your precious heart?"

"That's ridiculous." I fold my arms.

"Is it?" Her eyebrows rise. "Because that inscription says death by fire three times, and those cursed horn people really didn't want me to leave. I think it's pretty obvious. They want me in there with them, and they want it because I'm marked with a heart on my chest. Or did you forget that?"

"Liz." I step toward her as quickly as I can, my hands wrapping around her upper arms so she can't retreat. Or, you know, stab me with her sword. "You're my bonded. I would never throw you into a volcano. We'll go there together so I can *protect you*. I'd melt the entire mountain into the center of the earth before I'd throw you in."

"Do you really mean that?"

"Of course I do." I release her right arm and run the back of two fingers down the side of her face. "You can sense that I mean it."

"What if your dad—"

"My dad will have to kill me if he wants to throw you into that volcano."

She stares into my eyes for one beat, and then another. And then she presses her lips against mine. It's not our first kiss. It's not even our second or third. But it's the first time she has ever come to me and kissed me for no reason other than she wanted to do it, and that changes everything about it.

It feels an awful lot like approval, and that's something I've apparently craved without even realizing it. Her hands press flat against the muscles of my chest, and where she touches me, I start to burn. My hands wrap around her hips, dragging her closer, and she whimpers a little.

I like it.

A lot.

Her mouth moves against mine, and her body is pressed to mine from our knees up to our faces, and it still isn't enough. When her hand brushes up my arm and her fingers encircle my biceps, and squeeze, I can't help it. I kiss her harder, my tongue doing what she taught me before, and tasting the inside of her mouth.

It's better than anything I've ever tasted.

I could kiss her forever. I could drag her against me always, and it would never be enough. Something inside of me, the core of Azar, my desires to burn and destroy and *possess,* flares to life as her other hand strokes my chest, and I feel the heat start to emanate from me.

Liz pulls away just a hair, but I drag her back, desperate to consume her yet again.

"Your eyes." She's watching me as she whispers. "They're—they're glowing."

"There's more to this kissing thing than I realized," I say. "And if you ever kiss Gideon or touch anyone else like this again, so help me, I will roast them, and then I'll eat them."

Her laughter's the most blindingly beautiful sound I've ever heard. "What happened to 'mating has nothing to do with our bond'?"

The growl that rumbles through my chest is pure possession, and I don't even try to fight it. "I was very, very wrong."

"Wait." She leans closer, her eyes on mine until they drop to my mouth.

That stokes the fires inside me in a way they've never been stoked. "I can't wait, not for another second."

"But Axel, what does this mean—for Asteria, I mean?"

"Who cares?" I kiss the side of her face. Then I drag a kiss upward, to her temple. "She can mate with someone else—Hyperion. With my father. With a goat. I don't care."

Now she's laughing even more, and I'm about to do. . .I don't know what. But something *big*. My insides are on fire, and I'm desperate for more of Liz in every way—I realize that I want to mate with her, whatever that means. I want her to be mine in this form and in every form. *Mine*.

Until I hear them.

Rufus and Gordon are at the base of the hotel outside, calling my name. I'm going to roast them on a spit, and we're all going to feast on their insides.

Apparently human mating has to be done privately, which is a real drag.

16

LIZ

After Gideon told me he was quitting MMA for me —well, basically—I had about a million questions. I was too nervous to ask any of them, but I meant to as soon as he quit.

Before the world exploded.

Now that Axel says he's not planning to mate with Asteria, because of me presumably, I have ten million more. But I'm a hundred times more afraid to ask any of them than I was back then.

Not because I'm afraid of what it will mean for my future. At this point, I can't even imagine a future without Axel in it. But I'm afraid of what he might say. I'm afraid of what we might do. I'm afraid of what I may *become* if we keep going the way we're going right now.

That crazy old woman may think all of this is fascinating, and she may have shaken her head and cast away the idea, but I'm pretty sure that her first thought was that I might *be* Gullveig reborn or something, and that's straight up insane.

But what part of my life since the day the dragons arrived has been sane? What part has made any sense at all?

Only the moments I've spent with Axel.

And with my family. As they rush into the room, I can tell Axel's contemplating ways he could dismember them, especially Gideon, who looks like he's more than ready to fight my dragon prince. But Gideon and my siblings are two of the major reasons I haven't suffered a complete mental break during all this.

"Don't be too angry they're here," I whisper. "I need them. All of them."

Axel grunts.

When Fluff Dog shoots out of the box in the stairwell like a rocket of fur, she's running so fast that her wrap-around, curly tail's actually flying straight back. I crouch down and hold out my arms, and she leaps up into them. I bury my face in her fur ruff and then I start coughing.

"Why does she stink so bad?" I rub her head, but then I carefully place her on the ground. "What on earth happened on the way here?"

"She found something right outside when we let her loose, near the river," Coral says. "I had to pick her up and drag her away from rolling in it."

Dogs are so gross sometimes.

"I'll help them bathe her," Gideon says. "Since this is a hotel, it should be easy to find shampoo, at least." His smile's achingly familiar. It hasn't changed in the fifteen years we've been friends.

"Thanks." I find myself smiling back at him out of habit almost. "Sorry it's so cold."

"Maybe we'll find some bathrobes, too," Gideon says. "Hopefully they didn't take those when they evacuated."

"I'm trying to figure out how the humans knew to evacuate," Axel says.

Gideon's shrug is affected—he clearly had something to do with it, and Axel realized it before I did.

Actually, he's been getting better at playing human.

Much better. The way he's glowering at Gideon right now could be the opening scene of any love triangle in any fantasy movie ever made. Not that he's angry at him because of me this time, but still.

"Isn't it easier that they're not here?" Gideon asks. "You don't need to break up families by massacring party-goers who are dressed up for Halloween, at least."

How did we go from the Boo Bash to this in less than two months? I still remember worrying that day about what would happen if I ate a fun size Snickers. Even that small memory makes me laugh—as if a little sugar ever could have wrecked anything.

"Hey," Axel says. "Are you alright?"

"It's funny how it takes something like a dragon attack to wake humans up to what matters." I shake my head. "I'm profoundly screwed up. You should run away."

"Only if you're running alongside me." Axel's voice is low—only loud enough for me to hear.

"You probably run too fast for me to keep up." I think about how he did nine hundred sit-ups without ever tiring. "Sometimes I think that, underneath all those muscles, you're actually a cyborg."

His brows rise. "A cyborg?"

"Never mind."

"This place is cool." Sammy's trying to push one of the plush sofas away from the wall.

"Whoa, there," Axel says. "You're going to be sleeping on the other end of the hotel where there are smaller rooms."

"But Gordon doesn't like little rooms. He can only fit in them in his boring body."

"Boring?" I can't help smirking. Sammy still says the funniest stuff.

"You know," Sammy says. "No scales, no claws, and no razor sharp teeth."

"Are they razor sharp?" Axel asks. "I always thought his huge teeth looked more blunt, personally."

Gordon scowls.

This dynamic is new. The dragons are learning sarcasm and snark. I wonder what that will lead to, down the road.

"I think they're pretty sharp," I say. "I'd run the other way."

"Liar," Axel says. "You run toward every dangerous blessed you see. Why would you run from Gordon?"

"You're saying I'm dangerous?" Gordon asks.

Axel laughs. "No, I'm saying if she runs *toward* them, why would she run *from* you?"

"Alright," I say. "Let's get you all settled. Axel and I have to leave soon, but I want to make sure you're alright first."

"Leave?" Gideon freezes, turning around carefully. "Where are you going?"

"You know there's a volcano here," I say. "We have some recon to do there." I'm not about to tell him I've already been, and that I want to see whether more little demons will spew out if I poke it harder.

He would definitely not approve.

"I'll come." He turns and crosses his arms over his chest.

Axel snorts. "And if one of the demons attacks, you'll do what? Distract it with your soft human body?"

"*Demons?*" Gideon's entire face turns red, and he stiffens.

Whoops.

Now we'll have to pry him off Azar's leg when we try to fly away. I realize in that moment how much more annoying it will be here than it was in Houston for us to manage the Axel/Azar thing. Instead of being almost a hundred floors up, with only a handful of strike blessed even able to reach that level, we're now on the third floor of a building that's in the center of activity on the main river in Selfoss.

I'm glad we got the dragons out of Houston, and I'm delighted that the humans here evacuated. But making our own meals and him having to wander around as Axel until we can find a place where no one else can see us is going to be really irritating.

I wish we could, at least, tell Gordon and Rufus.

But Axel's reasoning is sound. They're loyal, and they'd be unlikely to see Azar as weak for his connection to them, *but* they'd also be a weak link. Any of the other dragons could simply filet them until they divulge his secret.

Not that anyone would know to do that.

But the more who know, the more ways the information can slip out. The only way to keep a secret is to really keep it. It takes me forever to convince Gideon that Axel was kidding about the demon, and then another twenty minutes to get them all settled on their side of the building.

Axel insists that I sleep for at least an hour, which annoys me, knowing that Hyperion may still be guarding the exit from the volcano, but I do need it. My eyes are burning. When he finally wakes me, which he does do after right around an hour, it's the early morning, and we're still stopped six times on our way out of Selfoss.

"I can't believe none of you ever sleep," I say. "It's wild to me."

By the time we're finally far enough from Selfoss for Axel to shift into Azar, it must be close to dawn. It's been long enough since we had our *moment* that I don't even know how to broach talking about what happened or what he said. It makes it easy to cling to his neck the whole way there without talking. And when we reach Eyjafjallajökull, Hyperion's still there, as I feared.

We left him there without so much as an explanation for hours.

What's the plan? It doesn't look like he's moved since we left, and shockingly, he doesn't even sound annoyed.

"Have you been here this whole time?" I ask.

I didn't want more of those little beasties escaping. He straightens. *I thought you'd be back sooner. What took so long?*

It's not like we can explain that we had to run halfway here before Azar could shift on either end. "It was my brother and sisters," I say. "We had to find a place for them to stay that was safe and large enough for Axel and the others." I'm kind of proud of myself every time I use Axel as though he's back there while we're here. "And we had to get the power turned on before the storm hits. Not everyone can make their own heat."

If he's annoyed, he hides it well. Maybe dragons are used to waiting around. *How are we going in?*

It's too bad Azar can't switch into his human form and just walk in beside me. It would be the easiest solution. But, *que sera*. "I'll go in first, and—"

Both Hyperion and Azar react immediately, trumpeting loudly. I'll take that as their refusal to allow that.

"But neither of you will fit through the tunnel," I explain reasonably. "And even if we brought one of the smaller earth blessed, they won't fit near the end. It gets narrower and narrower as you walk toward the center."

I can go back and send Axel, Azar starts.

I shake my head. There's no way Hyperion won't think it's strange if *only* Axel comes back. It would definitely raise questions.

As if that weakling could even help her, Hyperion says. *I know you like him, but. . .* He shakes his head and snorts, plumes of smoke puffing up from both nostrils. *We can just widen the opening.*

"It's long," I say. "You could take down half the mountain in the process."

So? Hyperion turns toward Azar, waiting to see what he says.

I'm actually impressed his much larger, much older brother hasn't yanked the reins of command from Azar. I figured that would take about two seconds, but he still yields to whatever Azar commands, at least, so far he has. Mostly.

But instead of worrying about preserving the mountain and the structural integrity of the volcano, Azar just says, *Get on my back where you'll be safe.*

"Safe?" I can't believe what I'm hearing. "Safe. . .while you and your idiot brother fire blast a *volcano?* What do you think is going to happen, exactly?"

We have nothing to fear from flames, little one, Hyperion says. *And neither do you. Not while you're with us.*

"What about the creatures trapped inside the lava? What about them?"

I doubt they can burn more than they already are. Hyperion's quite the comedian all of a sudden. *But if they do, I'm not going to worry. That one didn't look like he was following you to ask you a question. It looked aggressive.*

But they're obviously going to do whatever they want, and I don't have much room to stop them. I really don't want to confront the demons myself, so I climb up on Azar's back. As always, the second I've grabbed the handles of the saddle, he takes off, Hyperion on his tail. Both of them fly around in a large loop, and then come back toward the tunnel, blasting it with the full force of their firepower.

At first, the black rock turns bright red.

But then it explodes.

And they keep right on burning it, stopping periodically and circling around, possibly to recharge? Each time one section explodes, chunks of burning rock rain down overhead, but Azar must be doing something, because all of the chunks that come within a few feet of me turn back to black. When they pelt me in the head and face, and when they slam into my arms and legs, they're hot, but they don't burn me.

It's relatively slow going, but their flames are more tightly controlled than I realize, and before too long, they've opened up the side of the mountain, exposing the tunnel's path right into the cavern and its lava ledge.

"That's enough," I shout.

There's no way Hyperion can hear me, so I gather up all my mental energy and say, *It's done. You reached it.*

They both stop, suspended in air, wings flapping slowly, and watch as the red rock on either side of the tunnel flashes angrily.

"You realize that I can't possibly land on any of that?"

The bond's a bright green—humor, maybe? Happiness at least. He begins flapping his wings much harder, but he's holding the angle so that we don't fly in any particular direction. It takes me a second, but I realize that he's fanning the rocks.

And I'm removing the heat, one section at a time.

I always forget that he can do that. It makes me think about a law of physics, though. Energy conservation or something like that. "Where does that heat go?"

Think of us like flying furnaces, Hyperion says. *We can store up all that heat inside and unleash it whenever necessary.*

"That's handy," I say. "But how long will it take before —" Hyperion must be helping, because as I ask, the last of the red rock turns black. "You two are a little frightening."

But we'll never harm you, Azar says. *And with us around, no one else will, either.*

I notice that Hyperion doesn't bother echoing his brother's promise. I suppose if Azar trusts him, that's enough for me. Azar doesn't seem to trust anyone, really, and Hyperion did show up just in time to keep that horned beast from pouncing on me.

The very horned beasts that we're now here looking for.

Azar lands, and I slide off his back. The black stone under my feet is still warm—uncomfortably so—but it's not burning through the soles of my boots, so I guess that means it's fine. It surprises me a bit that Azar lets me take the lead, marching ahead of my two dragon guards into the cavern turned lava-viewing overhang.

But when the first horned creature spots me, it acts like it's nothing new. Like we didn't just blast our way in here. They're just milling around and churning, your typical demon-horned creatures. No dragons visible at all.

What is it we're looking for? Hyperion asks.

"Can you see them?" I turn around, studying the dragons' faces for recognition.

See what? Azar asks.

"You can't see the horned people swimming through the lava?"

Azar and Hyperion shake their heads, their eyes actively scanning the volcanic activity.

Strange, strange, strange.

"Alright, let's try this." I unclasp my cloak and unbutton the top of my tunic, handing the cloak to Azar.

What am I going to do with this?

"Hold it for me in case the beasts leap through the lava so I don't drop it and ruin my new pretty."

Azar rolls his eyes. He didn't do that a few weeks ago— I'm definitely teaching him bad habits. I'll worry more about that later. For now, I peel my tunic down enough to show them my birthmark.

Nothing happens.

The beasties don't even seem to notice.

At first.

I'm about to button up my cloak when one of them freezes, and he starts to shout—I can't hear anything for some reason, but the others react, and suddenly they're all pointing and milling around with their heads locked on me.

That's when I hear the first shout. *Hjartanu!* Followed closely by what I now know is probably the word *Gullveig!* Seconds later, the first dragon shows up, and I spin around to see what Azar and Hyperion think. "Now? Now do you see them? The dragons, I mean? They're back too." When I turn back, there are at least a dozen dragons, and some are even managing to leap out of the lava a bit.

I hear the sounds now—Gullveig and hjartanu, like you said, Azar says. *But I don't see anything.*

I could scream. "How can you not see them?"

Are they always there, but only some can see them unless they escape wherever they're stuck? Hyperion asks. *That would make sense, if they've been there all along, but most humans and apparently most blessed don't even know.*

Could it be that only brights can see them? Azar asks. *We should bring another here and then we can determine whether all brights are capable of making them out.*

Call to them, Hyperion says. *Maybe you're the key to freeing them, since you can see them. Your mark means something to them, clearly.*

It's worth an effort, at least. "Demon spawn," I say. "Why don't you come out? Come and see me." I step closer, even though their teeming and churning is making my skin crawl.

The heat from the lava bubbling and popping in front of me was already emanating outward in waves, but when I call them, the demon people and dragons fly into a frenzy. Their shouts increase in fervency and cadence, and more of them leap and shove their way toward the top of the lava.

"They can definitely hear me," I say. "But it doesn't seem to matter."

Try to leave, Hyperion says. *That's what motivated them last time.*

He's right. They became desperate when I ran away. I shout, "I have to go now. I'll come back."

They have no idea what I'm saying—they stop moving so frantically, and they're trying to listen, but several of them look confused.

Try our language, Azar says. *You said there are blessed among them.*

It's worth a try. I feel a little strange using the blessed tongue, which I can use thanks to the bond, but I can use it.

"I have to leave," I say. "I'll return."

The horned creatures may only speak Old Norse, but the dragons clearly understand my words this time. Like last time, they become agitated. They leap higher. They roar louder. And when they reply, I can understand.

Free us, they shout in dragon-tongue. *Release us from this place of torment.*

Are they all trapped inside the lava? Burning forever and ever. . .and for what reason? How has it not consumed them? Where do the dragons and horned creatures go when they aren't clamoring for my attention here? How many are there?

So many questions.

Why are you trapped? Azar could understand them too, and he has questions of his own.

The dragon heads all snap toward his location, as if they too can hear but not see. *Who's with you?* one of them asks.

"It's my bonded," I say, still in dragon-tongue. "He brought me here. We're looking for something."

What is it? One dragon, larger than the rest, has shoved the others back. He's flanked by two largish dragons and hordes of horned demon-people. *What do you seek?*

First, tell us how to free you, Azar says. *What would my bonded have to do in order to release you?*

The large dragon disappears and there's more frantic

churning. Horned people appear, disappear, and reappear. And finally, the large dragon returns, his lackeys alongside him yet again. *We're being punished here, punished for past sins that we had nothing to do with.*

That's a weird reply. "But what do you need me to do?" I ask.

Your death will free us, he finally says. *Gullveig must die to break the barrier.*

She's not Gullveig, Azar says. *You're mistaken.*

She's marked. Her death will free us, the demon dragon says again.

Absolutely not, Azar says. *You can burn in there forever.* He extends my cloak to me, held carefully between two talons. *Put this back on.*

What we seek is called the heart, Hyperion says. *Do you know anything about it?*

The large dragon smiles, and it sends a chill up my spine. *The heart is the barrier keeping us here, and she's marked because only she can remove it. Free us, and that barrier is yours.*

17

AXEL

I snatch Liz, my talons wrapping around her shoulders and underneath her armpits securely before vaulting into the sky.

I know Hyperion won't be far behind, but I have legitimate concerns that my idiotic bonded might walk right into the lava if I don't stop her. She had that look on her face, the one she gets when she's ready to sacrifice herself for someone else.

"Azar," she shouts.

No. I can't bring myself to say anything else.

"Azar." Now she's beating on my claws with her tiny, soft hands. The ones that would melt into goo so easily, that would never move again if she walked into that lava.

What do the dragons in that place know? They would say *anything* to convince us to sacrifice her if her death is what they believe will free them. They didn't even tell us what the 'mark' means or why they think that makes her this Gullveig person.

Azar. Hyperion's bearing down on my flank hard, and for the first time, I'm a little nervous he may not be on my side. *We need to talk about this.*

My concerns double. *They're criminals.* I fling Liz into the air and swing around to catch her on my back before Hyperion's close enough to try and snatch her from me. *We can't believe a thing they say.*

Agreed, Hyperion says.

Oh. He *agrees* with me. I slow, allowing my brother to slide in beside me.

We certainly aren't chucking your bonded in there because some trapped devil dragons are demanding it.

The tight feeling that had taken over my entire body begins to ease. *Of course not,* I say. *We have no way to know whether that's even true, that the heart is the barrier. They jumped right to offering us the heart—which conveniently happened to be the thing standing in their way—far too fast.*

Somehow it's all connected, Hyperion says. *They can see her. She can see them. They freak out when they see her birthmark, but that doesn't mean we should listen to them and free all the dragons that have been stuck here in a burning fire all this time, who clearly speak the same language as us.*

Now I'm uneasy again. It feels like he's agreeing with me, but only to play devil's advocate. *Hyperion, we can't trust them.*

Agree completely. We can't. We can test some things, however. When you took Liz and left, another beastie snuck through.

My blood begins to boil, and I turn to head back toward the volcano.

I blocked the cavern with a shield so she's still trapped, but we should return to make sure no others escape.

"How are they getting out?" Liz asks. "Isn't it weird that when I leave they're able to squeeze through?"

That's what I think we should look into. You obviously are connected to this barrier of theirs.

We need to find out why they're trapped, I say. *The last thing we need to do is release a plague of villains we'll need to contend with.*

"You'd think they might be immune to your fire-blasts," Liz says, "seeing as they're living in a pool of lava."

I wonder whether they're not in the lava, but somehow beneath it, I say. *Perhaps they're underneath the barrier and pushing against the lava.*

It would explain why they're scorched when they escape through, Hyperion says. *The female that escaped this time was smoking, and what looked like remains of clothing clung to her, blackened and charred.*

Hyperion's too keen on us investigating this, and he's in a huge rush. *Liz needs rest. It's time to head back.*

Father's deadline is tomorrow.

I want to burn something down. I want to destroy something—anything, really. I'm tired of being set impossible tasks and then being pressured into doing things faster, faster, faster. *We will not tell him about what they said. We have no evidence that it's even true.*

Those lava blessed are saying that the heart is there—that it's what is keeping them in that volcano, Hyperion says. *I don't trust them, but it's definitely the largest clue we've encountered by a wide margin. They speak our language, even. They might be able to tell us what happened in the first place and why we left the heart behind if it's so important.*

Dad should have told us that, I explode. *Why didn't he give us all the information in the first place?* We crest the ridge of the mountain range we've been following on the return trip to Selfoss. . .and that's when I see it.

"Whoa," Liz says. "What is all that?"

On the far side of the city, barely visible from our far west side, there are human forces gathered. Tanks. Long columns of troops, and huge machines like nothing I've ever seen them bring.

"Those look like huge crossbows," she says. "And what's that thing loaded into it?" She sounds nervous, and the bond is tight.

That makes me nervous. Their exploding weapons have never worked on us, but if the bright blue spears on the end of the massive crossbows are what I think they are, they might harm us.

Alert! I trumpet. *Hear me and report. The humans have mounted an attack.*

"It looks like an ice spear to me," Liz says. "Is that what it is?"

I swing in a wide loop around Selfoss, which looks untouched so far, and watch as blessed pour out of buildings, swoop through the sky, and stream out of the Ölfusá river and the ocean, far, far away.

The humans are ready, but they're not attacking. What are they waiting for? Why are they hesitating, allowing us to assemble our forces?

But then, as we're finally gathered, with storm clouds mounting on the horizon behind us from the impending storm, a dozen strike blessed fall from the sky, their bodies rolling, end over end, and then crashing into the ground below. When they hit, they explode, spraying lightning strikes all around, taking out dozens of the surrounding earth blessed as they die.

"What's going on?" Liz asks.

They're killing the human bonded, Hyperion says.

"How would they even know to do that?" Liz asks. But I can sense the moment she realizes the answer.

Gideon.

He must have sent them a message or left them one when we cleared out. And they're following his advice, and the gift we left them—sixty human-fused time-bombs to massacre the blessed.

"We need to figure out where the other human-bonded electro dragons are," Liz says. "It looks like they're killing the humans when the dragons are in the air, knowing that if they fall to the earth, prone as they are, they could die."

They've weaponized my people, because they know that killing the humans won't kill them outright. It'll just incapacitate them, but waiting until they're in the air makes them into weapons that are flying among us.

Who cares about them? Hyperion asks. *You and I can destroy the humans ourselves. We'll show them what happens to puny creatures who challenge Princes of the Flame!* He banks and heads right for them, fire already billowing out from his maw.

"We have to talk to Gideon first," Liz says. "If he—"

But I follow Hyperion too quickly for her to keep talking, Gideon's treachery the last thing on my mind. He's always been working on the human side, but stuck among us as he's been, I wrongly thought he couldn't harm us. I suppose I thought his loyalty to Liz would. . .

Actually, the truth is that he's so inconsequential, so powerless, that I never thought about him at all in a military context.

When the first blue spear arcs through the air, Hyperion dodges it easily. Ice-blue arrows rain down from the humans he's approaching, several of them making contact with and harmlessly clattering off the hard scales of his red hide.

Hyperion roars at the audacity of the humans, and he blasts the gathered troops, accelerating as he melts an entire line of our attackers. As he does so, I swing around, lining up to take my turn.

Liz is slapping the side of my neck. "Wait, wait, please."

I'm ready to fire, but she's still begging so piteously.

"Azar! We can talk to them. Don't just kill them all—it'll make everything worse."

They won't listen to me, I say. *I've tried. And they just murdered a dozen strike blessed and even more earth blessed.* But I swing past without flaming them, just swooping over their ranks with a furious roar.

"Do you trust me?" she asks. "I knew you'd keep me

safe by the volcano—" She cuts off then, and I'm not sure why.

As I swing back around, Hyperion begins his second pass, flaming a second line through the gathered troops. More blue arrows strike him and bounce off. Another spear zooms past him without making contact.

"Wait," Liz shouts. "It's Gideon! He's down there!"

He's chosen his path, I say. *It's time for us to take out our enemies. They* chose *to be our enemies.*

"No," Liz says. "This is the wrong decision. You have to at least try to talk to them."

They're armed with ice spears, I say. *The arrows won't work, but those spears might injure Hyperion or me. We have to take them out before they have a chance.*

"They'll come back with more," Liz says. "And better ones. It's what humans do. Roasting them isn't the right way."

I hear what you're saying, but you can't talk to someone who's attacking you. When I reach the front of the line this time, I'm taking out the humans poised to kill us. I'm not making my brother do all the work and take all the risk on himself.

But as we draw near, Liz leaps from my back, spinning round and round, her tiny, puny body plummeting toward the ground below.

The first match I ever fought in a sanctioned competition was a disaster.

My opponent was much, much larger than I was, and she had far more powerful strikes. She hit me, over and over, and all I could do was pull myself together and force myself to stand up again and again. I only beat her because, after acting like a punching bag repeatedly, I swung around unexpectedly and managed to get an arm bar she didn't see coming.

By the end, I was black and blue and generally looked like something headed to the morgue, but I won.

Ever since we stepped through the portal to Selfoss, my life has felt like that fight. I was almost compelled to that volcano, and I saw all those creatures, terrifying, pitiable, and trapped. Desperate.

I'm the only person who can save them, but doing so will be the end of me.

I'm not some legendary sister to Freya or wife of Odin. I don't reincarnate or come back from the dead. I'm just a normal human, birthed by a hippy and an uptight lawyer, raised with lousy dance lessons and group gymnastics classes in the suburbs.

Sure, I was kidnapped as a kid by a sex-trafficking ring, apparently. I survived that by murdering some people, which is pretty horrifying. But people move on from that. They recover from the trauma and live normal lives. They don't fling themselves into volcanoes to save demon-spawn and dark dragons who did who knows what to get trapped in the first place.

And normal girls certainly don't risk their lives by jumping off the back of a flying fire dragon, hurtling toward the ground at the speed of, well, maybe sound.

I may not be as normal as I'd like to think.

Thankfully, that's probably what allows me to spread my arms wide and stop, hovering about two feet from the riverbank below.

My head whips around immediately, checking to see whether Azar will still blast us all. The betrayal radiating through the bond, and the dark, blood-red color isn't promising, but he doesn't barbecue us.

But the humans do open fire on me.

On me! Another human!

Luckily, I'm able to stop the bullets as I release myself and drop to the ground. It's *bizarre* in the extreme, projecting a shining red shield out in front of myself that stops bullets.

"You're really still using those?" I shout. "They don't work against the dragons, obviously. Give it up."

But a whole contingent of troops is determined to prove me wrong as they advance against me, their guns significantly larger than standard issue, and the bullets firing in a continuous stream.

A roar overhead shows that Azar isn't keen on testing how many bullets my shield can withstand. This time when he swoops in a circle, he doesn't restrain himself, roasting the approaching troops into fricassee in front of me.

"I said stop," I shout.

I've either gotten much louder, or I somehow dragon-projected with that shout. However it happened, it's gotten the attention of literally everyone, and they're finally listening. The volleys of bullets stop.

"Elizabeth!" The voice is familiar—Gideon's running toward me. He's wearing army fatigues, and clearly he's a figure of some importance among them.

"It looks like selling out your best friend came with some perks," I snap.

His expression falls. "I never sold you out. I never would."

"Ice spears." I can't help shaking my head. "Kill him and I die too."

"Let me through." Gideon kept walking when the generals and commanders around him stopped, and now he's only a few paces away. He slams his fist into the red shield, grimacing a bit at the reverb when it blocks his entry.

"I have no idea how to let just one person through. If I drop it, they'll shoot me again." Shouting loudly enough to talk through the shield is annoying, but I'm not about to let them butcher me. It might give them the edge they need to take out Azar. I may want him to talk to them before massacring all the humans who are clearly here to attack, but I won't ever betray him. Not really.

"Stand down," Gideon orders.

Shockingly, the people around him listen, dropping their guns.

"Let me in so we can talk." He bangs the shield again, this time without even flinching, probably because he was prepared. We can do most anything if we're prepared for it.

I've learned that after a lifetime of training for fights, and I suppose Gideon has learned the same lesson.

"Liz, let me in." His eyes are sad, and that's what gets me. Gideon was the person I trusted most in the world—other than probably my parents. The dragons have taken that from me. Perhaps not intentionally, but my parents are gone to me. My siblings are constantly in danger.

And Gideon, my best friend, my supporter, my would-be lover one day. . .he's gone too.

But do I really trust him so little that I won't even release my shield? "We need to talk," I say. "I can get the dragons to stop attacking, but only if you tell the humans to stand down with the ice-spears. We're so close to getting the heart. It's here, in Iceland."

"Let me in," Gideon says. "And then we'll talk." He motions to the commanders standing a dozen paces behind, and he raises his voice so they can hear. "They want to negotiate a de-escalation. They may have found what they need. All the dragons may be leaving soon."

The white-haired man with the most medals on his coat nods.

"Do you have the authority to make agreements?" I ask.

"I've been named acting leader, because of the intelligence I provided."

"Because you betrayed them," I say.

He shrugs.

He's being honest in his role, at least. I drop the shield.

Azar roars from up above and dives toward us.

Every soldier whose guard had gone down lifts their weapon, and a dozen ice-spears pivot to aim for him.

"Wait." I throw my hands up. "Wait, Azar. Just wait a moment while I talk to Gideon." I grab my old friend's arm and yank him closer, and then I throw my shield back up.

Azar doesn't like it, and he bellows, but he veers back upward, circling around overhead like an irate guard dog. *I wish you'd fly a little farther away*, I say. *I know you're angry, but we have no idea what those ice spears might do. I can't risk you being hurt.*

I'm not leaving you, he says. *Not ever.*

Which makes me feel a little guilty for leaping off his back, but I had to save all these people. These idiotic, war-focused, human soldiers. They may be stupid, but I hope they won't die for it. They all have wives, daughters, mothers, and friends. I don't know them, but I know what they're risking, and they think they're doing the right thing. I can't just let them all be mowed down, laying yet another layer of hatred on the wall between dragons and humans.

"Listen," I say. "The heart's inside the volcano, and we're working on ways to extricate it that won't do damage to this whole area." It's not the whole truth, but I hope it's close enough to be convincing.

"As if they care about the surrounding areas," Gideon says. "What's the real hold up?"

"We really don't know how to get it out," I say. "But they can sense that it's there." Also a lie, technically, since we don't *know* it's there. Still, it's close to the truth as we know it.

"Listen." Gideon's voice is low and urgent. "The dragons left America, and in the wake of their departure, as people came back, all the people they had controlled are regaining their will, and everyone is *flipping out*. A terrible, scaly monster that we are figuring out how to kill is one thing. But humans who can take their will away with ease. . ."

"What happened to my mother?"

"It was not easy for the generals to keep her from being executed," Gideon says. "The public's calling for all of them to be killed, immediately. For war crimes."

"Is that why you killed the humans earlier who were linked to those electro dragons?" My hands ball into fists at my side. "You murdered ten people just so you could take out their dragons? Are they really just weapons to you? Because the humans who stayed were the ones who wouldn't even consider forming a partnership with their dragons."

"Which means their dragons were the worst of the lot." Gideon sighs. "Look, I know it's complicated, and I get that. But right now, killing those people to weaken their dragons is really the only weapon we have. Our enemy's a million times more powerful than we are, and they're mostly invulnerable to boot. Why can't you see the position we're in?"

"I see how strong they are," I say. "But they aren't even attacking humans right now. They never have, really. They came to search for something they need."

"No." Gideon grabs my wrists, forcing me to meet his eye. "You're missing the point. They're our enemy, Liz. They're not friends. They're not benevolent in any way. At best they're thieves. At worst, they're butchers."

"But they're not. They're reasonable," I say. "They aren't just gallivanting monsters, out to maim and destroy. The killing they've done has been necessary, because we keep attacking them. And now, here, they've harmed no one, and still, here you are, trying to kill them again."

"Iceland *begged* us to come," he says. "The people here are terrified, and can you blame them? Those are people's homes, in Selfoss, that they just waltzed in and took." Gideon points. "Your siblings wouldn't even come with me when I left. They're as bad as you—they're taking their cues from their big sister! They think Gordon and Rufus are really their *friends*, Liz!"

"They are their friends," I say. "And they listen better than you do."

A walkie-talkie at his belt starts making muffled beeping sounds. He whips it out and presses a button. "What?"

"Confirmation, sir. It worked."

"What worked?" I ask. "Who is that?"

Gideon shakes his head. "I wish I could tell you that, but Liz, you're in too deep right now. Anything you hear, he hears. You don't even realize they're the enemy anymore."

He steps closer and drops to a whisper. "Do you remember what I promised you? I said that I would never harm you, that I would always be on your side, and I promised to find a way out of this for you. For all of us." He's smiling now, but it looks sad.

No, not sad.

Tragic.

And that worries me. "Gideon, I'm not sure what—"

He jabs me in the neck, right in the carotid, and then he pushes the plunger on the syringe he must have had in his sleeve all the way down. "If there was another way," he whispers, "I would have taken it, I swear."

Everything in my body stops working right then, but as I'm slumping forward into Gideon's waiting arms, the red shield blinks out, and I watch, as the world slows down, as Azar shoots toward us.

And I'm helpless as the blindingly bright blue spear pierces his side.

19

LIZ

My head's pounding. It hurts so badly that I can't even form words.

"She's coming back." The voice is unfamiliar.

Foreign.

"That's a heartbeat," the same voice says. "I told you she'd be fine."

It's hard—so dang hard—but I force my eyes open. Gideon's holding someone by his collar. I blink, my eyes burning, and the image is still there. Gideon's shaking the smallish man now. "You told me it would be immediate. Why did it take more than an hour to get her back?"

"I told you she had to be cold."

"She *was* cold!" Gideon's roaring now, and I'm worried what he may do to the poor man.

"Not within the parameters I set, and frankly, even those were outside of what—"

"It was a bloody war zone!" Gideon's rattling this poor man's brains. "We did everything we could, but one of the stupid earth dragons smashed—"

"Gideon?" My voice sounds like two pieces of sandpaper being rubbed together. "Where are we?"

He turns toward me, releasing the lapels of the man's white coat. "You're—your brain's fine? You know who I am?"

My hands move then, both of them coming up to press against the fronts of my eyes. "If this horrible, painful pounding is normal, then sure. It's working."

"She'll be pretty dehydrated," the white coat man says. "To reverse the metoprolol, we had to push glucagon and epinephrine—"

Gideon waves his hand through the air. "Don't care as long as that's not medically alarming."

I slowly force myself to a seated position, and that's when I realize what's missing. "Where's my bond to Azar?"

Gideon's face transforms in that moment, from handsome to dizzyingly beautiful, because he's beaming with real joy. "It worked." He crouches next to my bed, his hand reaching for mine. "I freed you from him."

He freed me.

Instead of allowing him to take my hand, I ball mine into a fist and slam it into his jaw, sliding off the bed on the side opposite of him, yanking leads and an IV needle out of my arm as I do. Blood sprays outward, splattering all over the man whom Gideon was just borderline strangling.

"You can't take those off," the white coat man says, poking at now-alarming machines frantically. "You're awake, but your system—"

"Fix it," I shout, ignoring the doctor. "*Fix it!*"

"I can't fix it," Gideon says. "Even if I wanted to, you can't be bonded to a dragon who's dead."

I knew he was going to say it. I *knew*, but it still didn't prepare me to hear the words. It can't possibly be true. "No!"

"He died *after* you did," Gideon says. "And that's why his

death didn't kill you! I did it—I found a way to save you, just like I swore I would." He's shaking his head. "I killed you first, and the trauma sent him crashing into the ground. We lost a lot of good men, but we killed hundreds of dragons, including one of the invulnerable flame ones. You have to see that this is good news for all humanity."

I'm not even listening to him anymore. If Azar was really dead, I'd know it, right? I crouch on the floor, my hands flung up in front of me to block out his words. And then I close my eyes and reach for Azar.

"Your mother's free too, now. And her dragon's almost surely dead." Gideon's still trying to get my attention, but I can't even look at him. If I do, it'll be like accepting that he's right. It'll be like acknowledging that he really did what he always wanted to do.

That he freed me.

By slaying my captor.

Except Azar wasn't my captor, not anymore.

Gideon would call it Stockholm Syndrome, the feelings I have for Azar, but it's not that. It isn't.

And I can't feel him *at all*. Not a location. Not a single emotion from the bond. No colors. No pain. *Nothing*. It's like it's just. . .all gone.

"Where are we?" I stand up and look around the room. It's small—just two beds, one of which I just vacated, a bunch of machines, Gideon and the other man, the frantic one in a white coat, who's still telling me I need to lie down and let him redo the IV.

Delusional.

"Where *are we*?" I demand. "Someone tell me."

"Your dragon's brother immediately followed us," Gideon says. "But I knew he would—he wasn't weakened by losing a bond-mate like his brother. We had a plan in place, though."

"A plan to do what?" I step toward him, angry enough to strangle my oldest friend. "A plan to ruin *everything?*"

"Liz, it had to happen," he says. "I can't believe you're not grateful!"

"Grateful?" I take another step, shifting around the edge of the bed.

That's when I see them—the edge of my swords, gleaming up at me from the other side of the bed I just vacated, like they stripped me of my weapons and then placed me on the bed. Which is probably exactly what happened.

Swords that can pierce dragon hide.

Gideon can tell me all day long that he killed Azar—I believe that he succeeded in destroying our bond by killing me—but I won't believe that Azar's dead until I see for myself. Until I see his massive, red corpse, I'm assuming he's alive and that he needs me.

"I can't stay here," I say. "I have to return to Selfoss."

"I'm not even sure whether they're there anymore," Gideon says. "The storm hit moments after I killed you, and after. . ." He coughs. "After your bond was gone, we rushed you away. In all the madness, Hyperion followed us to Reykjavik in the middle of a snowstorm. Liz, it was like Mother Nature was on our side, and we lost him, but he razed that entire city to the ground, killing over a hundred thousand innocent humans."

"Hyperion and Azar weren't killing anyone," I shout, still advancing on him. "Mother Nature wasn't on your side. No one was! You attacked them, unprovoked, and you're celebrating a victory right now for a war that you started."

He keeps backing up, just happy that I'm engaging with him, I think. But it's working. He's moving backward, which allows me to move toward the swords. "They would have attacked us, given enough time," he says. "They did it in Houston, and it was only a matter of time before they did it in Iceland, too. Everyone knew that but you."

"Azar made them leave half the bonded humans and all the enslaved ones back in Houston." Another step. Closer still. I wish my knees weren't wobbling and my heart wasn't pounding. I lurch another step forward, and spots dance across my vision for a moment. "And we were so close to getting what they wanted, and then they'd have left forever."

"Taking you with them," Gideon says. "And if you think I was going to allow that to happen, you don't know me at all."

My vision clears *just* in time.

"You really need to lie down again," the doctor says. "Until you've been given the full dose of—"

"Enough," I say. "Tell me it was a lie. Tell me you didn't really succeed in killing him." Then I can go back, and I can help them remove the heart, and—

But Gideon, his jaw locked, pulls a phone out of his pocket. He taps a few buttons and flips it around, and I watch as the scene I saw from below, bleary and exhausted and apparently about to die, plays out in full color glory on a tiny screen in front of me.

The first ice-spear that hits him appears to just piss Azar off. But the next dozen are enough to knock him to the ground. After that, he disappears into the earth. Less than a minute later, fire erupts from the earth like a small volcano, leaving nothing but a blackened crater behind.

"I didn't want to show you that," Gideon says, "but all they found when the pit cooled enough was chunks of red, scaly flesh, seared and smoking." His shoulders slump. "What else will it take to convince you?"

I dive down and grab my swords, but standing up again while holding them is harder than it should be. Their tips wobble. "You've convinced me." I step closer, the edges of my blades pressing against Gideon's neck. I realize that tears are streaming down my cheeks. "I won't feel the least bit guilty when I decapitate my oldest friend, thanks to how *clear* you were."

When the door bursts open and soldiers stream through, all of them with guns aimed at my head, my disgust only increases. A tall man in the doorway grunts. "You told me she'd be on our side, Evans. You swore it on your life."

"She will be." The movement of his neck as he speaks causes pressure against the edge of my blade, slicing his skin. The scarlet of the blood reminds me of Azar's scales, which enrages me, and I want to press harder. *Harder and harder and harder.*

I want to kill him—it was his idea, this whole thing. He orchestrated Azar's death himself. He knew what it would do to me, and he did it anyway. "I hate you, Gideon Evans. I'll hate you until the day I die."

"Seize her." The troops move toward me slowly, waiting to see whether I'll really kill Gideon, I suppose. He hasn't made a single movement to stop me, and he never does. Not right up until they take my blades and cuff my hands behind my back. Not when they haul me away, over the doctor's vehement protests, and stuff me into a locked room without even a window. I sit on the bed, noting only a small collapsible table and a bucket I assume will function as a chamber pot, a few seconds before the lights go out.

Just before the lights go out, I notice my hair has changed color. It's not gold. It's not red, either. No, it's a color I haven't seen since the day of the Boo Bash—my hair is back to being brown. For some reason, it sets me off.

I'm not sure how long I'm bawling in the room like a teenage girl whose boyfriend dumped her. But at some point, my rage begins to eclipse the pain, and that's when I start to make a plan.

First on my list of tasks is to figure out where I am, so I can somehow get back to the dragons. If Azar really is dead, they'll kill me. That would actually be a big relief. My heart hurts so much that death would be a welcome mercy.

But if he's still alive?

We're coming back here, and we're going to destroy every single soldier in this military encampment.

Okay, maybe not all of them. They have families, and they didn't do this. But Gideon and the tall man are both going down. I'm delusionally wondering whether Hyperion might bond me and help me reach my goals of justice and revenge, if Azar really is dead, when the door opens.

It's the last person I expect to see, to be honest: my dad. His silver hair's neatly combed, as always, and he's wearing a black pinstripe suit, like it's just another day in the office. His wry smile is the same one he gave me when I told him I wasn't going to college.

"Button," he says.

I completely descend once again into tears.

He sits next to me on the bed and pulls me against him. "It's been a very hard two months."

Something about that understatement makes me laugh, uproariously. "You think?" Tears are still leaking down my face, and I feel entirely unhinged. "I alternate between wanting to kill Gideon and all the generals and just wanting to kill myself."

Dad's sigh fills the tiny room, even more than the light coming from the open door. "You kept your siblings alive, and you freed your mother."

"They might be dead now, thanks to Gideon, and he's the one who freed Mom, not me."

"He freed you too, even if you don't see it yet."

"Dad, I know they sent you to calm me down, but—"

Dad drags me against him for a hug, and then whispers

against my ear. "If you don't calm down soon, they'll kill you."

Gideon doesn't have as much power as he thinks. I'm sure he thought that he could protect me, but my dad knows. The powers that be won't allow me to leave here, not ever. Not if they think I'm a risk to them or of telling the public the truth of what's happening and what they've done.

If I'm not on their side, I'm a traitor, and that's enough for them to kill me out of hand. I wonder what they're telling the world about Reykjavik. But I know that if I want to make it back to Selfoss, I need to convince them that I'm on their side. I'm not a very good liar. But I wasn't very good at a lot of things. . .until I had to be.

"Thanks," I say. "I needed that hug. I think it's hard for me to accept that the shackles bonding me to that creature are really gone. You know?"

"Do you mean that?" Dad asks.

"Of course," I say. "Doesn't Mom say the same kind of thing?"

Dad nods slowly. "She does, but when her dragon died, she didn't try to kill the one who orchestrated it. She kissed him."

Mom kissed Gideon? That's a strange image. "Well, I'm not sure that I'll be kissing anyone any time soon, but I have realized that he's not the bad guy." I nearly choke on those words, but the sooner I come around, the more believable it will be.

"You're probably still a little groggy from that stuff they gave you to stop your heart."

"I hear I was out for a long time," I say.

"They couldn't revive you until they were sure that Azar was dead—they couldn't risk your bond surging back into place. And then they had to get you away from the mess before they could do much, too." Dad chuckles, and it sounds so forced, I can't imagine that anyone would buy it. "They brought you here in a refrigerated cabin on a plane, you know."

"They did?" I ask. "Where are we, anyway?"

"You know, there aren't many hospitals in Iceland, so they didn't have many options, but thanks to that other red dragon taking out Reykjavik, they were stuck bringing you to Njarðvik."

A man in a uniform bursts through the doorway. "Alright, that's all the time we have." He's scowling. I'm guessing Dad wasn't supposed to tell me that we're still in Iceland. I wonder how far Njarðvik is from Selfoss. . .

I leap up to hug him—even if they're using him to try and manipulate me, he passed me a message to be careful, he clearly still loves me, and most of all, I'm happy to see him.

"I was so scared when it all happened," he whispers. "Thank you for keeping your siblings safe, and for everything else." He has tears in his eyes when he releases me, and I wonder whether Mom really did survive. If so, he's probably thanking me for that, for keeping her alive when she wanted to die.

But when Dad leaves, it's back to a dark room and no company.

That's fine, because I start working on a plan in earnest. My swords are somewhere close, and if I can recover them and get free, all I need to do is find an earth dragon and. . .

I have no idea who's leading the earth dragons now. Even when Axel was their leader, several of them tried to kill me. That was before he had gone public with our bond, however, and long before everyone thought I had bonded Azar.

Even thinking about it guts me.

I spend at least half an hour curled into a fetal ball, sobbing, before I manage to sit back up and clear my mind.

I still don't have any real evidence that Azar's dead. So what if they speared him? So what if he exploded? We don't know anything about dragons, and I didn't see his head on a pike.

So that means he might have survived.

Something about the numb feeling where the bond should be nags at me, but I can't allow that fear to weigh me down. Not when little Sammy, brave Coral, and effervescent Jade are still with the dragons. I do consider, for the first time, what their situation might be. They refused to go with Gideon, and he had a whole plan in place. He must have been frustrated, but the US Army was coming.

So he left them.

The man I thought would protect my own family like he'd protect me, left them to die. Because if Azar really did die—would the dragons kill them? Or would they try to force bonds on them? Thinking about it makes me sick. If they blame me for Azar's death, they might just kill them out of hand. Or if they want to punish them since I'm not handy. . .there's no telling.

I felt like I knew Azar, but I often have no idea what the other dragons are thinking. Even Azar's motivations frequently baffled me. They're so different from us.

And they're here for the heart—which is now very close.

Hyperion must be gnashing his teeth that he didn't just chuck me into the volcano when he had the chance. Above all the others, he must hate me passionately. I was the weakness they used to attack his brother. I could have been used to get them what they wanted, and now I'm gone. Gone, back with the sea of millions and millions of humans.

If I were Hyperion, I'd want me dead last week.

Except, of course, he will want me back to chuck into the volcano. There may be a way for me to leverage that, even if Azar's gone, to get my siblings back. I hate thinking like that—the rage always swells up when I do—but above all else, I've always been a pragmatist. If Azar *is* dead, I can't afford to just curl up and die, or attack anyone recklessly. If he's gone, I have to at least try and save my siblings before I do anything else.

At some point, all the adrenaline works its way out of my system, and I sleep. A light tapping on the door wakes me, and this time, my visitor is my own mother.

"Oh," I say. "You're here too, after I worked so hard to get them to leave you behind."

Mom should race across the room and hug me. She should stroke my face with one hand and coo, because those are all things she has always done. She's a hippy, and she's an activist, but above all else, she's a mother.

Her words from before come back to me, then. *And who better to protect children from monsters than. . .a monster.*

She hangs back near the door, shifting and edgy. "I'm so happy to see that you're alright."

Only, she doesn't look happy. I sit up, my body turning toward her. "Are you?"

She swallows. "Of course I am." That actually sounds genuine. "I was worried that you might blame me—be angry with me. I know that losing Azar must be hard for you in a way that being freed from Ocharta was not for me." She clears her throat. "After all, your bond was different than mine. You were entwined, and he wasn't awful to you."

She has no idea, but unlike Dad, I can't trust her to understand. "I'm fine."

"Are you?" She steps closer, the light from the hallway beyond illuminating her silhouette. "Gideon did the impossible, you know, saving all of us. Freeing us by killing us and then bringing us back from the dead. It was all his idea."

I'm sure it was. "I'm glad you're free." That much is true, at least.

I realize then that the walkie-talkie, that's what he was waiting on. He used the first round of humans that they killed to take down the electro dragons as his guinea pigs. Once he had confirmation that they'd been able to bring those humans back, then he was willing to kill me in the same way.

Ugh.

"Did you go back to the volcano?" Mom's voice is deceptively light, but I can tell from the intensity of her eyes, even in the terrible lighting, that she was asked to find out this information.

"Mom, really?"

She trots across the room until she's standing in front of me, and then she drops to one knee, her hands reaching for mine. "I wanted to see you. I asked them to send me to talk to you."

Still, she's here to try and get information from me. "Sure." I snatch my hands back.

At least she has the decency to look hurt. "Are you alright? I've been worried you'd struggle with it—the freedom."

"My bond wasn't like yours," I confess. "By the time Gideon killed me, I wanted that bond."

Mom's inhale is sharp, but she recovers well. "And now?"

"I'll be fine with enough time. Like most things, humans recover, right?"

Mom rocks backward, propelling herself up to her feet. When she turns to sit next to me, she leaves a whole person's space between us. That, more than anything else, shows me just how broken we've become. A mother and daughter, too uncomfortable to even embrace after surviving a shared trauma.

"I went to the volcano." I decide that offering them a

bit of information might build some goodwill. "I think you may have been right. I may have imagined the people there to make me feel better about what happened."

Or at least, my brain may have interpreted the chanting from the lava as coming from the type of humans I'd normally see. I'm still not sure about that one. But the closer I can keep my lies to the truth, the better they sound.

Mom reaches for my hands again, and this time I grit my teeth and let her touch me. "I'm so sorry you had to do that alone."

I wasn't alone, I want to shout. At least, not the second time. Azar was with me—he's always with me. He kept me safe in ways she never could, never did! But shouting would do me no good. As long as I'm shouting and angry, they'll never release me. In fact, they might kill me for it.

"I'm happy you've calmed down," Mom says. "They're breaking camp soon, now that you're healed, and they'll be flying us all home."

"Soon?"

Mom's eyes narrow. "Another, larger force will be coming to begin a second assault on the remaining dragons, but before that happens, we'll be leaving."

Which means I'm running out of time to get out of here.

"If you were to give them some information they could use, they might trust you enough not to imprison you when we get back home."

Imprison me.

It's worse than I thought.

"What kind of information are they wanting?"

"Anything you know about the heart," she says. "Anything you can share about fire dragons, especially. They may have killed Azar, but there's another, even bigger fire dragon that poses a significant threat. Unlike your bonded, he hasn't selected a human, which means he'll be much, much harder to kill."

I hate that I was the liability that cost Azar his life. Not that I believe them about him being dead, not entirely.

I'm still holding on to hope that maybe he didn't die. Maybe he just turned into an earth dragon and, I don't know, burrowed or something. None of the other dragons know what he can do, so obviously the humans would have no clue.

I try not to think about the chunks of red scales he left behind.

"You should get some sleep," Mom says as she stands. "There's something Gideon wants your help with in the morning."

Gideon wants my help? "With what?"

Mom shakes her head. "That's for him to share, or not."

I can't help standing as she walks toward the doorway—I'm too nervous not to. "Any word on Sammy, Coral, and Jade?"

Mom freezes, and then she walks out without saying a word. I guess that's my answer.

If there is news, it's nothing good.

20

LIZ

The night before a fight, I always have to take a Xanax, so it's no surprise that after telling me that we're leaving soon and that Gideon's going to come talk to me, I can't sleep.

At all.

It doesn't help that I have no idea what time it is, where I am, or how long it'll be until someone walks through my door. It also makes using the stupid chamber pot they gave me a little nerve-wracking. Other than a few bottles of water and a soggy sandwich, they haven't given me anything to eat or drink, either.

When I think about what Gideon did, I'm still filled with rage—he said he'd protect me, and he tore me away from Azar against my will. He killed Azar—or at least, he tried his very hardest, even if he didn't succeed. I'm still desperately hoping that he didn't. He also coordinated with the humans to make weapons specifically calculated to bring Azar down.

And he used me to do it.

He can say he did it to save me, but his priority was

killing Azar all along. He left my siblings with the dragons, knowing he'd be killing me and attacking the dragons.

But I'm rational enough, thanks to all my time in solitary confinement, to understand that my only shot at escaping, at reaching my siblings, and at finding out whether Azar really is gone, is to play nice. Instead of giving head to my desire to strangle Gideon until the light leaves his eyes when he does finally show up, I focus on the fact that I'm hungry, smelly, and irritable.

"Hey." He cracks the door and looks around the room. "They did not exaggerate what this room looked like."

My tone is flat, but I'm not yelling, and I'm not throttling him. "What are you here for?"

"Good to see you too," he says.

"I'm not attacking you," I say. "But if you thought I'd smile and gush after being killed, revived, and then locked up, you've lost your mind."

Even in the low light streaming past him from the hall, I can see Gideon's frown clearly.

"I've been locked in this room for who knows how long, without light or anything to do, read, or see, and I've been a good girl. I haven't tried to fight my way out, I haven't banged on the walls, and I haven't tried to find a way to kill anyone who entered."

"You spared all three of us, huh, your mom, your dad, and me?" His expression's pretty patronizing for someone I vowed to kill the last time we met.

"I should take a swipe at you right now," I say. "You're being kind of a jerk."

"But you won't really hate me forever."

It's funny how humans are more likely to believe what we want to believe than anything else. I specifically refuse to consider what that might mean in regard to Azar.

There's no way Gideon will believe that I've done a one-eighty, so I settle for hanging my words on my emotional upheaval. "I was ticked off, okay?"

He snorts. "That you were." He takes one step closer, looking me over. "You look less angry now."

"If I dance and sing with a smile on my face, can I get a shower?"

"Is that your top priority right now?" He steps closer still. "A shower?"

"I didn't think you'd offer to loan me a tank so I can head back to try and rescue my brother and sisters. Is that on the table?"

"A tank?" He shakes his head. "It's not, no."

"A jet, then?"

He laughs. "No, I doubt the army will be handing you any kind of expensive machinery in the near future."

"But you, they trust. They put you in charge."

"Not in charge anymore," he says, "but I'm on a critical advisory board, because I've proven myself to be useful. And I'm still a patriot."

I want to insist that I, too, am a patriot, but I'm not sure I'm capable of outright lying to him, especially if they have cameras that will analyze my face. "My mom says you need my help."

"Not help, so much as we have an opportunity for you to lend a hand."

"So. . .my help. Or did the meaning of that word change during my sojourn with the dragons?"

Gideon rolls his eyes. "Still a smart aleck."

"No." I stand. "Just smart."

"Why are you standing?" He narrows his eyes.

"Oh, did you want my help with some sort of quantum physics that could be done while I remain seated?" I ask. "My bad. Last I checked, my brain wasn't very impressive, but I'm pretty handy with physical things. I just assumed."

I sit. "Alright, hit me with the details of the math problem that has you stumped."

He arches an eyebrow. "You could tone down some of the snark."

"And that would make me seem more like myself, would it?"

"I guess not." He points at me. "But I need your word that you were just upset and freaking out earlier when you tried to kill me, and that you're back to yourself."

"If I had tried to kill you, you'd be dead," I say.

"You made a decent show of it." He looks pretty hurt.

"What if I can never go back to who I was?" Trying to only lie a little bit is hard.

"We need to know whether we can trust you."

They must not have many other choices, or my word would not be something that they found very reassuring. "You need something, or you wouldn't be here at all."

"I've been authorized to lead you out of here, on a short leash, mind you, and if you come along politely, you can get a proper meal *and* a shower." He touches his ear with one finger, and I realize he's wearing an earpiece, getting commands even as we speak. "But then we'll need your help with something in return."

"With what?" I ask. "Because if you think that I'm going to scrub toilets or, like, do something degrading or embarrassing then. . .you're right. I would do most anything for a shower at this point." I force what's probably a pained smile.

Gideon clearly suspects it's an act, but he isn't sure. "Nothing like that." He gestures for me to follow him. "Come on out. You can shower, eat, and change into nicer clothes. And then I'll show you what we need."

"Whoa," I say. "You're going to pay me before I do the work? That's not how life works."

"This time it is," he says. "Your willingness to help us is enough to get you paid."

I don't look the gift-shower in the mouth. I just follow him out. By the time I'm clean, fed, and finally warm, I'm just as upset as I was before, but I feel like I'm hiding it better. It's hard to act like you're fine when you've been pooping in a bucket.

"Alright, what do you want?"

"When we brought you here, you had two swords strapped to your back."

Oh.

"Swords that, rumor has it, are able to pierce dragon scales."

I shrug.

"Is it true?"

I nod.

"We're able to move them."

That makes me a little sad. I was hoping they'd be like Thor's hammer or something.

"But when anyone tries to grip the hilt, it's like the end of the sword becomes insanely heavy, and they fall to lodge, point first, in the ground. They're very difficult to pry loose each time."

They're jacking up my swords with their experiments—ugh. "So, none of your soldiers are worthy?" I can't help teasing him a little, and he'll never buy that I'm fine if I don't.

"Our scientists think it has to do with magnetic resonance—something they've also been able to detect in connection with some of the earth dragons, so they'd like to see what happens when you try to pick them up."

Now that I'm no longer bonded to Axel, he means. "They think I could use them because I was bonded to an earth dragon?"

Gideon's frustrated. "None of the scientists can agree,

and to make matters worse, most of them weren't even willing to travel here, this close to the dragons. A lot of their studies require soldiers to do things and then report back or show them what's happening via a video feed."

I can hardly believe what I'm hearing. "You've rejoined the humans, and now you're running experiments for some eggheads in Washington over webcams?"

Gideon frowns. "Will you come pick up the swords, or not?"

"You just want me to pick them up?"

He nods.

I don't see how that could hurt any dragons. "Fine." And who knows? Maybe I'll get my hands on the swords and break free.

But as Gideon cuffs my hands behind my back and marches me out of the suite where I showered—we're clearly in a hospital—out of the building, and around the corner, I pass hundreds of soldiers.

I also pass at least fifty ice-spear crossbows.

The sight of them sickens me.

And now I'm going with Gideon to help them study more things they think might kill dragons. It wasn't that long ago that *I* wanted to kill dragons. I understand the desire, but this time, thanks to me, the dragons didn't even attack. I like to think that I'd have taken that as a sign that we might get along with them and *not* massacred any of them.

As Gideon and I walk up to a huge domed tent, I struggle to take in the scope of it. Where do you even get a tent that's the size of a Costco? "What is this place?"

"It's our research and development headquarters."

"Wouldn't it make more sense to have this back in the US?" I ask. "I mean, especially if the scientists are all back there."

As we walk through the doors, I finally understand why

it's here. This is where the dragons are. In massive enclo-
sures with electrified perimeters, there are two water
dragons and four earth dragons. In the first one, a dark
brown earth dragon that looks like a frilled neck lizard is
pacing back and forth.

When it sees me, it stops and hisses, the frill around its
neck standing out. I remember his name—Phileas. I think
that's it. He shrieks loudly, slamming his massive front feet
against the ground. He even slams against the side of the
pen, being electrocuted for his trouble. I can't help cringing
a little when he falls to the ground and starts writhing in
agony.

Next to him, there's a bright yellowish-brown dragon
that looks like a horned toad, wide and squatty, and covered
with dark blotches. The horns at the front of his head
curve backward, almost reaching his back. His nostrils
flare, but otherwise, he doesn't move. I don't recall his
name, but he was on a few different perimeter sweep crews
with Rufus at one time or another.

The blue dragon the closest to me is on her back, tubes
and lines running into her from all sides. Her eyes are
closed, and somehow they've managed to penetrate her
scales. She looks sedated. There are whole sections of her
hide that have been removed, and internal organs glisten
underneath. A dark, reddish-brown goo is leaking out of
the open areas and puddling on the ground beneath her. I
can only tell she's female from the extra layer of facial
horns that all the female water dragons seem to have.

The other blue dragon's the color of a sky on a spring
morning, and she's lying, listless, on the ground. Her
tongue's hanging out just a little, and her eyes are glazed
over.

One of the earth dragons is stuck under what looks like
a glass dome, and it's coiling and twisting and moving
around constantly, like an angry grass snake that's big

enough to eat the pest control truck. Its eyes flash—but as I've never seen it before, I don't even know whether it's male or female. The earth dragons don't seem to have any kind of head frills that delineate, and unlike the electro dragons, the females don't have daintier heads, either. There's something spread all over the floor of its enclosure, and I don't know what it is, but when one of its coils touches the powdery stuff, its scales smoke.

"What's happening in here?" I can barely get the words out. "What are you doing?"

Gideon leads me past those dragons to the last one, the one I could barely see. It's dark brown—almost black—and it looks like the quintessential Chinese dragon, with a large, square head, covered in long and short whiskers that shift and change, with two large, impressive front legs, but no back legs. Its powerful body tapers down near the end of its body into a very long, very muscular tail with a pronounced spiny ridge that runs down its back all the way to the forked end. When it sees me, it hisses loudly.

"We're learning all we can about the dragons now that we've created the technology to contain a few."

They're torturing and experimenting on them. I want to ask him whether it feels *wrong* to him. I want to ask how he can sign off on this kind of treatment. But I can't. If I do, they won't let me near my swords. They won't give me any chance to escape. I'll be stuffed back in that tiny cell and left to rot.

Or killed.

Clearly the people here know how to eliminate any threats with extreme prejudice. As we walk past each dragon, I note clumps of humans gathered around computer screens, as well as several soldiers with crossbows slung over their backs, monitoring.

I don't want to make it obvious, but I've counted at least eighty people in here, half of them soldiers. And presumably, they feel somewhat confident in their ability to keep the beasts contained in their cages.

"Here are the blades." Gideon finally stops in a small enclosure with small, temporary walls just beyond the last dragon cage. "As you can see, they're sunk into the concrete floor."

He's right. Both of them are face down, and sunk at least six inches into the concrete foundation.

"Not many human blades could even penetrate concrete, much less sink in on their own like this."

I blink. "And you want me to, what?"

"Hello, Ms. Chadwick." A man with light brown hair, neatly combed, wearing a white lab coat stands up and salutes. "Thank you for coming to help us."

I want to tell him I'm not going to help. I want to tell him to go to check out a local volcano, but I don't. I grit my teeth.

"Can you remove them from the concrete?" Gideon asks. "That's the first question."

I look at Gideon, wondering how much they think I'll really do for a meal and a shower. "Let's see." I grasp both hilts and a sense of excitement runs up my arms and down my spine. I may no longer be bonded to a dragon, but something about these blades still feels *right*. I pull and twist, and they slide right out, like they were stuck in a vat of cold butter.

"That's impressive," Gideon says.

"We applied nearly five hundred pounds of force on them earlier," the scientist says. "They didn't budge." He's eyeing me with undisguised curiosity. "I wonder what it is about you that makes them shift."

"Please tell me you recorded the stupid fields or whatever," Gideon says.

"Right." The man shoves his glasses up his nose and turns around. "Yes, of course." He sits again, and starts typing into his computer. Then he pushes back and stares. "It wasn't magnetic. That seemed the most obvious answer, but of course, magnetic field surges would run the risk of destroying lots of computer components, if they were strong enough, so maybe the lack of them is for the best."

"Yeah, if you have one main computer that's controlling all these pens, the last thing you'd want to risk is that thing burning out. You'd probably have some pretty angry dragons on your hands."

Gideon frowns.

The scientist laughs nervously. "Right? Plus, if the computers fritz, we have a lot of electricity flowing into pens that could go in another direction. Being on the end, we're right next to the control panel, so we're in the worst place in the room."

"Well, if that's all you need." I turn around, like I'm going to walk off. I know they aren't going to let me leave with the swords, but I can't keep myself from testing how they'll react.

"Funny," Gideon says. "Those swords are now the property of the United States Military."

"Right," I say. "I mean, spoils of war, right?"

Gideon smirks. "Something like that."

"Because last I checked, I was a US citizen, and they're *my* property. Since the government can't even use them. . ."

"That's the other thing we wanted to see you do." The lab coat man stands up and gestures at the pen closest to me, the one holding the nearly-black Chinese-looking dragon. "So far, we've only been able to penetrate the water dragon's scales, and only because we found a combination of phosphorus pentoxide and sulfuric acid that dehydrates them, and once we accomplished that, their hide became brittle enough to saw through."

I wonder whether he can hear himself. "They're living creatures," I say.

He shrugs. "But they want to harm us. They're the enemy. If we don't find out how to kill them, they'll continue to kill us instead."

I can't help my shudder, and I know it's not winning me points with Gideon. "What do you want from me precisely?"

"We want to see whether these blades really will slice through dragon skin," Gideon says. "And then we want to study how they do it."

"You managed to pierce Azar with an ice spear," I say. "Can't you just do what you did there?"

"We believe it only worked because you weakened him when you died," Gideon says. "Our attempts with Hyperion have not been successful."

The last thing I want to do is hand them the key to killing Azar's brother, but if I say no, they'll lock me back up for sure. What I'd *like* to do is use the swords to break the dragons free, but with the sheer quantity of bullets these guys are carrying, bullets that may not take out a dragon, but would definitely harm me, there's not much I can do. . .

Unless I could take out the control panel and plunge them all into temporary darkness. Then maybe, with the dragons' help, I could escape. The question I can't answer is. . .are the dragons on my side? Or do they hate me for my role in all this?

I can guess how the water dragons feel. I got their big boss killed, and now I'm here with the humans who did it. I wouldn't trust me at all. But if I can free one of the earth dragons, could I convince them to take me back? Would any of them be in good enough condition to do it?

That's the gamble.

Was Phileas slamming against the pen because he wanted to kill me, or because he recognized me and was happy to see me? Actually, now that I'm thinking it through, what are the odds he was slamming against the enclosure out of joy?

Not great, Chadwick.

"Which dragon are you wanting me to test these blades against?" I arch one eyebrow. "And are you wanting me to, like, slice one, or gut one?"

"You really do think they'll cut through the scales?" the white coat asks.

I shrug. "They have in the past."

"But only when you were bonded to that big dragon, right?" He narrows his eyes. "So we'll be testing whether it was the blades, or some sort of magic from that bond."

"It could be the magic of the blades," I say, "but that still won't help you."

"Unless they attach the blades to the end of an ice spear," the scientist says.

My stomach sinks. If I don't steal the swords, they'll try to use them against Hyperion. They only have them because of me. So his death would also be my fault. "You do realize that once you destroy all the dragons here, more will come, right?"

Gideon frowns.

"Only a fraction of the dragons in existence are here on Earth," I say. "They sent an advance force to try and recover the heart. It's not an attack. It's a mission. But if you slay them, they'll send more, and you can bet that the second round will focus first on an attack." I mean, I don't know that, but it's a decent guess.

"Did Azar say that?" Gideon asks.

I'm not about to start telling him everything that Azar told me, but the humans should at least be warned about the idiocy of what they're doing. "You're poking a bear."

"They're here to steal from us, though." Gideon folds his arms. "Will you test the blades, or not?"

"I asked which dragon." Now my lips are pursed, and

I'm glaring. If they're keeping track, I'm not doing the best job of showing them that I'm on the human side. I try to blank my face.

"Which one do you want to try attacking?" the scientist asks. "Maybe the one surrounded with the citric boric acid mixture. With your boots, you won't even notice it, probably."

I pretend to be examining the dragons, but really, I'm looking for the central control he mentioned. At first, all I see are a bunch of boxes, soldiers with guns, and the support poles holding up the tent structure. But then, just behind one of the largest piles of supplies, I see it. There's a large grey box with wires coming from the ground and feeding into it. It must control the electricity to the whole place.

Unfortunately, from literally any dragon cage, there's no way for me to reach it. Even hurling one of the swords, it's not possible for me to strike any part of it. If I still had my very limited, uncontrolled telepathic powers, maybe I could come up with some kind of Hail Mary, but my bond's gone, and so is everything else.

I checked in the shower, desperate for anything that still ties me to Azar or Axel. . .and the backs of my shoulders are entirely smooth and clean, like I'd never been bonded at all.

I have no idea which dragon to try and maim.

"It's not rocket science," Gideon says. "Just pick a dragon."

The one right by me has no back feet. How fast can it really move? Phileas is fast, but I'm pretty sure he'll try to eat me. I wonder whether I can still talk to them without my bond. Was my ability to communicate something I could do because I'm a bright? Or because I was bonded? I could hear Ocharta before I was bonded, but probably just because she was projecting.

Maybe I could ask them whether they're mad, but what would I say exactly? 'Hey there, do you hate me? Are you wanting to eat me for killing your boss? Or do you realize that I didn't mean to hurt Azar?'

Actually, I don't even know when they were taken. They may have no idea what happened that day, like I knew nothing when I woke up. Or even if they know Azar died, I have no idea what they think about Axel. No one knew he was Azar, so in their mind, they may think he's just missing.

"This one," a voice from the front of the dome calls. "She should start here."

It's my mom.

My mom the hippy, who won't eat the flesh of any living creature, wearing army fatigues, complete with laced up combat boots and a handgun clipped to her belt.

I couldn't be more shocked if she was chowing down on a roasted turkey leg at the Houston Livestock Show and Rodeo.

"He's been aggressive," Mom says, "and we keep having to gas him."

Gas him?

That sinks in about the same time as I realize that my mom's here, working for the military in their dragon-torture research facility, or she wouldn't know what they 'keep having to do.' I suppose it makes sense. She and the other bonded are about as close to experts about dragons as it gets, but it's still *my mom*, the pacifist. The vocal supporter of all things liberal. She's here, advocating that I, what? Stab a dragon?

"Actually, I know Phileas, so I'm not sure that it's the best idea for me to—"

It's your best chance. The words are faint, like the volume on my speaker's turned down to ultra-low, but the message is there. Mom's thought is clear in my mind, like a bell.

My mouth dangles open.

She scowls and shakes her head tightly. "Isn't that for the best? If you know him, maybe his guard will be down."

"They understand us," I say. "They speak English."

Mom looks annoyed. "At least if you go too far with him, it'll be a loss that makes them easier to contain." She shrugs. "And if you splay him wide open, we can study his insides."

He's also the strongest.

What's she doing? What's my best chance? To kill him and convince them I'm trustworthy? Why does it matter that he's strong?

"I really don't think they understand us," the scientist next to me says. "If they did, we wouldn't have so much trouble with them. We've been explaining what we're testing each time. They probably only understood you because of the bond."

"That's what I told them," Mom says.

She told them. . .what? That they speak English? Or that they don't and that the bond made communication possible? Because if so, that's misinformation. She's seen them communicate with Sammy, Coral, and Jade. Gideon has too, for that matter.

"Just do it," Gideon says. "Any cage is fine."

Pick this one. Stab me. The message is faint, but it was as clear as my mom's, and it came from the Chinese-looking dragon right next to me.

21

LIZ

It takes everything I have not to snap my head sideways and give away the fact that she just spoke to me by talking right back.

Gaia, she says. *That's my name. Stab me to show them you can, and then help me escape.*

Well, at least one of them still likes me.

I'm faster than the others, and I burrow better, too.

Burrow. Of course. If I can get them free, and somehow get through the side of the tent to dirt. . .maybe we could burrow away from here.

The humans are all staring at me. Most of them seem to think I'm a half-wit. "I'd rather practice on one who's calmer than the aggressive dragon in the front, at least as an initial experiment."

I step toward the closest enclosure, and I start to climb the steps, but the scientist jogs after me, reaching for my wrist. "When you reach the top, wait for me to tell you it's safe. I'll turn the power down for a split second, and then you can duck through. You'll still want to avoid touching the wires."

"How strong is it?"

"Way, way stronger than any electric fence you've ever encountered. It would scramble your brains in a heartbeat."

Fabulous. Once I reach the top, I pause. White Coat nods, and I step over the bottom wire and below the top one. A shiver runs up my spine once I'm through, possibly relief that I wasn't fried, or possibly trepidation over this confrontation.

I'll make it look like I'm your opponent. The giant earth dragon snarls and takes a swipe at me, her whiskers rippling as she moves. She's careful not to brush the edge of her cage, I notice, and I wonder how much learning that lesson hurt.

I duck, and then we circle, but eventually, Gaia backs up a little too slowly, and the edge of my blade scores her leg.

It bleeds, a very similar brownish goo to the water dragon being cut up for parts like a bug tacked to a board. When a large drop hits the mat, it doesn't splatter. It spreads, like tacky glue. I don't turn away or drop my blades, but I raise my voice. "Satisfied?"

"Splay her wide open," a gruff male voice behind me says. "I want to see what's inside."

The corner of my lip turns up in a snarl, but I choke down on it.

You never chose to betray Azar.

I shake my head, letting the humans think I'm replying to them. "I'm not sure I can do that," I say. "It might kill me in the attempt."

"You don't seem to be very helpful right now," the man says. "I'm not sure what we'd lose if you fail."

"She can use the blades," Gideon says. "Which means that—"

"We can strap them onto the spear whether she's alive or not," the man says. "More than one way to skin a cat."

What a lovely turn of phrase.

I risk a glance around, noting that nearly all the soldiers and scientists in the entire dome have gathered around to watch me. Murmurs are rising from all sides, some of them shocked that there's no magnetic field involved. Some are arguing over why I can use the blades when no one else can. Others are talking about the nature of dragon blood.

Most of the soldiers just want to watch a dragon die.

My mother has come closer, and I notice she's standing right by the main control panel. *I'll kill the power. You leave— save them. Do whatever it takes.*

I thought maybe she was here to protect me, to be on my side. But she's not. Again, she's here to send me on the path she thinks only I can take. I'm tasked once again to be the monster that protects her other children. Her non-damaged ones.

It hurts a little. I'm not going to lie.

But I'm not in a position to quibble over any offer of help, no matter where it comes from. Normally, I'd worry about what helping me might mean for her, but I refuse to do that. I freed her, and now we're right back here, with her sending me to do what she can't.

I need to get back to the blessed.

Gaia nods.

If I free you, you'll take me?

People who haven't spent the time I have around the dragons might not see it, but she smiles. It's enough for me. "Die!" I shout as I spring toward the dragon, but at the last minute, I avert my blade, just missing her side.

Mom unholsters her gun and fires it into the open panel. Sparks fly.

And then the room goes dark.

I'm sure my eyes are as bad at adjusting as everyone else's, but the dragons don't suffer from that. Gaia's giant maw opens, and then closes around my middle, and suddenly, I'm being carried in a dragon's mouth as she bounds over the wires containing her and barrels into a mass of milling humans.

Someone fires, but the gruff man starts shouting. "No! Not until we can see—no friendly fire."

Let's go, Gaia says. *Elizabeth Chadwick has freed us.*

The other dragons bound out as well, all but the one who's missing whole chunks of her scales. She remains utterly still.

Gaia stops by her just as someone flings open the tent flaps.

"We've lost power," the gruff man—a white-haired general—shouts. "Call everyone—tell them to blow them up as they leave. Containing them before was too costly."

Phileas leaps toward the flap, tearing the opening twice as high, and then barges through. The sound of bullets flying is nearly deafening from the area outside the tent.

We can't leave her, Gaia says. *Not like this.*

"What do you want me to do?" I ask. "I don't know how to wake her up."

Kill her, Gaia says. *It's what she'd want.*

But I can't bring myself to do it. "She might get out— she might yet be freed."

Gaia roars, and then she barrels through the hole, followed quickly by the other water dragon, and the other two earth dragons. Phileas has already made a hole—or I'm assuming that's what created the giant wormhole in front of us—and Gaia dives for it.

I'm not sure how this would go if I were riding on her back, but being crushed between her teeth as we slither across the wet, cold, and in some places, frozen portions of earth over the distance we travel is remarkably uncomfortable. I don't dare ask them to stop, but the second time her teeth pierce my skin, shooting horrible pain up my left side, I cry out.

You're injured?

Her voice in my head is much stronger now—clearer. *Your teeth aren't dull.*

Stop ahead.

Phileas turns, his expression furious. The frill around his head ripples. *We can't stop. Not until we've reached Selfoss.*

Gaia sets me down. *I'm going no farther until I've made Prince Axel's bonded a saddle. If I return her damaged, he'll be very angry.*

She's not his bonded anymore, Phileas says. *Prince Azar took her.*

I heard she was bonded to both, Gaia says.

"Wait," I say. "Is Axel still alive?"

Gaia frowns. *Do you have cause to believe he perished?*

"Did he?" I ask. "Have you seen him?"

We were captured in the conflict, Gaia says. *Shortly after Prince Azar's death. We don't know—did the humans say he was dead?*

My heart sinks. When I heard them mention Axel being alive. . .my hope surged. Which is stupid. If Azar died, so did Axel. If he didn't. . . "Maybe Azar and Axel are both fine."

Gaia's eyes are sad. *If Azar had survived, he would have come after you.*

Maybe. Maybe not. Without our bond, how would he know if I was alive?

But the more I think about her words, the more they sink into my soul. If Azar was truly alive, would he wait to feel our bond? Or would he be searching *everywhere* for me?

If he were alive, he'd have come for me.

It feels true down in my soul.

The weight of that drops me to my rear in the dirt, and I start to bawl.

Leave her, Phileas says. *Prince Axel's better without her. They've broken the bond—I heard one of the scientists say it. His life will be better without a human to protect.*

He can decide that for himself. Gaia shifts into a human form and back so quickly that I barely register it's happened by the sound. Then she waits for a moment for me to get up, but when I don't—too depressed to even try—she gives up on waiting for me. She snatches me up with her mouth again, and they move out.

Burrowing through the earth toward Selfoss is dirty, slow work. It gives me plenty of time to think. When they discover that Axel's gone too, what will they do with me? Will they blame me for his disappearance too? And what have they done with Coral, Jade, and Sammy? If it weren't for the three of them, I might just curl up and quit.

But Mom's right.

I'm probably the only human who stands a chance at entering the settlement and trying to save them. The blades are barely still clutched in my hands, my muscles tired and cramping from holding them so long.

"Can you make something to hold my blades?" I finally ask. "I'm not sure how much longer I can hold them."

Humans aren't designed well, Gaia accurately states. *Your god should have given you talons.*

So true. If I met the god who made me right now, I'd have some choice suggestions. Talons might not be the top of the list, but they would be on it.

A moment later, Gaia stops again. *You seem to be in a better mood.*

Not really, but I have renewed purpose, and maybe that's the same thing.

I've made you a saddle. Are you strong enough to use it?

I demand my chance to bear her. The giant green snake's eyes flash, and I realize it's another girl.

She trusts me, Gaia says. *I'll keep her.* She shifts again, this time more slowly. I'm shocked to see her move from her lovely dragon shape into the squattiest, roundest human shape I've ever seen in an earth dragon. It's a big surprise, honestly. Clearly their human form doesn't really tie to their dragon form. "Here." Her voice is deep and gravelly, like my old high school gym teacher, who—antithetical to her job as a PE coach—smoked two packs a day. "Put this on."

It's not a very well-designed sword scabbard, but it was created by a dragon, so I shouldn't be surprised, I guess. It's large, heavy, and unwieldy, but I finally get the thick straps of blackish leather tied around my waist, and I slide the swords into place. They do appear to be at least secure, even if they'd take way too long to unsheathe, and there's no real way for me to jog and wear them.

Before I can thank Gaia, the serpent shifts into a human shape that would make Jessica Rabbit jealous, complete with a shimmering green ballgown that's slit almost up to her thigh. She winks at me before shifting back into her snake form, this time wearing a saddle that appears to be harnessed to her head so it can't slide away.

You two are pathetic. Phileas takes off again, not willing to wait any longer.

Gaia switches back again, her saddle much more elegant this time than the last. She's learning, at least. *Ride me.*

Both of them are now looking, expectantly, at me. How do I resolve this without causing a fight?

We don't have time for petty arguments. The horned toad dragon has a high, almost squeaky voice. *Just ride Gaia. She's faster.*

"But she's also been carrying me this entire time. I'd rather not wear her out." I step toward Gaia, and I touch her side gently. "Thank you. I'll never forget how you saved me."

She tosses her head a little by way of response.

But then I turn toward the green snake, who leans down so I can easily climb into the saddle.

I'm Agrippa, she says. *And I'm just as fast as Gaia.*

When we finally set off again, it's like she's trying to prove it. Even when Phileas insists that we all switch positions so he isn't stuck doing all the burrowing, Agrippa has no trouble keeping up.

I'm not sure how hard it is for them to travel underground, but we must do it for a hundred miles before they deem it safe to surface. They may not mind, or they might even *like*, being surrounded by vast tracts of cold earth, but I'm shivering, miserable, and filthy when we finally surface. I can't wait to breathe in a lungful of fresh air.

Until the icy air hits me. They didn't exactly give me a coat back at the hospital, probably to keep me from wanting to run away, but it's absolutely *freezing* aboveground, and moments after surfacing, I brace myself to ask them to go back under.

We are making better time, but I might freeze to death up here. I'm shivering uncontrollably, and my fingers have gone entirely numb.

But before I can say anything, Agrippa notices. *You're cold.*

"Keep going," I say. "I'll be fine." Or I'll freeze to her back, and I won't need to hold on anymore.

We have miles yet to go. Phileas stops. When he does, the others do too, gathering closer. The water dragon hasn't said a word yet, but the others start to argue over what to do.

Finally, though, Phileas shifts. He's not very tall, but he's surprisingly good looking for such a crabby dragon. His face is hawkish, almost too severe. His high cheekbones look just right with his brilliant yellow eyes, and his hair surrounds his head in a strange sort of stiff, thick halo—a bizarre echo of his frill in dragon form. "Here." He thrusts something at me, much as Gaia did with the sword scabbard.

When I take it, I'm surprised to find it's a cloak, not

unlike the one Azar gave me, only it's made of cloth. Bright red cloth.

"Thank you," I say.

"It's bright red—so you don't forget who you killed."

Oh, yes. Frilly dragon's ticked.

"I never would have done it had I had a choice," I whisper.

He spins around so fast that I can't even react when his finger jabs me in the clavicle. "You leapt from his back. I saw you. You had a choice—you could have stayed on *our* side instead of trying to protect your people, the ones who were attacking us."

He's right about that.

"Have you ever done anything, thinking it's the right thing to do at the moment, but regretted it later?"

He shifts back without answering me, and I realize that he doesn't mean to answer. This time, once I've wrapped the cloak around myself, I climb up on Gaia's back, and we're off again. I'm not sure how far we go—the cloak doesn't help as much as I'd hoped it would—but then I see something that's far more chilling than the air.

A crater in the ground.

"Wait," I shout.

The earth dragons won't go anywhere near it.

"Please," I beg. "I have to look at it." Gideon's words ring in my ears. *Chunks of red scales and flesh.* I shudder compulsively.

I'll take you. It's the first time the water dragon has said a word, and all of us turn to look at her. *You refused to kill Wisteria, not because you were afraid, but because you wanted to give her whatever chance she might have to survive.* She nods slowly. *I'll take you to the dark place.*

"Dark?" I peer at the crater, but it doesn't look dark. Just deep.

The energy around it is dark, the water dragon says. *Do you not see it?*

It must be like the 'bright' thing. They can sense something about us, and here, they can sense the opposite. It's not promising.

There's no way to make a saddle for a water dragon. They can't shift forms and create one, so I'm stuck scrambling up her silky smooth scales, slipping and sliding a half dozen times before I finally grab the ridge on the top of her back. I'm not sure I could ride her very far, which makes me wonder what they do with their bonded, but when she starts to move, there's no room for me to think about anything but holding on.

And then we're at the edge, and when she stops, I nearly go flying over into the enormous hole. As it is, I slide off her back and fall to the ground below, my hands landing along the edge of the burned and blackened lip of earth.

Inches from my hand, there's a bright red scale, crusted with something sticky and brown.

"No!" My shout's sharp and almost involuntary as I clutch the scale to my chest. Tears stream down my face again, and I have trouble breathing. "No." I shake my head. "No. No, no, no!"

I think I accepted that he was dead in the tunnel. As much as I'd clung to hope, I knew in that moment, that if he had been alive, he would have come for me.

And he didn't.

Still, seeing the red scale, the impenetrable red scale, alone and bloody, makes it real in a terrible, horrifying way I can't yet fully process.

"Elizabeth," someone behind me says.

I shake my head. "Just leave me for now. Please." I know the earth dragons want to get back. I know they have people to report things to, but. . . "I just need a *minute*." I squeeze the red scale so tightly in my hand that it begins to slice the skin of my palm, and the pain actually feels good.

I deserve it.

I deserve all the pain in the world for my idiotic mistake—leaping down among the humans and trusting Gideon. Wanting to be the one who brokered peace between the two worlds. It was hubris. I was practically begging for this to happen.

"Liz." This time, I hear the urgency in the voice, and I realize that it's a voice I know. I turn slowly, not quite sure how it can be. . .

But it's Axel, in his human form, standing in front of me.

Healthy.

Whole.

I'm covered with grime from riding a hundred miles in a tunnel. I'm exhausted and weak and nearly frozen to death, but I'm here.

And so is he.

Alive.

"You have to leave." He beckons for Gaia. "Take her back to the edge of the human encampment, immediately."

22

AXEL

The worst has happened.

Liz has returned.

"Absolutely not," Liz says.

Apparently dying didn't change a single thing about her.

"You can't stay here," I say.

She struggles to her feet, and seeing her so weak, so dirty, and so very cold breaks my heart. "Why not?" Tears are streaming down her face, leaving dark runnels through the dirt that's coating her entire body almost uniformly. She looks like, well, like she's been burrowing through earthen tunnels, which I assume is how she reached me.

She freed us, Gaia says. *Please don't make me return her.*

Until I came to Earth and met this human, my body worked perfectly fine. It was strong, and it allowed me to do all the things I needed to do. I had the ability to destroy my enemies. I could defend my allies. But ever since I met Liz, my ability to do what needs to be done has been eroded more and more. Even now, seeing her in front of me, I'm wavering.

She saved you? How? We're no longer bonded, and she's weak again. Weren't there thousands *of humans?*

Only she could use the heart swords, and she betrayed her people to set us free.

"Technically it was my mother who shorted the control panel, but I did gratefully hitch a ride on the way out." Liz sounds tired, and I want to reach for her.

She came back for you, Gaia says, *knowing that Azar was dead. You clearly matter to her a great deal. Don't be angry.*

The earth blessed have been hurt for a while, thinking that she abandoned me for Azar. They were proud that one of them bonded a human, and to see her disappear with the giant red flame blessed, prince or not, hurt their pride. But I can't keep her here, in danger, just to mollify them.

You must return to the humans, I say, just to her. *It's the only place you'll be safe.*

"I'm not safe anywhere," she says. "If you haven't figured that out yet, you don't know me at all. If there's trouble anywhere at all, I find it."

I shake my head. "That's not what I mean. Hyperion's enraged now that Azar's gone." I glare, but now that she can't feel our bond to even guess at my emotions, I'm not sure whether it helps. This form has always been my least terrifying.

Losing Azar, losing my ability to control flame and shift into that form, hurt a great deal. It felt like half of me was ripped away—like I'm not a whole being any longer. But losing the bond to Liz, that part of me where our bond used to be—it *aches* and *throbs* actively. I long to reach out for her again. I can sense the pulse of her power, even now, but I can't do it. I can't risk her life like that. I won't survive losing her a second time.

"I still have your blades, and I'm not giving them back." She folds her arms under her chest, her eyes flashing gloriously.

I allow myself a moment to look at her—dirt, grime, and terrible clothes notwithstanding, she's the most beautiful thing I've ever seen. I want to drag her into my arms, kiss her until she can't speak, and then bond her all over again.

But I can't do that.

I won't.

"Where are Gordon and Rufus?" she asks.

Gaia, Agrippa, Phileas, and Wilhelm all turn toward me at the same time, all clearly wondering the same thing. Rufus and Gordon are well-liked. They always have been the best of the earth blessed. They're almost always with me, too.

"They're busy right now," I hedge. "I'll tell them you miss them if you'd like, but you can't stay—"

You aren't my prince. If you won't keep her, I will, Plumeria says. *She refused to kill my sister, because she holds out hope for her rescue. She never betrayed us, and I like her.*

"You can't keep her." I'm sure my eyes are flashing, but in this stupid human form, there's no way I'm going to have a hope of scaring any blessed. I shift without thinking, barely larger in my earth prince form than the medium size water blessed in front of me. *You may not keep her. I forbid it.*

Plumeria straightens, her body expanding as she moves toward me. *She's brave, she's strong, she's powerful, and you don't own her anymore,* Prince. *I'll keep her if I* want *to keep her. Unlike your kind, water blessed can bond any bright.*

She's going back, I bellow. *You won't even think about bonding her, or I'll destroy you and feed your body to my subjects.*

Plumeria's assessing whether Liz is worth the fight, her head tilting, and her eyes narrowing, when the other four earth blessed circle around to flank me, showing her that I won't have to make good on my threat alone.

But if I bond her right now, you won't dare harm me. She smiles.

With that epiphany, she's won—she's right. I won't dare harm her once she's bonded Liz.

"Forget all the bonding, staying, going nonsense," Liz says. "I want to know where my siblings are. If you really don't want me here, I'll just collect them and be on my way."

She looks angry enough to slice me up with those swords.

Let me bond you, and we'll find them together, Plumeria says. *I'm sure I can find plenty of strong water blessed who would be good options to bond them when they're ready.*

Liz shakes her head. "You're stunningly beautiful, powerful, intelligent, and brave. If I were looking for a new blessed to bond, I would choose you in a heartbeat." She smiles at Plumeria. "But if Axel won't rebond me. . ." She shakes her head, and sniffs. I realize that she's fighting back tears. "Then I won't bond anyone."

You can't retrieve your brother or sisters, I finally say. *In fact, even being this close is very, very bad.*

"Why?" she demands. "Where are they?" But she already knows. I can see it in her eyes.

Hyperion took them.

She flinches—my strong, brave spitfire flinches. She's beginning to understand what I truly learned a week and a day ago.

Loving someone leaves you powerless.

"Then I'll go after them."

I explode toward her, barely stopping without touching her, my face lowered so it's on level with hers. I shake my head slowly, forcefully. *You will leave now. You* cannot *go after them.*

"Say it," she says.

She already knows the truth. I can tell. Even without the bond, I know her. *You're the one he wants. He's holding them hostage to get to you—just in case you're still alive somewhere.*

"And if I don't go?" She lifts her eyebrows.

I hate how smart she is. I *hate* it.

Azar was the only thing that kept Hyperion from hurling Liz into that volcano when those demons demanded her. With them gone. . .

"Axel, if I don't go there and face Hyperion, then what?" Her jaw is set, and I know what she's saying.

Going there would mean dying, I say. *You can't go.*

"But if I don't go," she says. "He'll eventually try throwing them in, won't he?"

I wish I could argue with her logic, but I can't.

"Where are they, exactly?"

Hanging over the volcano in a cage, I finally admit.

"Can they see the. . ." She cuts off and looks around.

Everyone here knows about the demon creatures in the volcano, I say. *It's not a secret. I don't know whether your siblings can see them, but the creatures pay no attention to anyone who comes near or hangs over the volcano. They've only ever cared about one person, and so Hyperion only cares about one person.*

"I'm sure he's plenty upset he didn't chuck me in when he had the chance."

Then you understand why you must go, I say, just to her.

"I understand why that's what you want me to do." She steps closer, and lifts her hand to the side of my face, caressing my golden scales. "But Axel, I won't leave my family, and I won't leave you. If you truly ever thought that was an option, you don't know me at all."

You must go. I huff. *I've ordered it, and if Gaia and Agrippa and Phileas and Wilhelm have to drag you back, kicking and screaming, so help me, they'll do it.*

She steps forward again, ducking around my head, and wraps her arms around my neck. When she squeezes, my stupid, traitorous heart lurches. I yearn for this moment to continue, but it can't. I won't allow her to become bonded to me, not now that Azar's dead.

There aren't many things in this world that can harm me, even now, but the idea of having her here but being unable to protect her? That's the worst nightmare I can imagine.

And it's staring me in the face.

The one who wants her dead is far too powerful for me to resist.

Running away is our only option.

But when Liz finally releases me and steps back, something strange happens. I start to feel a weird sort of *pulling* sensation, as if something is sucking away at my very soul.

Axel-Azar, Prince of Flame and Earth, she says just to me, *you are mine. You will always be mine. Whether you can set the world on fire or just set my heart aflame, you are* mine, *and I won't give you up.* She reaches up and grasps my face, turning it toward hers, and the pulling feeling intensifies.

I thrash back and forth, trying to dislodge her, but I can't break free.

Or maybe, deep down, I don't really want to.

"I can't exist in the world without you," Liz says. "I know that Hyperion will find me. Bonding you again is cruel, because it'll just hurt you later. I should leave you here and go to find him alone, but seeing you, I can't do it." A tear rolls down her cheek, and her voice breaks. "I can't, Axel. Please don't hate me for needing you so much."

I could never hate her.

Never.

From the moment I saw her, all I've wanted was to restore the bond between us. A small part of me even hopes that, once we're bonded again, the part of me that the ice spears sundered will return. Could restoring our bond heal me? Could it return me to my former glory? Could Liz be the key to Azar's return?

One tiny second of weakness, and my shields drop, and the blazing light of our bond, the shining strength of it, snaps back into place. Both of us bow backward, writhing, but not from agony. From the blinding brilliance of that connection screaming back to life.

I'm stronger.

I'm smarter.

I'm faster, more resilient, and more powerful. The bond strengthens me in every single way. I should have known it would happen, that the renewal of our bond would be glorious. But as the earth dragons nearby gasp, and as Plumeria groans, and as more earth dragons draw near with exclamations and questions. . .

I realize that no one could have missed our bond settling back into place—Liz and I just went from nothing straight to entwined. Of course the re-forging of that bond would resonate, and no matter how much better it makes me, it's not going to be enough. But even if they didn't feel it, the visible change of her hair from brown to gold is enough evidence.

Every blessed here knows.

When Hyperion wheels overhead, trumpeting, I want to grab Liz and burrow deep and fast into the ground. My earth dragons would leap into his path and slow him down, sacrificing themselves for me willingly, but their attempts would be futile. Nothing I do will be enough to keep her safe.

Not from him.

Not from the power of the flame, a power I used to command myself. Not from the brother who used to protect me above all others.

The brother who doesn't even know me anymore.

Elizabeth Chadwick. Hyperion lands with a loud thunk, the earth around us trembling as he settles his enormous bulk into place. *I've been hoping and wishing that you might yet be alive, and now, here you are, like a gift-wrapped offering the humans sent just for me.*

"Here I am," she says, her chin thrusting upward. "Take

me, and release my siblings."

Oh, I don't think so, he says. *You already cost me my favorite brother, you know, so don't be angry with me if I kill yours in front of you, just to even the score.*

Don't do that, I say. *It won't help anyone.*

You. Hyperion's eyes flash and smoke pours from his partially open snout. *You, my brother's self-proclaimed best friend, who was* nowhere *to be found on the battlefield, or even for hours after. You're a coward.* Hyperion snorts, blowing half flame, half smoke against me and shrouding me in black. *You have the audacity to rebond her, when I ordered all of you to bring her to me the moment you find her? She killed him!*

"He only did it so he could drag me to you," Liz says. "I have these swords yet. I may be small, but I'm feisty."

And will you, Axel? Hyperion asks. *Will you drag her to the volcano for me?*

Why would she say that? She must know that the moment we reach that horrible place, he's going to fling her into the lava. She may have cheated death once, but it's not likely to happen again. *She's not Gullveig,* I say. *She won't be reborn. You'll just be murdering her for no reason.*

Hyperion stalks toward me, and I scramble backward, watching to make sure that Liz isn't anywhere near his tail or flank as he pursues me. *How do you know about Gullveig? What else did my brother tell you and why?*

For the first time in my life, I fear something else more than I fear my own secret being revealed. Everyone knows that Hyperion has been kind and understanding to exactly one creature in all of history. One blessed.

Only one, ever.

He didn't tell me, I say. *I was there all along.* I straighten and stand my ground. *I'm Azar—I always have been both Axel and Azar. That's why I wasn't at the battle. It's why I was never seen with Azar, not once, in spite of everyone knowing that we're best friends. We're the same, and when the humans speared me, it destroyed my flame blessed half—but I'm still me.*

Hyperion arches one eyebrow at me.

I'm still your little brother. And now I have to pray that divulging my secret is enough to save her.

That flaming idiot. The very second his horrible brother shows up, he outs the secret he's kept for so many years I don't even know how long it's been. It's a secret that could put him in grave danger—especially now that only the weak half of himself survived.

After he divulges it, the dragons that have gathered—dozens of earth dragons, a few more water dragons, and even two electro dragons—freeze, turning slowly to wait for Hyperion's reaction.

I wait, too, tensed and nervous.

Will he attack to see how weak his brother is now? Will he embrace him? Or will he do something else entirely, something I can't even imagine? I sense Axel's apprehension along the bond—it's a stormy grey.

But then, Hyperion, who has been utterly still, starts to laugh.

Dragons don't really laugh. I've heard it only a handful of times. . .but apparently Hyperion didn't get the memo. He's not just laughing. He's completely falling apart with laughter.

Suddenly, as quickly as it began, he snatches me around

the waist, wrapping his talons tightly, and launches into the sky. All the times Azar shot into the air without warning prepared me, and I don't even vomit in my mouth. Of course, it could be the fact that, in the past week, I've had hardly anything to eat, but I'm proud of keeping my composure.

Being among the humans so much has clearly warped his brain, Hyperion says. *As if I'd ever believe a lie that idiotic.*

It's a relief, really, that he thought Axel was kidding.

Did Azar—he chokes up a little, I think—*ever tell you about the prophecy?*

"You mean the one where he was chosen to save all of you?"

Hyperion's snort this time shoots flames at least three feet out in front of us. *Trust Azar to tell you only his part of the story.*

"There's more?"

I was first hatched, you know, to his last hatch. I was the very first egg to hatch after our departure from Earth.

"I knew you were older." We're headed for the volcano, clearly, but for some reason, Hyperion isn't in a hurry. Either that, or his top speed is quite a bit slower than Azar's. From what I've seen, that's not likely to be right. So clearly, he has something he wants to tell me without an audience.

Not just older. I was the first subject of a prophecy from that crazy oracle, the one who died when we left—Freya.

"Wait, the oracle who prophesied about you and Azar was named Freya, and your dad's named Odin?"

Hyperion grunts, picking up a little speed. Apparently my questions are irritating.

"Those are the names of two Norse gods," I say, "who were supposed to be married."

There's no way my father would have abandoned his mate, even if she was crazy.

"Why'd you leave in the first place, if the prophecies said you'd return?"

Father vowed we wouldn't ever return, but the oracle was the only blessed who dared disagree with him. She told him that his departure was doomed, and that his first-hatched son would be the one to destroy all the blessed.

Oh, shoot. That's a pretty awful prophecy to have hanging over your head from the day you hatch. "I'm sorry," I say. "But for what it's worth, it doesn't seem to be true." At least, not any truer than her claim that Azar would save them. That'll be hard to do, given that he's been destroyed.

Everyone else thinks that, anyhow.

My father attempted to kill me several times, Hyperion says.

"Are you kidding?" I try to lean away from his massive talon-grip so I can see his face, but he's too huge. His head's just too far away for me to make out any part of his expression from here.

It's not a jest. He's silent for a moment, and the volcano appears out in front of us. Instead of dropping to prepare for a landing, he starts to circle. *Azar's water blessed nanny, Euphrasia, stood between my father and me long before Azar was ever hatched and asked my father whether he was sure that his murder of his first-hatched wouldn't bring the destruction that was promised.*

The same dragon who saved Azar also saved Hyperion?

She's also the one who told me about the companion prophesy to mine, that although my destiny was to destroy our people, another would be hatched, my younger sibling, who would be capable of saving us all.

"You, too? Or just the people?"

The exact wording is, He who is first hatched of flame, heir of the fire-king, shall herald the doom of all the blessed, casting them back into a darkness that shall consume them for all time and evermore.

Yeesh. "That's pretty rough."

But the prophecy given for Azar was, He who is last hatched among the deserters, the final remaining heir of the fire-king, shall redeem the blessed above and below, and shall cleanse them of their stain and drag them through the darkness and back into the light.

"If I'm being honest, his sounds pretty rough, too."

He was supposed to save *them.* Hyperion's voice is ragged, even in my head.

He sounds like he's in real agony, but I don't have time to think about consoling him. We're diving now, right toward the cavern full of demons. "Has it occurred to you," I shout, "that throwing me in the pit may be the very thing that dooms all of you?"

We're doomed already, he says. *Without Azar to lead us, without Azar to guide the recovery of the heart, we'll all slowly die. You're our last remaining hope.*

"I mean, that might be a little melodramatic. The whole world hasn't been searched. There are plenty of places it could be."

It's here. I can sense it.

He can't sense anything. He has no idea what the heart even is, but I don't bother arguing with him. It's like arguing with a brick wall.

If a brick wall wanted to kill me and had talons, fangs, and blew liquid napalm.

"We don't even know whether the heart really is part of the barrier. Those horned people could have been lying." Azar said this already, but I feel like it bears repeating.

Hyperion lands, the entire shelf of obsidian that forms the floor of the former cavern trembling from the force of his weight. *I've considered that, but . . .* He sets me down. *If I'm wrong, all we've lost is one useless human.*

"No!" Sammy's not hanging over the lava, like Axel said he was. He is, however, in a cage, suspended from the remaining section of ceiling in the far corner. Coral and

Jade are both in the same cage, their feet dangling through the bars. I have no idea where the dragons even got such a thing—unless the other humans helped them craft it.

"It's fine," I say. "Don't worry."

Why do humans feel compelled to say that when it's clearly not true?

A strange sort of clanging sound draws my attention to Gordon and Rufus where they're chained with massive metal collars, the chains bolted into the ground.

"Can't they free themselves?" I tilt my head. "Earth dragons, right?"

They wouldn't dare to defy me, Hyperion says. *The chains are to remind them that I've ordered them to wait here, guarding the tiny humans until you're brought to this place.*

"What if I'd died?" I ask. "Would they have simply starved up there?"

Hyperion shrugs. *You're alive.*

He's right about that, I suppose.

We were feeding them, Rufus says. *Prince Axel made sure of it.*

Yes, the weak Prince of the Earth was willing to defy me to defend your tiny whelps, Hyperion says. *That gave me hope that he thought you might be alive.* Hyperion's smile is terrifying. *But now, it's time for you to pay for their release.*

"If I walk into the lava voluntarily, you'll release them?"

Hardly, he says. *If your sacrifice fails to free the heart, we'll try them next. But if your death retrieves it, they're free to go.*

I unsheathe my swords and lunge for him then, unwilling to simply walk like a lamb to the slaughter, especially when he's not even willing to release my siblings for it.

He's unprepared for me to attack, apparently, because one of my blades strikes him right in his massive chest. . .and slides right in. A massive shiver runs through him, and then he bats me away with a paw the size of a semi-truck.

I'm not an untrained idiot, though. I know how to take a blow, even if it's a million times stronger than the others I've endured. I duck and roll, losing the blade that's now lodged in his chest, but I'm not significantly injured, at least. When I hit the far wall, I flip and stand, waving my remaining sword. "How's it feel?" I ask. "Being the one getting stabbed for once?"

If I didn't need you, I'd melt you into goo.

"But you do need me," I say. "Did you really think I'd make it easy for you?"

His lip curls and he rushes toward me, but his left side, where the blade's still lodged, moves slower. Markedly slower. It allows me to duck under a ledge and roll across to the other side. The horrible monster can't roast me, not if he wants to serve me up as a snack to the bubbling lava.

I manage to evade him twice, rolling toward the ledge, in a calculated ploy. If he comes at me, hoping to bump me in, I could feint and shove him toward the lava instead. I'm not sure what it would do to a fire dragon, but I bet it's not lovely being burned, even for them.

Only, he realizes what I'm doing and his brain cells finally engage. He has something that will push me the way he wants immediately. Something that doesn't fight back.

He saunters backward.

My heart sinks, knowing I'm about to be forced to walk in the lava on my own after all.

He may not be willing to promise me he'll spare my siblings, but the chance that they'll be spared when my death frees the heart is better than watching him kill them in front of me.

How about I throw them in first? He's smiling at me while he reaches for the cage. *After all, I'm not out anything by doing that. If they don't free the heart, they don't free it.*

No! Gordon yanks his chain out of the ground and slithers at mach speed toward Hyperion, sinking his teeth into the massive fire dragon's leg. As if he's stuck on the top of a steep precipice, Rufus looks stricken, the blood draining from his face, but he straightens.

Before Hyperion can incinerate Gordon, Rufus yanks his chain free and races toward Hyperion's other side. He's opening his mouth to strike when the fire dragon back-hands him, sending Rufus careening toward the lava.

Axel bursts around the corner at the top of the path into the cavern, his sides heaving, and blocks Rufus's body just before it slides over the edge. *You're angry with my blessed for defending my bonded? Your anger is misplaced. Release them and attack me.*

I'm helping the blessed, Hyperion bellows. *How are all of you too stupid to see it? If we can recover the heart at the loss of just one irritating, unfaithful human, why would you fight me over that?*

You laughed before, but it wasn't a joke. Axel stands upright again. *Since my hatching, I've hidden the truth—I have two affinities. I've been flame and earth blessed from the start, and only Euphrasia knew my secret.* He pauses. *Until I inadvertently bonded Liz. Why do you think an earth blessed was able to do the impossible?*

Hyperion pauses. Then he blinks.

I kept the secret because I was afraid to expose the truth. The blessed don't welcome weakness at any level, but to be a prince of flame who was also a prince of earth? Father would have put me down.

You were always weaker, Hyperion says. *I defended you in spite of that.*

So that you could be free from the curse of destroying us, Axel says. *Not for any other reason.*

At first. Hyperion nods slowly. *That was my reason at first, but in time, I became fond of you. You were weak, but you thought differently than the rest of us. Now I understand why. You were both strong and weak. You were bright and dark. You could fly the heights and burrow into the depths. You truly belonged to no place at all.*

Axel doesn't argue. He simply begs. *Don't do it.*

It could be my eyes—they could be failing me. The waves of terrible heat from the lava at our backs wash over me constantly now, and I can hear them calling to me.

The demons have seen me, and they're chanting.

Not *hjartanu,* not anymore. No, ever since seeing me, they're chanting *Gullveig* again. For whatever distorted reason, they think I'm somehow connected to the Norse goddess who was burned thrice and rose again.

But whether I'm imagining things from distress, or whether I'm losing focus because of the tremendous heat, I could swear that I see a tear roll down Hyperion's massive face. It drops and disappears into the dusty floor. *Maybe it is my doom, to destroy all of us.* Hyperion's voice is broken. *But I can't spare her, not even for you. We're dying off slowly, and she's our only hope.*

We have no idea whether that's true, Axel says. *We don't know what we're doing.*

I went back to see Father after you died. Hyperion's head bobs, and his body slumps. *He told me that he had left the heart as part of a barrier. He told me—*His head snaps up. *I wish I could spare her. I wish I could hope for another way, but this is the only way.*

His massive, powerful arms grab Gordon and unfurl him, and then he aims him at us and chucks him with all his strength.

Axel tries to duck, throwing one of his strong, golden limbs around me, but it's no use. The force behind Hyperion's throw is too great. Gordon plows into us, knocking me, Axel, and Rufus over the edge at the same time. My hands pinwheel, and my eyes meet Axel's, just as we slam into the lava.

� 24 ✸

LIZ

I think we all like to imagine that if we were placed in a situation where we were tortured, or forced to endure in miserable circumstances, we'd bear up under the strain. I recall a time when Sammy was quite small and he told me what he'd do if bad guys ever came for us.

He jutted out his bottom lip, and in his delayed, slurred speech, he told me how he'd punch and kick the bad guys to keep the rest of us safe. As an MMA fighter, I've always been the strong one. The fearless one—quite literally, in fact. I've fought past broken limbs. I've ignored a shattered nose. Twice.

I'm frankly lucky that I had good enough insurance for them to put me back together after the misery I've endured.

I thought that the dragon venom I survived months ago was the most exquisite pain I would ever experience, but this is different. This is pure flame and heat and it pulses through what feels like every *atom* of my body, dragging me down to an elemental level.

My nerves cry out in agony.

My lymphatic system shuts down.

My respiratory system screams in protest.

That's when it gets *worse,* because somehow, the beasts have reached me. Great, horned creatures of muscle and sinew and fangs. I kick out at them, but they don't slow, even when my heel knocks one in the jaw hard enough that I feel the crunch.

They snarl and snap, and when the first one's mouth connects with my shoulder, clamping down, I realize that they mean to *eat me.* Panic breaks through the pain that's been rendering me mostly inert, and I kick like a donkey, swinging with my arms, flailing with my legs.

But it's useless.

There are dozens and dozens of them, converging on me in the boiling lava, and consuming the flesh that hasn't yet burned. Finally, blessedly, my world, nothing but misery, and fire, and anguish, blinks into peaceful surrender.

And I wake up in a room of nothing but light. There aren't beds or chairs or windows or doors. Everything's white. Everything's peace. Everything's calm. I'm lying down, but not on anything I can see or feel. I sit up easily —nothing hurts, nothing even twinges, and I swing my legs over the edge of. . .well, of nothing at all.

I'm wearing a white caftan, and my arms and legs are mostly bare, but no part of me is so much as scraped, much less burned. I blink, and when I do, there's a figure standing in the center of my view, starkly alone against the endless sea of white light, but walking slowly toward me.

I flinch at first, but as she draws nearer, I can see that she's not at all what I expect. She's absolutely lovely—tall, strong, bright, and stunning in her beauty. It's as if someone set out to paint the strongest features humanity had ever known, but blended them effortlessly and in perfect balance.

She's perfection in light.

Her bright golden hair streams around her shoulders,

but as she shifts, I see darker colors, and even hints of the brightest red. Her hair is everything and nothing at all. It's light in all of its shifting shades and glory. Her deep eyes are such a dark brown that they're nearly black, but not in an absence-of-light-way. No, her eyes are the blue of the ocean depths, the verdant green of spring crops, the in-between hazel of a cat's eyes, the rich grey of tempered steel, the deep loamy brown of the southern clay, the sparkling golden of champagne, and the startling richness of a raven's wing, shifting as she moves.

When she speaks, it's in the dragon's tongue, which shouldn't surprise me. *I'm Freya, wife to Odin, heart of the barrier.*

The heart's a *person*? It feels right somehow, like I should have known that all along.

"I need you to come with me," I say. "The dragons are all dying—or rather, they can't have children. They're slowly dying with no way to reproduce."

This time, instead of speaking to my heart, she matches my vocal speech. "You're the chosen sacrifice of your people, Elizabeth Chadwick, marked from birth to be granted entry to this place."

I shake my head. "No. That can't be right. I never have any idea what I'm doing, and most every choice I make turns out to be wrong."

Her smile's profoundly sorrowful. "No choice is right or wrong. Each decision we make carries a price and a conse-quence. But your choices will determine—"

"That can't be!" I shake my head. "You don't under-stand. I'm not representative of my people." Tears begin to well up and then leak from my eyes. "I'm not the right person. I'm monstrous—even my own mother thinks so."

"Your mother sees her darkest, strongest, most fearful traits in you. She's afraid of her own reflection, not of you, child," she says.

"Is Azar's father, the dragon, really your husband?"

"I don't know who Azar is." Freya's smile this time isn't sad, it's wistful. "But you're focusing on things that don't matter. It's time for you to choose. Only our choices matter." She waves her hand through the air, and the white room disappears. She disappears. Even I disappear in my white and light, and my soul's slammed torturously into my body in another time, another possibility.

I've returned to the locker room to retrieve my water—my coach is in a rush for me to join him, where he's waiting in the hallway. He's angry I even came back in here, because we're set to walk into the ring in the next few minutes. But I'm not the only one who's not ready for this match. My opponent's in here too.

Gisela Lopez is hunched over, her face in her hands. "I told you," she whispers. "I'm going to win, Mom."

The tinny sound of her phone's speaker phone rings out loudly, easy to hear, even from where I'm standing across the room. "I begged you not to fight again. I told you it's my last wish. Your sister needs you."

"It's not your last wish." Gisela's voice is iron. "I'm going to win the money tonight for the enrollment fee for the clinical trial. You're not going to die yet. You *can't*, Mom."

I snatch my water bottle off the ledge and pivot, desperate to get away from what I just saw. She wants to use the fifty thousand dollars prize money to pay for her mother's medical care? Ugh.

"What's wrong?" When I reach him, Coach is frowning. "You look like someone squashed your kitten."

I shake my head. "No, nothing like that."

He drops a hand on each of my shoulders. "You're here, Liz. This is what we've always wanted, what we've trained for, and you can do this. You can *destroy* her. Remember what we practiced. Her kicks may be killer, but when you duck around them, she leaves herself open for the choke."

We've gone over and over the tapes. He's right.

I can do this.

When we walk out, the crowd goes insane. The media has been hyping this one as a scrappy underdog taking on the establishment. Gisela has been a fixture within the MMA for a while. She's a solid fighter, but she has some gaps that result in her losing almost as much as she wins.

She's flashy, with her insane roundhouse, so the MMA keeps her around, but she's always as likely to go down as she is to take down her opponent.

Today, she's going down. When she walks out to mixed shouts, I realize that she knows it.

But she's walking out anyway, her face desperate, because unlike me, she's not fighting for position, prestige or glory. She's fighting for her mom. Like me, there may not be much else she can do to make money. There may not be many options for her—I can't help thinking about how powerless I would feel in her position, if I *needed* that money.

My coach is shouting. "Focus, Liz. You look for that opening, and you stay clear until you see it."

I nod, and as she walks in, I put everything but the fight out of my mind. If I hadn't walked in when I did, I would know nothing but the fight. I would only know what I'd prepared. I can't save her mom. That's her job.

But I do know.

If I lose this match, my MMA career may be over before it starts, but if she loses. . . I can't even imagine losing my mother. It would wreck me. And her mom's saying she has a sister to care for, too.

That makes me think of Jade, of Coral, and of Sammy.

What wouldn't I do for them if Mom died?

I shake my head, and as she comes after me, I sink into

the fight. Not thinking. Moving. Reacting. Closing the gap. Then I see it—my chance. She's lining up to kick me, and it's painfully obvious. She's too slow. She's old, at least, for this sport she is.

I can dodge her strike easily.

But I don't. Her heel connects with my solar plexus and sends me sprawling on the mat. In that split second, everything slows. My coach's face looks almost frozen in place, spit spewing at me as he shouts, his mouth twisted, his nostrils wide.

You must choose—the power to dominate, or the strength to endure.

The words that spread through my mind make no sense. Who's speaking? Why did time slow down? What's the power to dominate and the strength to endure?

And endure what? The misery of losing? The shame of my career ending before it's begun?

Or I can destroy her, how? From the ground?

But when time snaps back, I see it. She's overbalanced, and even from the ground, if I snap upward, I could topple her. The hold would be easy to make, even now, from the ground.

I could still dominate her.

My career rolls before me, as I come from the bottom to take my position alongside the greats like Amanda Nunes and Ronda Rousey. I can do it—in that moment, I know it.

Or I can endure the shame, the humiliation, and the misery of defeat, but I will know that I didn't steal someone's mother's last hope. I'll know that, deep down where it matters, I'm whole and complete.

I don't take the window.

I let Gisela Lopez pin me, and I prepare myself to endure, my conscience clear. But instead of hearing the shouts and jeers and cheers of the crowd, I'm thrust back into a room that's nothing but light and whiteness.

Interesting, Freya says. *I wouldn't have expected you, a warrior, to choose the strength to endure.*

I lift my chin. "You don't know me."

Her laughter's light and bright and painfully beautiful, like everything else about her. *You're right. And you're wrong.*

Again, I feel the sensation of falling as I'm slammed into another scene, another snapshot, and then. . .

I'm in chains.

Axel's in human form beside me, also in chains.

Shift, I command him. *Do it. It won't hurt as badly.*

His eyes find mine, and a pulse shoots through the bond. *I'll feel what you feel. Always. We're doing this together.*

No. This time, unlike the last, I can still feel that it's not me—I know this is a dream. It's a vision. It's not real.

Get me out, I scream. *Freya!*

You put yourself here. It's your bond—your decisions—your fault that he's here. If it weren't for you, his Azar half wouldn't have died. You dropped down among the humans to save them as they attacked his people. You released your shield and let the one named Gideon inside to kill you.

A human I don't recognize—burly, large, and brutal, with hard eyes—is holding a bull whip. It's a horribly large handle, but his beefy hand still manages to encircle it. "You'll do as I ask, now." His hand falls then, and the whip's tattered and bone-shard adorned end arcs toward Axel's back.

His bloody, mangled back.

Shift! I shout. *Please!*

Axel's body shudders when the nine-tailed whip strikes, but he doesn't cry out. He simply grunts, and when he looks at me, he shakes his head. *If I do, he'll whip you instead.*

The savagely terrible man strikes him again and again, blood spattering away from Axel's ruined back. Each time,

I see the desecration growing, and each time, Axel merely grunts. But then, after the fifth strike, or maybe the sixth, Axel coughs, spitting up blood.

I'm desperate this time. Beyond desperate. *Make it stop!*

You have the power to stop this right now, Freya says. *Only you can stop it, in fact.*

How? I'll do anything. Anything at all. I already know it in my bones—the guilt I feel over what I've cost Azar is overpowering. I'll do anything to make the damage stop.

He never had to die, the flame blessed prince. He chose it. Freya's voice is calm. *He could have given up his memories of you, released his hold on the bond, and that part of him would never have died.*

That makes no sense.

I agree. He should have given up his memory of you. You had already died—by abandoning his ties to you, he would have remained strong enough to fight the humans. His grief made him weak.

Another crack sounds as the ends of the whip turn yet another section of his back into hamburger. The man wielding it is laughing. "No matter how brave you are, brother, she's next. Eventually, in that weak form, you'll die."

Axel grunts.

In that moment I realize that since the time we met, I've done nothing but weaken Axel. Azar. All of him. I'm an anvil around his neck and always have been.

So what if he loses his memories of me?

He chose to keep his memories of you and live as Axel, Freya says. *Would you take that choice from him now, just to restore his strength?*

Yes! Do it.

You're sure?

The whip comes down again, and for the first time,

Axel flinches and cries out, and the man holding the whip grins. "Cry for me, brother. Cry."

Azar chose to die rather than sacrificing his memories of me. He chose to keep me and lose himself, but now he's not the one making that choice. *I am.* What would a monster do? What should I decide?

But when the whip comes down yet again, and when Axel groans, low in his throat, I can't even think about what it means about me. I can't contemplate right or wrong. There is only Axel and the pain I've caused him.

I can take it all away.

Will he know what he's lost? I ask.

Freya shakes her head.

Then do it, I say. *The only person who will suffer will be me.*

So be it. Freya smiles.

There's a bright flash of light, and I'm back in the light room.

"You're a real conundrum. You'd choose to spare a stranger—strength of resilience to overcome rather than power to destroy, but when faced with the misery to endure the trials for love, you choose to erase it."

Tears well up in my eyes, and I collapse into a ball on the non-floor of this strange place. "I can't abide the choices that I make harming him."

"Isn't that his decision to make?"

I shake my head, forcing myself to look at her. "You made it mine." Even here, even in this place, I can feel the shining bond between Axel and me.

Her smile is serene. "Even now, you don't change your mind."

The bond dissolves, fading away like acid-eaten rope. I collapse to my knees, so gutted as it disappears that I can't breathe. I can't see. I can't even think. A pitiful moan escapes my lips, and just before it's gone, I hear it.

A pained roar that must be Axel as our bond

evaporates.

He didn't want to bond me again, but he refused to give up his memories of our time? Refused, knowing it would mean that he lost Azar forever?

There's another bright flash, and then I'm standing high in the air, on nothing, as always in this place, watching Rufus and Gordon below us. They're thrashing and roaring and moaning as the horde of demonic beasts consume them, bite by bite.

"The cursed have been starving for millennia, you know." Freya's voice is quiet. "They were always a little depraved, but it's only grown far worse in our sojourn in this barren place."

I swallow. "But what—"

She shakes her head. "No more ignorant, uninspired questions. I can't take it."

"I can't just watch them. I'm not like you. I don't relish the pain of others."

She turns slowly, her eyes sepulchral. "Is that what you think of me, that I relish any part of this?" The pain in her eyes is raw, and yet, she stands, tall, strong, and severe. "I have hated every moment of my life since the forging, and here I have remained, hating myself and hating Odin for abandoning me. I choose to maintain my position every single day, every single moment, because it's the right thing to do."

"What is this barrier?"

"The blessed," she laughs. "Is that still what they call themselves?"

I nod.

She points. "And these, my subjects, are the cursed." The horned creatures truly do look cursed.

"It hurts less in that form," she says. "So most of them assume their humanoid shape, but when they sense that you're near—their only possibility of escape—sometimes they can't help themselves." Freya grabs the skin of my arm and pinches, hard.

I cry out.

The demons below whip their heads upward and snarl. Three of them shift, before my eyes, into the black, burned dragons I saw before, swimming through the lava. Their trumpets of excitement sound more like the wails of the dying.

"Don't worry. They won't harm you while I'm here."

"But you're what the dragons need," I say. "You're the heart, right?"

She laughs.

"I don't understand."

"Everything in this life requires a sacrifice, just as restoring Azar's power, his flame-blessed lifeforce, required the loss of something equally powerful—his love-forged connection to you."

"What happens to me now?"

Freya doesn't smile this time. "You have one more decision to make before I'll know."

Great. "What now? Do I have to choose which of my siblings to save? Or do I have to skin another innocent child to save them?"

Freya's laughter is bitter. "You'd do that in a heartbeat."

She's not wrong. It would erode my soul, firmly establishing that I'm the monster my mom believes me to be, but I would. For Sammy, Coral, and Jade, I would do it. "You already know I'm a monster."

Freya slowly shakes her head. "No, your actions are more complex than you give yourself credit for. You're always willing to sacrifice yourself, and monsters don't do that. You've retained your memories of Axel, while his memories of you are now gone."

"How is that fair?" I ask. "I thought mine would disappear too."

Her smile is nearly feral. "You must remember or the choice would be rendered meaningless. You can't suffer without knowing what you've lost."

"You're a horrible person."

She shrugs. "A monster, perhaps. The queen of the cursed." She points to Gordon and Rufus. "You already know that the earth blessed are different."

"They can reproduce," I say.

"They paid the price when we created this barrier. Their strength, their abilities—they gave them up to contain the cursed in this place. More than any other blessed, they loved the humans and wanted to keep them safe."

The cursed hurt the humans? "I don't understand."

"I'm aware." Freya sighs. "You can save Gordon and Rufus, and you can restore to the earth blessed their power, their strength, and their glory."

I'm waiting for the catch.

"But then they'll be afflicted like the others."

"What does that mean?"

"They'll know longer lives, they'll be on par with their companions, but they'll never know the joy of offspring. They'll lose their ability to shift and their empathy for the humans."

Axel.

He'd never be able to take a human form either.

When I agreed that Azar would be restored but his memories lost, I was counting on the opportunity to recover them, or at least recreate them. I was convinced that I could penetrate that massive ego, that stubbornly insistent brain of his, in much the same way I did in the past.

But that will be gone.

He won't smile at me from his gorgeous human form. He won't brush his hand down the side of my face, or ask me to teach him to kiss.

He'll simply be my enemy.

But if I made this choice, the earth dragons wouldn't be fodder any more. Azar wouldn't need to hide that he's Axel, because Axel won't be a liability.

"I'm not qualified to make this decision," I say. "They need to make it."

"They can't," Freya says. "You must make it for them."

It hurts.

Worse than the demons taking bites, more than the lava burning through my skin, my muscle, and into my bone. It hurts more than losing myself—making this life-altering, binding decision that will take from the earth dragons something vital.

"I don't know them well enough to decide," I say.

"They won't all agree," Freya says. "You'll be a savior to some and a monster to others. That is always the case."

"What about the fire dragons, the water dragons, and the electro dragons? What happens to them when they can't eat the earth dragons anymore?"

Freya shrugs. "Unknown."

I can't decide.

But I must.

Gordon and Rufus are being eaten, even now. "If I choose to restore them, will they be safe?" I think about Sammy and his love for Gordon. "The earth dragons will be able to bond humans and care for them, too?"

No more games of cards, but Gordon won't be chained to the ground at the foot of Sammy's cage. They won't be weak—they'll once again be strong.

Freya nods. "They'll be as the others. No shifting, no groveling, no being consumed or mistreated."

But the dragons are here to regain their ability to procreate.

"You're the heart—now that I've found you, can they all regain their ability to have offspring?"

Freya points at Gordon and Rufus. "The decision you are set to make now is placed before you. Sufficient the day the sacrifice presented."

"What about the demons?" I ask. "If I restore the earth dragons, will they be freed?"

"I keep them here," she says. "The earth blessed sacrifice fueled it, but they will yet remain."

It feels like a curse either way. They'll either continue as they are, weak and abused, but able to procreate, or they'll become strong like their brethren, but lose that chance at a future. They chose the initial sacrifice, if Freya is to be believed. They chose the weaker part, to trap the demons here in this place.

I shouldn't take that from them.

But Axel is their leader, and I'm not at all sure what happens when life resumes. If he's weak, if he's partially human, I might be able to win him over again. I might be able to restore what I've lost.

In coming here, he disclosed his secret.

When we return, he'll be seen as weak. Hyperion already does see him that way. There's one way I can protect him from that liability, while simultaneously sealing off my chance at ever winning him back. I should be thinking about the earth dragons as a whole and what they would want.

But I can't think of anyone but Axel. I never have been able to make the decision that's right when the decision that's right for my loved ones is an alternative.

So I choose to skin the innocent child, just as a monster should.

"Fine," I say. "I choose strength. Restore them all—make them powerful like the others."

"Interesting," Freya says.

And then there's a flash so blinding that I can see nothing but light.

AXEL

When I'm expelled from the burning place, my oldest brother's waiting for me.

Azar? Hyperion sounds incredulous for some reason.

What was I doing in that strange place? Small creatures kept trying to gnaw on me, distressed as they were with the heat.

Hyperion's mouth gapes open. And then he makes a strange, choking, coughing sort of sound. Flames and smoke spew from his maw.

What's going on? Behind my brother, small humans are crouched in a large metal cage, hanging from a hook in the remains of a ceiling over the edge of the ledge on which we're both standing.

Welcome back, brother. I suppose you were telling the truth.

The truth of what? I hate this disoriented feeling. *When did you arrive? The last I remember was telling you farewell before departing for Earth.*

You really must be both Azar and Axel, Hyperion says.

I've feared this moment my entire life—Euphrasia always impressed upon me the importance that no one ever discover that I have two affinities. *Why would you say that?* I shake my head. *That's insane.*

You told me yourself. Hyperion steps closer, his head tilted sideways as he studies me. *Do you not recall it?*

Two loud crashes behind me have me spinning around as Gordon and Rufus come flying out of the same lava pool that I recently evacuated.

You're alive? Hyperion looks as if he can hardly believe it. *But where's Liz? Is she not with you?*

Liz? Who's he talking about? Why would someone named Liz be with us? I wish I could even recall why I was in the burning place, but the more I think about it, the more blank it feels.

Prince Azar! Gordon slithers toward me, but as he approaches, I notice he's bigger than I recall, and his legs are now massive. He's still a bundle of dark brown coils, but his legs look as if they could propel him forward easily as well. When he stands, it's clear that he's definitely larger than he was.

Much larger.

And as he straightens, something unfurls behind him. Large, shining wings of walnut— darker even than his scales. And his face is now framed by dark, sharp horns. He looks less serpentine and more, well, more like a warrior.

What happened to me? Gordon asks. *Did Liz do this?*

My desire to rend something grows. *Who's this Liz? Why do people keep asking after her?*

She's your bonded. Rufus walks toward me, then, and it's clear that he's grown as well. Not by quite as much, but still to nearly double his former size. He too has wings, and his colors are both brighter and richer.

I can't be bonded, I say. *We've only just reached Earth.*

He's clearly lost part of his memory, Hyperion says. *But don't worry, brother, we'll catch you up on things.*

I turn toward him and snap, *I don't need you catching me up on anything. I'm fine.*

Well, I'd still like to see it, Hyperion says. *Shift for me, into your earth blessed form.*

I want to refuse, but he already knows. It appears that I must have, inexplicably, confessed my biggest secret to these three. Instead of arguing further, I shift again.

But when I take the form of Axel, it's different. I'm nearly as tall as I was as Azar, and like Gordon and Rufus, powerful wings unfurl from my back. I spread them and marvel a bit at their golden weight and length.

It looks like that little girl won you all quite the upgrade. Hyperion looks almost angry. *Perhaps I should have leapt into the lava with her.*

But where is this mysterious Liz, my alleged bonded? I've no sooner wondered about her when, from the depths of the lava, a creature erupts, exploding upward and outward, and then brilliant, feathered white wings spread out behind her, and she flies up, up, up into the air, rising steadily above the ridge of rock that curls around the top of the children and disappears from view.

"What on earth was that?" one of the small humans asks. "Because it looked a lot like Liz, but it had dark hair and *wings*."

"That old woman who came to us just before the dragons took us was telling me a story," another small human says. "She said that before, when the dragons were on earth, their bonded humans weren't human."

What were they? I ask, curious in spite of myself.

Gordon slithers toward the cage, but the children don't shy back in fear. Instead, Gordon raises up and bites the door of the cage, releasing them. The children slide down his back like it's some kind of game, the little male staying on his back while the others scramble off and rush toward Rufus.

What's going on? I hate feeling lost.

These are the sisters and brother of your bonded, Liz, Rufus says. *You ordered us to protect them.*

Who is this Liz? I demand, tired of hearing her name over and over.

She killed you, Hyperion says. *She sided with the humans, and they used your bond to weaken you. Then she returned, and you all went into the lava, and now she's back, or she was. . .* Hyperion looks upward, at the bright blue sky.

I'm certainly not sitting around here any longer, feeling stupid. *I'm going to find her,* I say. *I think she owes me some answers.*

Find out whether she brought the heart, Hyperion shouts from below. *Because if she didn't, I'm dragging her back here and throwing her back in.*

EPILOGUE: LIZ

When I emerge from the lava, I'm sailing through the air, and without thinking, I spread my wings—*my wings??*—and fly. My siblings appear to be safe down below, next to a much larger, beefier version of Axel, but then, I can't quite figure out how to stop flapping, so I keep going up instead of down.

At least Gordon and Rufus 2.0 appear to be caring for the kiddos, so hopefully while I figure out this flying thing, they'll be alright. I sweep around and head the only direction I know to go from here, toward the place that Azar has carried me several times in the past.

Not that he'll remember any of that.

I start winging my way toward Selfoss, and as I do, I pass not one, not even two or three, but dozens of dragons. All of them, like me, are flying for what looks like the first time. There are shouts of joy, exclamations of apprehension, and even some dragon swear words.

I'm shocked that, even without being bonded, I can now both hear and understand them. Now that I think of it, I suppose I could also understand Gaia and Phileas and the others, even before I rebonded Axel. Maybe it's a once-bonded, always-dragon-aware kind of thing. Watching the earth dragons frolicking is a little calming to me, and it helps me to process the fact that my bond is, once again, *gone.*

I'm still a little surprised when I discover that I've flown, with my large, gorgeous feathered wings, all the way to the home of that old Icelandic woman. When I land in front of the steps up to her porch, it's as if she can sense I'm there.

She opens the door with a whoosh and steps out onto her small porch. "Where's the dragon?"

I shake my head. "I'm not bonded to him anymore."

"You traded your bond for wings?" She's frowning. "You're a bigger idiot than I thought."

"Not intentionally," I say. "But I suppose I did."

"Was it worth it?" she asks. "Giving up your dragon just to become a valkyrie?"

"A what?"

"I'm assuming that's what you are. They're the only winged warriors in Norse mythology." The old woman grunts. "You must have met Freya?"

How could she know that?

"Don't look so shocked. You were human before, and you return as a valkyrie? Only the queen of the valkyries could effect such a transformation."

"She's the queen of—but are there more people like me?"

"Not that I've met." The crone cackles. "But who knows what Freya will do now."

Before I can ask her anything else, a dark spot blocks out the sun.

It's Axel—flying toward us.

That means the things I recall of my time with Freya really happened. I transformed the earth dragons. I wonder whether they know it was me who did it.

You're Liz, Axel says as he lands.

"Who's the gold dragon?" the crone asks. "You sure have a lot of dragons chasing you around."

She has no idea.

You have much to answer for, winged human. Axel looks as though he has never seen me before. It appears that Freya's little tests carried real consequences. It makes me wonder about the first one, though. That's a fight I never even had—so how can the choice I made have any bearing? And I forgot to ask her about the people I saw standing around when I was a child, chanting. Next time Hyperion chucks me into the lava, I need to take a checklist.

"I'm ready to answer your questions as well as I can," I say. "A lot of what happened doesn't make sense, even to me."

The crone's watching us, her eyes wide and curious. Other earth dragons have noticed that Axel's here, and they've begun to land all around us, slowly flapping their wings even once they've landed, as if they're worried they might disappear if they stop using them.

"But maybe we should go somewhere more private," I suggest.

The earth blessed will only follow me wherever we go. I can feel more of them approaching even now. You may as well speak openly here.

Nice try, Axel. The last thing I'm going to do is risk breaking down and sobbing around all the gathering dragons and a strange old woman who already knows too much.

Then something he said to me once surfaces in my memory. He told me that he'd first been drawn to me, because unlike the other humans, I wasn't sobbing and scared. I had attacked him.

If I want to convince him to like me again, I need to channel that same energy.

Only, before I can even open my mouth, a gorgeous silver dragon lands next to Axel. *Where's Hyperion? I heard he took* her *to the volcano to throw her in.*

Axel's head whips around. *Asteria? What are you doing here?*

Asteria frowns. *I've been here, idiot. Why would you ask me that? You should be answering questions, like what in the world is happening to all the earth dragons?*

My eyes nearly bug out of my head when the bigger, burlier version of Axel shifts in a burst of red smoke into Azar.

Asteria, who until this very second believed Azar to be dead, nearly falls over backward, stumbling to get away from him. *What's happening?*

I'm Azar and Axel and always have been both. Now that Axel's no longer weak, I'm no longer going to hide it.

Asteria shakes her head, clearly struggling to process the information. *But you died.*

I most certainly did not.

I decide this is as good a time as any to sneak away and make sure Coral, Jade, and Sammy are doing alright. I launch into the sky, but I make it no more than two dozen yards before Azar flies up alongside me and plucks me from the air with one giant claw, his talons wrapping around me carefully. *My brother plans to throw you back into the lava, but I have questions for you first, winged human. I'm not ready to part with you yet.*

It's hard, but as he flies away with me, I shove down the hope that starts to spring up in my breast. He's not saying he won't take me back to Hyperion because he cares about me. He just wants answers.

Even so, it's a pernicious thing for humans.

Hope.

No matter how many times it gets squashed, it just keeps rising up.

**I hope that all of you enjoyed Entwined!! it was SO much fun to write. Embroiled is outlined, but it has to patiently wait while I write some women's fiction books, and my last horse shifter book... BUT it's coming up later this year, so don't worry. <3 You'll get to hear Azar roar and Liz berate him for it before you know it. Preorders help me a LOT, so if you can manage to preorder it for me, that's awesome. It'll also ensure that you hear if I manage to get it out early, which I'm always aiming to do.

If you don't know what to read while you're waiting, you might try my horse shifter romances, starting with My Queendom for a Horse.

Or you could want Displaced—a urban fantasy romance series that's already complete.

And as always, if you have time to leave me a review anywhere (Amazon, Nook, Apple, GoodReads, Bookbub, Kobo, Google Play... you get the picture!) it really helps! THANKS for all the SUPPORT!

ACKNOWLEDGMENTS

Mostly, I'm grateful for my three girls. No one in the world is more excited about my books than they are. (Although, Tessa insists on waiting on the audiobook...)

My husband is also amazing.

My two sons are often inspiration for my ideas.

My editor Carrie is a rock star.

AND ALWAYS AND FOREVER: I love my fans so much. I have the best readers in the world. Thank you so much for loving my fake people and fake worlds. May we play in these fantastic places forever. YOUR support makes my job possible. If I could, I'd give every single one of you a dragon of your own.

ABOUT THE AUTHOR

I have animals coming out of my ears. Seven horses. Three dogs, three cats, thirty-ish chickens. I'm always doctoring or playing with an animal... and I wouldn't want it any other way. But Leo (my palomino) is still my very favorite.

When I'm not with animals, or even if I am, I'm likely to have at least one of my five kids in tow, two of which I'm currently homeschooling.

My hubby is the reason all this glorious madness is possible. He's the best parts of all the amazing men I write (although he's bald and his six pack sometimes goes into hiding because of cookies.)

I also love to bake, like to cook, and feel amazing when I find time to kickbox, lift weights, or rollerblade. Oh yeah, and I'm a lawyer, but I try to forget about that whenever I can.

I adore my husband, and I love my God.

The rest is just details.

(But one detail you might want to know! I have an active reader group on FB called the Bridget Baker Binge Readers, and I have a newsletter you can sign up for at www.BridgetEBakerWrites.com! I'd love to have you sign up for either thing!)

Awoken (3)

Capsized (4)

The Sins of Our Ancestors Series:

Marked (1)

Suppressed (2)

Redeemed (3)

Renounced (4)

Reclaimed (5) a novella!

A stand alone YA romantic suspense:

Already Gone

I also write women's fiction and contemporary romance under B. E. Baker.

The Scarsdale Fosters Series:

Seed Money

Nouveau Riche (2)

Minted (3)

Loaded (4)

The Finding Home Series:

Finding Grace (1)

Finding Faith (2)

Finding Cupid (3)

Finding Spring (4)

Finding Liberty (5)

Finding Holly (6)

Finding Home (7)

Finding Balance (8)

Finding Peace (9)

The Finding Home Series Boxset Books 1-3

The Finding Home Series Boxset Books 4-6

www.ingramcontent.com/pod-product-compliance
Lightning Source LLC
Chambersburg PA
CBHW050756190726
48285CB00005B/1688